Ida's Trunk

A Dakota Farm Girl Goes West

Patty Cresalia

Ida's Trunk
© 2022 by Patty Cresalia

Editorial Committee, *From the Valdres Valley of Norway to the Red River Valley of the North and Beyond: A History of the Oihus Family, 1580-2020.* Grafton, N.D.: Privately Published, 2020.

Scriptural passages are taken from the Holy Bible, New American Bible, Washington, D.C., United States Conference of Catholics Bishops 2002.

Title page painting: 1996 rendering of Ida's home in Nash, North Dakota, by Patricia Schistle

eaglesnestparable@gmail.com

Dedication

Ida's Trunk is dedicated to my grandmother, Hazel. All her life, this good-natured woman quietly attended to the demanding domestic needs of the family farm. Her history and the articles within her trunk stirred my imagination, motivating me to write the story of Ida, the mother that Hazel never knew.

My grandmother
Hazel Ottoson Lykken
1915, Age 13

Table of Contents

Section 1: The Beginning

Section 2: The Promise

Section 3: Tender Moments

Section 4: The Journey

Section 5: Los Angeles

Section 6: Passages

Section I

The Beginning

Preface

September 30, 1912

It was late, and Hannah had been fidgeting since crawling into bed. Finally, unable to sleep, she rose and perched on the edge of the mattress. Her head was pounding as her thoughts reeled in turmoil. Arne, asleep beside her, was roused by her movement. In a hissing whisper, he challenged his wife,

"Answer me this, Hannah, what good will come of telling the child any more than she already knows?"

Hannah crossed her arms and replied, "You see how the girl pesters me with questions! Furthermore, whenever a letter arrives from Canada, it sets her off to fretting. She rereads the words until the paper falls apart. Besides, I promised."

"You are certain she is old enough to hear the story?" Arne questioned gruffly, not wanting to restart an old quarrel.

"Yes, I am," Hannah pressed on. "Caroline and I have discussed it. We both feel that now is a good time with the farm work slowing. I just want you and Anthony to know it will happen."

Exasperated, Arne made a sound clearing his throat to speak, then shut his mouth and rolled over to face the wall. He decided there was nothing helpful to add to this late-night conversation.

The following day dawned with a clear sky. Hannah's grand-daughter, Hazel, was sitting at her upstairs bedroom window in the little gray farmhouse. She loved this vantage point when the first rays of the sun streamed into her bedroom. It only lasted a few minutes, but she treasured how the light bright-ened up her walls covered in pansy-patterned wallpaper.

When the cooing of a mourning dove drew her attention, she spotted the bird pacing on the roof of the potato house. Two weeks had passed since those frantic days of the potato harvest. Everyone in the family needed to do their part. It was so important that Alma, Clarence, and she even missed school until the crop was stored. They stooped and crawled as they moved down the field rows filling the wooden slatted baskets with spuds. It was dirty and hard work. Hazel was relieved when it was over. Even though the potato harvest was gruel-ing, she was glad that the earthen dugout was filled again with enough potatoes to supply their plates for a year.

Beyond the dugout was one of her grandfather's recently gleaned wheat fields. The dry yellow stubble was ready for burning. Each year, her grandfather and Uncle Anthony ran a harvesting crew. Their mighty steam engine and separator were waiting in a neighbor's field two miles away, ready to har-vest the final field of oats for the season.

Finally, Hazel lifted her eyes to the cottonwood trees down by the Park River. A few days ago, the majestic trees had been crowned in gold. But now, they were giving up their leaves to the tugging of the wind. Soon, all their branches would be barren.

Hazel turned from the window. It was time to begin the day. Lately, she'd scribbled out a list of her plans for the day, including chores, homework, and anything else of interest. She took her red pencil and a scrap of paper and wrote "Saturday" in bold letters on the top. Then she began to write. *Today is my birthday; I am ten years old!* Her list continued and included baking a cake with her grandmother, helping Aunt Teana, Uncle Anthony's wife, peel apples for sauce, and memorizing the poem.

Hazel began reciting a few lines of the September poem as she wiggled into her shoes and braided her hair. The poem's words sounded musical to her ears and spoke of familiar things.

September
by Helen Hunt Jackson

The golden rod is yellow;
The corn is turning brown;
The trees in apple orchards
With fruit are bending down.

The gentian's bluest fringes
Are curling in the sun;
In dusty pods, the milkweed
Its hidden silk has spun.

Hazel smiled confidently; *only five more verses to learn before Monday.* All at once, she remembered one more item for her list, which made her smile. Suddenly propelled with anticipation, Hazel moved quickly, tying her shoelaces, putting on her apron, and making her bed. After straightening the coverlet. she centered her doll on the pillow.

When all was in order, Hazel paused to survey the room. The narrow cot, the small table, and the large trunk she used for storage constituted all the furnishings of her tiny closet-sized room. It was all she needed. In a large household, she was grateful to have a room of her own.

Eagerly Hazel set out in pursuit of Caroline. She stomped sideways down the eleven steep steps between the floors with her fingertips to the walls for balance. Her grandparents, Arne and Hannah, were sitting at the kitchen window and were startled when Hazel burst through the kitchen door. Arne briefly lowered the *Grafton Times* to peer over the top of the paper, raising one eyebrow.

When Hazel saw her grandmother's warning scowl, she gulped. Quieting her voice, she asked, "Where is Caroline?"

"Here I am, Hazel. I'm grinding coffee. Whatever do you need?" piped up a cheery voice from the pantry.

Moving to where she could see Caroline, Hazel sputtered, "Did you do it? Did you wind the clock?"

Caroline smiled, "Of course not! We know you have been looking forward to doing it yourself. Happy birthday, Hazel!"

―⁓―

Later that morning, Hannah summoned her daughter, Caroline, and Hazel to the sitting room where they gathered in front of the sideboard. It was here, on the open shelves, that Hannah kept her best dishes safely on display. The clock sat on a lower shelf next to a row of well-read books. The small library included the family Bible, *Luther's Small Catechism*, Arne's books concerning veterinary care of livestock, and a stack of *The Youth's Companion* issues.

Hazel eyed the clock, watching the pendulum swing back and forth. When she turned ten, Hazel had been promised that she would oversee the weekly winding of the "wedding" clock. The moment had arrived.

After pulling forward a chair for Hazel to stand on, Caroline opened the glass door of the oak-framed timepiece and drew out the key. Turning Hazel's hand palm up, she laid the small brass key into it.

"You must always keep the key with the clock," Caroline reminded as she began to instruct and point. "Use the turnkey in both holes. Turn it slowly, just a few times. Never force it. You will get the hang of it."

After the clock was wound, Hazel closed the door and whispered to the clock, "Now, it will always be my job to care for you."

Circling to face her aunt and grandmother, Hazel mustered a firm voice, "And you also promised to tell me the story. I want to hear everything!"

Introduction

The winter of 1881 was a legendary season of blizzards. The bitter wind chills remained well below zero, gripping the entire Midwest. As the season turned to spring, Arne and Hannah Oihus welcomed their first daughter into the world. Anna Ovedia Oihus, or "Ida," was born March 10, 1881, in a small sod house on the Dakota prairie near the tiny community of Nash in Walsh County, North Dakota. Ida's Norwegian parents were "Old-Timers," early homesteaders who came to work the land. They arrived in 1880 with hopes to prosper, which began by staking a land claim under the Homestead Act.

Beyond the farming enterprise, the Oihus family took on active civic duties in the growing Farmington Township community. The family attended the Lutheran church in nearby Auburn, received mail at the Nash Post Office, and purchased supplies from the larger town of Grafton, eight miles away. When Ida was ten, the railroad company laid tracks near the family homestead, diagonally crossing her Uncle Anthony's farmland. The train tracks connected surrounding communities and provided the essential means for a farmer to get his crop to market.

Beginning at a young age, Ida worked alongside her mother, eventually becoming proficient in managing the farm household. When available, Ida attended school in the one-room schoolhouse located less than two miles from her home. She completed her studies through the eighth-grade level.

Ida would likely have remained in the family home to live an unremarkable life but for an opportunity that redirected the course of her life. Ida was my great-grandmother, and *Ida's Trunk* is her story.

CHAPTER 1

A Job for Ida

Uncle Anthony's expectations

Early one spring, when Ida was finishing her eighth-grade examinations, Uncle Anthony approached her parents with a proposition. "I've heard Ida is not planning to go on with her schooling; I wondered if she would like to housekeep over at my place?"

Ida's mother, Hannah, interjected, "So, you've finally decided to listen to me. It's about time; as I said, you need more help raising Eddy. It would be good for him to have the influence of womenfolk around."

"Yes, as always, you are right, Hannah," Anthony scoffed. "I know you think we are bachelors living in squalor over at my place, but I still have reservations about getting help, especially from a woman. However, between the farm work and supplying the boys with food, I admit extra hands would be good."

"You and Eddy are constantly at odds," remarked Hannah. "All boys go through a time when they think they are so smart that they can make their own rules, but Ida has been around her brothers to see how Arne and I put up with their tiresome ways. She can be a help to you."

"There is nothing wrong with the boy, Hannah. Maybe someday, he won't be so cocky, and his grumbling tones will not grate on my nerves. Though I won't deny that I am not a patient man," replied Anthony, sounding annoyed.

"Well, we agree on that," Hannah retorted. "Yes, you may ask Ida. If she agrees, let her do the job and don't interfere. It will not be easy, Anthony," warned Hannah grimly. *You have not even let me into your domain for some time,* Hannah thought, cringing as she imagined the present condition of his kitchen.

Ida was thrilled when Uncle Anthony approached her with his idea. She liked school well enough, but Ida was a homebody. While her fellow schoolmates aspiring to become teachers, nurses, or business owners were making plans to attend Grafton High School, Ida was not. No longer interested in being in a classroom, Ida was relieved that her parents weren't pressing the issue. Ida silently reasoned, *It would be a problem in winter anyway. I would have to board in town, and that would cost money.* She had also overheard her parents talking about saving money to send one of her brothers to the agricultural college in Fargo, and she knew her choice not to continue in school meant they would be able to do so that much sooner.

Ida liked helping her mother with domestic duties and the other work necessary to run a family farm. As a child, Ida had helped Uncle Anthony plant and water the seedlings on his tree claim. Over the last decade, she had watched with satisfaction as the growing seedlings became a stately cottonwood forest of young trees. She also loved solitary walks on the shady deer paths next to the Park River. Because she was known to enjoy her own company in places of quietude, others sometimes considered Ida a reserved, independent kind of girl.

So, when Ida agreed to work for her uncle, she already knew the situation would suit her. She was confident in her abilities to do the job he wanted. In addition, Ida rarely went to nearby Grafton or Auburn to shop or look at window displays, but it still pleased her to think that she could earn, or rather save, money.

"Will you be able to manage without me, Mama?' Ida asked.

Hannah promptly replied, "I will expect more from your sister, Caroline. It is the way of family. It is good you have an opportunity to work."

"Anyhow," Ida continued, "I will not be far away. If you need me, I will come."

The next day Ida began the daily trek across the pasture to work for Uncle Anthony.

—⁓—

Twenty years had passed since Ida's father, Arne, and his younger brother, Anthony, had left the family farm in the established community of Oakland Valley in Franklin County, Iowa. In 1879, with a spirit of adventure driving them, the brothers rode the train north into the Dakota Territory. The reports and stories of the rich loam that could produce exceptional wheat yields echoed in their ears. Under the Homestead Act of 1862, a hard-working man had a chance to claim his own land.

Arne and Anthony knew the stipulations to satisfy a claim were demanding. They would be committing five years to live on and improve the virgin land for agricultural use. It was not enough for a hopeful farmer to be a dreamer. He needed to formulate a plan and gather the resources necessary to execute the work. Beyond a horse and plow, there were other critical and practical items like seed, a shovel, food, nails, tar paper, lamp oil, and money for the unexpected expenses. Often settlers relied on sharing labor and equipment until the land became productive. At the end of five years, many who tried to achieve a farming livelihood in the harsh Dakota climate had failed. So it was with determination that the Oihus brothers proceeded onward.

The tracks ended in Fargo, North Dakota. Arne and Anthony continued their journey, following along the west side of the Red River on horseback. One hundred and twenty miles later, they arrived at their destination. They stopped on the unsettled prairie near the hamlet of Grafton. There, the brothers encountered other early settlers—Norwegians, Swedes, Germans and Poles—camping along the Park River.

After exploring further, the brothers felt even more certain about taking a calculated gamble and moving to the area. After the 500-mile trek northward, the brothers returned home to make preparations. In the spirit of this looming new beginning, Arne and Anthony decided to change their surname from Christopherson to Oihus to honor the heritage of their Oihus family roots in Norway.

The following year, well-equipped with supplies, Arne and Anthony returned to the Grafton area and immediately filed for adjoining land parcels northwest of Grafton on April 21, 1880. With spring upon them, the brothers began the strenuous work of plowing under the thick Bluestem grass to plant wheat without delay. They built sod houses by cutting earthen strips from the prairie and placed fence lines to define grazing areas. In time, they constructed large, protective barns for their working animals.

Soon, Arne married. He met young Hannah Skaufle during his travels north of Fargo in the boomtown of Caledonia, where she had lived since arriving from Norway in 1873. Her father was a day laborer hired by the Hudson Bay Company who oversaw moving goods past the rapids of the Goose River confluence with the Red River. In Arne, both Hannah and her father recognized ambition. After Arne prepared a suitable home, he returned as promised to make her his bride. Their first child was born in the soddy. In time, Arne built a log cabin for his growing family. After fifteen years of marriage and several more children, they made their home in a two-story wood-frame home built around 1895.

Across the way, Anthony was also making progress working his tree claim and farmland. His single-story plank house consisted of a common room with a combined kitchen and living area, a storage room, and two small bedrooms. Anthony, fifteen-year-old Eddy, and a hired man, Ernst, lived in the house.

Nearby, Anthony's substantial barn towered over the modest home. As time went on, Anthony purchased farming tools, equipment, and implements with his hard-earned cash. A wagon, plow, harrow, cultivator, and stone boat with wooden gliders stood in a neat row near the barn. The "boat" was handy for hauling heavy loads like grain sacks or removing field rocks.

Well-cared-for horses, and cows milled about the corral and pasture. It was a hard life, but those who recognized the opportunity, such as the hard-working Oihus folks, got ahead little by little.

Ida was the first of Arne and Hannah's seven children. By her rank, Ida naturally became her mother's helper as the family grew. She learned the skills expected of a young woman, including everyday cooking, baking, cleaning, sewing, and repairing clothing. The milking, caring for poultry, and nursing orphaned animals like piglets and calves also fell under Hannah's duties. In addition, Ida was familiar with seasonal duties such as butchering, gardening, and preserving the produce in the fall. These critical tasks were necessary for a family's survival through a cold North Dakota winter.

Before Ida started her job, Anthony cleared a corner in the kitchen near the pantry for her use. After placing a chair and a new broom into the tiny space, he inserted two pegs in the wall to hang up aprons and her coat. The first day, Anthony, Ernst, and Eddy sat at the kitchen table waiting and watching as she made her way across the pasture. The men had shoved aside the dirty dishes and various tools on the table—including a hammer, pliers, and a sharpening stone—in anticipation of a meal.

"Maybe I should wipe off some plates," mumbled Ernst as he stood up to wet the corner of a rag.

"Yes, that would be helpful," replied Anthony. Turning to Eddy, he said, "Go draw a fresh pail of water. I suppose she will need more if she begins to clean right away."

When she arrived, Ida greeted the three men warmly

as she stood at the door. Looking around, she was appalled. While Anthony kept his farmyard tidy, his living quarters were severely neglected. Focusing only on the area around the stove and the nearby ham and bowl of eggs, Ida tied on her apron and went straight to work, very conscious that the men were watching her every move. She had to ask several questions, including where they kept the frying pan and butter. Anthony briefly went over the stove's operation as the frying pan heated. When she asked, "How do you draw out the hot water from the reservoir?" her uncle looked puzzled. Surprised, she wondered if he used hot water for washing or anything at all!

In a short time, Ida efficiently plated up three servings of steaming hot food and placed them in front of the men. Pleased that the first meal was so eagerly received, Ida poured herself a cup of coffee and sat down. It was a satisfying feeling to watch as they devoured the food. But when they had finished, they sat eyeing each other and playing with their forks and knives. Finally, Eddy spoke up, "Is this all, Ida? I could eat a lot more."

Ida's face began to burn as she realized she had not prepared enough. Immediately she rose to fix the second round of ham and eggs. Later, with the men off to work, she collected her thoughts as she washed dishes. *I never saw so many eggs eaten at one time except at harvest. At home, we only get one egg apiece. Papa sometimes gets more, but only if there are enough.*

In reflection, it was a rough beginning for everyone when Ida started working at the house. Slowly, and one meal at a time, Ida learned what the men liked to eat and what work was expected. The day she made beans and ham, they ate hardly anything but consumed all the biscuits. When she finally got a chance to eat herself and took her first bite, she immediately spat out the beans. While smelling savory and comforting, the beans were hard and crunchy.

Frustrated by her efforts, Ida returned the pot to the stove. When she added water, it left the stew tasting bland. Ida retrieved more ham, diced up another onion, and tossed in some salt. Before she left later that afternoon, she tasted the soupy mixture again. She frowned, "I'll ask Mama about this…something isn't right. The beans are finally cooked, but this is surely too salty!"

At home, Ida questioned her mother about the meal. "What didn't I do right?"

"Beans take time to soak and cook, no matter what you do. It takes practice, but you'll get it," Hannah advised helpfully. "If the beans are too old, they will never soften. Adding the molasses or vinegar to the beans before they are soft sometimes makes them tough."

"And the salt? Your beans are never as salty as the ones I made today," said Ida.

"You must taste your food as you go along. An easy cure for saltiness is to add a potato to the pot next time. It will take up the salt."

"That would have been easy. I'll remember that," returned Ida. Feeling empowered, she retrieved a notebook and began that very day to fill the empty pages with helpful information and recipes. On the first page, she wrote:

1) If something is too salty, add a potato.
2) Make extra. Men eat more than you expect.

In time, Ida learned her way around Uncle Anthony's

expectations. Sometimes when she arrived, either a chunk of raw beef or chicken was waiting for her. If apples were left out, it was a hint for her to make pies. While she worried about setting out enough food for their voracious appetites, she quickly learned to keep plentiful amounts of bread and butter on hand.

While the men looked forward to having meals provided, Ida was determined to thoroughly clean the house. After the long winter, she warned them that she was going to wash their filthy sheets and long underwear. Ida considered it a reasonable plan, but Anthony had a differing opinion. He had been on his own for many years and had his own way of prioritizing. The animals and fieldwork always came first. In his mind, food was necessary and should be simply managed. Clean clothes and sheets were fine, but during winter, plowing, planting, and harvesting, laundry simply was not a priority.

When he proposed that the spring washing could wait, Ida furrowed her brow and asserted, "If you want me to keep this house, then don't tell me what to do. If you want clean clothes for Sunday services, I *will* wash them today."

When Ida stood her ground, he thought, *It seems like I'm the one doing all the compromising.* Anthony shot a glare of exasperation her way. Grunting and shaking his head, Anthony pushed back from the table, his chair scraping across the floor. Setting down his empty coffee cup with a thud, he snapped, "Eddy, set up the washing tub and bring a stack of wood. When you're done, you will turn your long johns over to *her.*"

"I'll bring the water," offered Ernst hurriedly, stuffing the last bite of his egg sandwich into his mouth. Then, after gulping his coffee, he rushed outside but not before catching Eddy's attention with a nod for him to follow.

Later that day, as Anthony milked, he grumbled to himself, "What next, Ida?"

Earlier in the day, Ida had glared at him upon seeing a trail of muddy footprints through the house, and he heard her mutter, "They don't even try to scrape their boots!" He decided he would just have to take the bad with the good.

—⁓—

A few days later, Ida arrived to find small jars of seeds lined up on the kitchen table. Her uncle spoke up. "Ida, you need to get the garden going; the time of frost has passed. Eddy will be helping you. I noticed the weeds have already shown up."

"Oh," Ida replied, raising an eyebrow. "I'll get started after breakfast." Inwardly, she realized she hadn't considered that tending the kitchen garden would be an additional duty to housekeeping.

It took several days for Eddy and Ida to prepare the ground. They grunted their way through the hard labor of pulling out the old weeds and the remains of the plants from the year before. After digging and turning the rich black soil, they took turns raking the ground smooth. Ida was pleased with what she saw as she eyed the plot of ground. Picking up a stout stick, she and Eddy drew straight lines through the dirt and planted seeds for carrots, beans, beets, and the like. After the seeds for the row vegetables were in the ground, Ida showed Eddy how to plant the squash, pumpkin, cucumbers, and other vining plants into small mounds of dirt.

Uncle Anthony arrived after the garden was planted and

handed Ida a sack of seed potatoes, each with the potential to sprout a new plant from each eye. He asked her to cut each potato into three or four pieces, preserving the best "eyes" for new potato plants. Eddy took the pieces out to the freshly plowed rows in the field adjacent to the farmyard where Anthony had already planted rows of corn. If the growing season was good, they would have plenty of food to last the year. Potatoes and corn were the staples served in some form at every meal.

As time went on, Ida relaxed into the rhythm of her work routine. Her little notebook grew fat as she added recipes for soap and cookies, a diagram of the garden, and the seed planting dates. Eddy was especially keen to report to Ida as the seeds sprouted and took on more defined leaves. Both Ida and Eddy groaned when they noticed hungry bugs attacking the tender stems and devouring the leaves.

As the summer progressed, Anthony and Ida came to terms, and the household developed a sense of enjoyable comradery. One day, Anthony even commented to Hannah how useful it was to have Ida around and noted that her cooking had improved since she first began. When her uncle declared, "I don't think I would like going back to my old ways," Ida beamed. It was the nicest compliment he could have uttered.

CHAPTER 2

Harvesttime

There are no acceptable excuses for not working during the harvest.

"*That sounds like* the crew coming now," Arne said, listening to the approaching sounds of chains rattling and wagons creaking, accompanied by the signal barking of the farm dogs. "Oscar, saddle up and send out the word," he commanded.

It was mid-September, and Arne had become increasingly impatient over the wait. He held that a farmer had nothing worth showing for his efforts until his crops were off the field and ready to be sold or stored. The Dakota weather was also a constant source of angst: wind, rain, hail, and temperature were all unpredictable and uncontrollable. All those factors either helped or hindered a successful wheat crop yield. A farmer might hope for a perfect growing season, but while ambitious, it usually was a foolish expectation. Several scattered rainy days added to the harvesting delays throughout the surrounding area this year, but Arne's foul temper of the past days began to dissipate as he walked out to greet the driver of the massive steam engine. He even paused to admire the show of power by the six draft horses pulling the engine into the farmyard. The heavy steam engine was followed by other horses pulling a threshing machine and additional supply wagons.

Every year, local farmers banded together to hire a threshing crew to help get the wheat out of the field and into storage bags. The self-sufficient Arne paid for this service grudgingly, knowing it cut into any profit he made. He and Anthony often talked about owning their own outfit. Still, the initial outlay for equipment was pricey, so they would wait for better times.

Once again, reason reminded him that the efficiency of the modern farming equipment was evolving. A better machine meant they gleaned more from the dried stalks. Despite the improved harvesting equipment, wheat still demanded much personal effort from everyone involved.

The threshing teams often came from places outside the area, even as far away as Minnesota. The close-knit crews tended to be German or Polish-speaking and spoke in their native tongue. Spending the growing season living out of their wagons, the men were hearty souls. The timing of their arrival was crucial, as was the order in which each farmer's land was worked. Moving from farm to farm, the crew would set up camp in the farmer's yard or a nearby field. In the best of times, the complicated and coordinated efforts of a year of farming finally came together at harvest. The farmer and his family worked alongside the hired crew using his own horses and wagons, water, and food supplies.

Arne, Anthony, Ernst, and the older boys had cut and

bundled the shocks of wheat two weeks prior. After bundling, nine or more shocks were placed upright together into tipi-looking formations scattered throughout the field to dry in the blazing summer sun. As the farmer awaited the threshing crew's arrival, the wheat "cured." The men and older children spent hours roving the fields, turning the shocks and picking up bundles blown over by the prairie winds. When the wheat kernels hardened sufficiently within their protective stalks, the grain was ready for threshing and storage.

The threshing crew of twenty-five to thirty-five men presented additional work for the women who provided continuous rounds of food and drink. The men and women worked strenuously during the long days of summer's hottest weather. It was always a challenge to get the job done, especially when younger children needed attention.

Before the thresher's arrival, Hannah and her older daughters coordinated the cooking with Ingrid and Mabel, the two sisters hired to run the cook car. This kitchen on wheels was designed to be pulled into the fields by a team of horses. Operated by skillful women, the well-equipped cook car had a full-size stove, a large dining table, and even a day bed for the rare moments of rest. The hosting farm was expected to supplement the meals by providing bread and bakery items, milk, butter, and vegetables. Keeping ample water nearby was also necessary for drinking and washing.

The harvest was a social time for the neighboring women as they moved from task to task, each meal ending with abundant dishes to wash and stack for the next meal. At night, even after a long day of fieldwork, the young people gathered at the table in the cook car to talk and play card games by the light of a kerosene lamp.

Depending on the weather and the size of the fields, the stay at one farm lasted from a few days to a few weeks. The grueling work was not finished until all the farmer's grain was sewn into bags, ready to sell or store. On this day, the temperature was already climbing, and it was only eight o'clock in the morning.

———

A coughing fit roused Ida from her sleep and left her gasping for air. *How come it is starting up again?* She fumed. Summoning the energy to rise, Ida sat up only to realize her head was whirling, and she felt extremely weak. The tickle in her throat became a coughing fit once again, and she winced in pain. Disappointed, Ida dropped her head back into her pillow.

When Hannah heard her daughter stirring, she called Ida to present herself. Ida rose and climbed barefooted down the steep steps. As she reached the bottom, she began to cough again and had to sit down.

"I can see how poorly you feel, Ida. Of all days, shame on you for getting sick!" chastised Hannah, coming to where Ida stood looking wilted and flushed. Concerned, she reached out to touch Ida's face.

"Can Caroline take care of the butter and bake bread today?" asked Ida in a wavering voice. She knew no excuse was acceptable for not working on a threshing day. Everyone was expected to share the work effort. "I think if I could sleep a little while longer, I'd feel better."

"We will manage, but it certainly is not like you to get sick," frowned Hannah. "Off to your bed. I'll try to check on you later."

It was almost a week before Ida felt strong again. When she finally made her way over to see Uncle Anthony about her work, he was shocked by her frail appearance. "You look kind of pale, Ida. Best shorten your day," he instructed.

Another week passed before Ida felt like her usual self once again. The grain harvest was over, and the threshers had moved on. As she looked around, enjoying the pleasant day, she let her thoughts run on about the work waiting for her. After some consideration, Ida decided she would turn her attention to the garden. The weeds had grown unchecked during her absence.

It is a relief to have already canned the peas and put up all those jars of pickles. Maybe Eddy will have time to dig the carrots while I pick the beans. If I mention it, the others will gather the plums and apples, especially if they want them for pie this winter.

In late fall, her uncle butchered a pig, and Ida had to season the meat and put it into the smokehouse to cure. In addition, she had blodpudding and sausage to make. She also prepared a plentiful supply of soap using the rendered lard, lye, and water.

—⁓—

Before Thanksgiving, an unexpected storm arrived, bringing snow and leaving drifts around the barn and the house. After a week of reprieve, another snowstorm confirmed that the Dakota winter had begun.

Ida could not go as often to work for Anthony during the winter months. As the temperature dipped to zero and below, it was unsafe to be outside for long, so the women and younger children stayed close to the woodstove. Hannah constantly reminded her children about dressing in layers as she mumbled, "This place does not hold the heat like the soddy or the log home."

Arne and his older boys spent the cold winter months doing chores and making repairs on equipment in the barn. The horses and cows generated enough heat to keep the barn tolerable. By the dim light of a lantern, Arne taught Albert and Oscar the necessary skills for maintaining the farm equipment, such as properly sharpening plow blades and repairing harnesses and bridles.

In one corner of the barn, logs were piled high, ready to be split. Besides keeping the livestock fed, feeding the home's stove was the main chore of winter. After chopping, the wood pieces were stacked on a sled and pulled close to the kitchen door. Moving as quickly as possible, they filled the wood box in the kitchen with armloads of wood. Even with the sweat effort of splitting and hauling wood to keep the stoves stoked, the house rarely felt warm as the temperature plunged.

One winter day, Ida stood at the frost-encrusted window and sighed as she watched the snow swirl. "I don't know what to do; I'm tired of being inside and useless. I guess I'll go sleep the afternoon away."

Overhearing her comment, Hannah was not amused. In fact, she realized her girls' sour moods and bickering were grating on her nerves. After pulling out a stack of fabric scraps, she called them to the kitchen table. As they cut quilt pieces and strips of fabric for braided rugs, Hannah reminded them of the pastor's recent sermon on idleness. "He reminded us that we must be on guard against tendencies to be lazy."

Ida's cough returned often and persisted through the winter confinement. At night, the sound of her daughter's hacking traveled through the floor grates right to her mother's ears. Hannah often rose from her bed to prepare and apply small poultices made from dry mustard and flour to Ida's chest. "It will open your lungs, Ida. Just do it!" Hannah insisted.

When Ida's skin became irritated and even burned by the mustard, her mother relented, saying she should stop applying them, but she still maintained they were helpful. When Ida started to experience night fevers, Hannah brewed willow tea to bring some relief.

Even Arne was concerned and applied his experienced veterinarian skills of bloodletting using his father's old spring-loaded lancet. He believed the practice was curative as it helped balance body fluids, including blood, bile, and phlegm. Ida was terrified of the painful procedure but trusted her father, especially as he insisted it was beneficial. Both times, her father called Uncle Anthony to hold her down as there was nothing to be given for the pain inflicted. But after removing a full cup of blood each time, it became doubtful that it made a difference. Ida remained sickly, and as time went on and as her cough came and went, it wasn't easy to decipher if home treatments helped.

CHAPTER 3

A Grim Diagnosis

What is wrong with me?

Finally, during a spell of milder winter weather, Hannah insisted, "Ida, I've had enough of your coughing. Today, your father is going to town, and we will go with him to do some shopping. We will go by Dr. Gamble's office and see if he is in. Perhaps he can prescribe some medicine for you."

Once in town, Arne and the women separated. He went off to look for some nails, flux, and leather strips while the women worked their way down Hill Avenue to the doctor's office. A small bell jingled when they opened the heavy door, announcing their arrival. They stepped into the small waiting room and found it vacant.

"I'll be right there!" boomed a voice from a back room. Momentarily, Dr. Gamble appeared. He greeted them, nodding, "Mrs. Oihus, what brings you in this day?"

Hannah took the lead and briefly began, "Dr. Gamble, this is Ida, my daughter. Arne and I are worried because she has a cough that won't go away." Turning to the young and apprehensive woman, he motioned for Ida to follow him. She nervously looked back at her mother with panic in her eyes. Hannah encouraged, "Let me take your coat, Ida…do as Dr. Gamble says. It will be all right."

Upon entering the exam room, the physician said, "Ida, first I will ask you some questions, and then listen to your lungs. Here, take a seat on the table." Mutely, Ida sat and watched Dr. Gamble take a piece of paper and pen in hand. "How long has this coughing been going on?" he asked.

"Well, I think it got started in the summer. We were threshing, and I felt so poorly that I could not help. I just felt weak, and then it went away."

"When your coughing returned this time, did it feel as bad as last summer?"

"No. Now when I cough, sometimes it hurts. But I feel better after I cough up stuff."

Picking up a stethoscope, Dr. Gamble explained, "This will help me hear your lungs, but you must remove your shirt."

"Oh!" exclaimed Ida, flushing as she put her hand protectively to her throat.

"Here is a cloth to cover yourself if you like," offered the doctor as he handed her a square of muslin and turned away to give her a bit of privacy.

Ida stood and undid the fashioners on the front of her top. Then she struggled to slip her arms from the tight sleeves and fitted bodice. When Dr. Gamble heard her whisper, "Alright, I'm ready," he turned and saw her settled back on the exam table. Her eyes were downcast.

Using his most calm and reassuring voice, Dr. Gamble

held up an instrument and offered, "Can I show you how my stethoscope works?" Opening the side pieces, he settled them on her ears. Then, holding the working round diaphragm to her chest, he moved it until he saw her face light up. He could tell she was listening to her heart beating.

"My heart? That sounds so loud…so fast," commented Ida in surprise.

"Now, let me have a listen. You see, it is nothing to worry about." Dr. Gamble proceeded with his exam, which included listening to her heart and asking her to breathe in and out several times, fast and slow. Then he reached down for her wrist to take her pulse. He gasped when he noticed a festering wound on her wrist. "Ida, this looks sore. I will show you how to care for it before we're finished."

Ida winced in pain as Dr. Gamble thoroughly cleaned her wrist wound by soaking it with antiseptic, then applying an ointment. Finally, he dressed her wrist in gauze and instructed, "Make sure you clean and dress this sore every two days. I'll give you extra bandages."

"I will do as you say," Ida murmured.

"If it is not looking better soon, you need to come back so I can check it. I have finished your exam and will speak with your mother while you dress. Come to my office when you are ready."

When Ida joined her mother and Dr. Gamble, she felt alarmed when she saw their grim faces. Her mother had a handkerchief in her hand, and her eyes were red. Immediately a sense of dread washed over her. "What is it?" she demanded. "What is wrong with me?"

Dr. Gamble urged calmly, "Come, sit down, Ida, and I will try to answer all your questions."

———∾∾∾———

After leaving the doctor's office, Ida and Hannah began making their way back down the block to the livery. When they reached the drugstore, Hannah said, "Let's go in. I need to buy a few things."

Inside, Hannah went directly to the counter and addressed the waiting sales clerk. "I need camphor, two yards of muslin, and a bottle of this remedy," she said, handing him the note from Dr. Gamble.

As the clerk filled their order, Hannah turned to Ida, "The muslin is for you, for more handkerchiefs." After paying for their purchase, Hannah and Ida went to find Arne. Turning off Hill Avenue, they could see him standing with a small group of men. His voice was echoing loudly amid a heated exchange. When Hannah caught his attention, he stopped talking and motioned for them to wait while he brought the wagon around. When they began the return trip, no one spoke until they reached the railroad track crossing. Taking a deep breath, Hannah announced, "I took Ida to see Dr. Gamble while we were in town."

Arne snarled in return, "How come you didn't tell me?"

"I did what needed to be done," returned Hannah sharply. "You know all that we have tried—the bloodletting, poultices, laxatives—nothing has helped."

"What do you expect me to say, Hannah?"

"Our daughter is sick, Arne. There is little to be done except for rest and treating her symptoms. Doc Gamble says Ida

has the consumption." Hannah's voice trailed off to nothing-
ness.

—⁓—

Later that night, as Ida washed the supper dishes, Arne noticed her bandaged wrist. "Did you hurt yourself, Ida?"

Ida looked to her mother, unsure of what to say.

Hannah spoke up, "Dr. Gamble does not approve of bloodletting. He says Ida's wound is infected, and he treated it."

Arne, indignant, demanded, "Let me see, Ida."

Ida obediently moved to the table. Arne unwrapped the
wet bandage and examined the poorly healing wound. Looking at her father's face, Ida insisted, "It is getting better now,
Papa."

"How about the other place?" asked Arne more softly.

"Oh, that one is all better. Dr. Gamble said it is just taking
time to heal because I am not healthy."

"Tell your father the rest of what Dr. Gamble said to you,"
Hannah piped up from where she stood at the stove.

"He said I must catch my coughs in a handkerchief so
others don't get it. I need fresh air in the room where I sleep.
When I am tired, I need to rest," Ida repeated dutifully. *He also
told me I am infectious, and I won't get better. You don't want to
hear about that, and I don't want to say it out loud.*

—⁓—

A few days later, still under a heavy cloud of melancholy,
Ida was determined to push past her desire to stay in her warm
bed. After dressing quickly in the cold bedroom, she quietly
slipped out the kitchen door. The morning air bit at her nose,
but the sky was clear overhead, and the sun would be up soon.

Ida wanted to escape the paralyzing pall cast over her by Dr. Gamble's diagnosis. Yesterday's conversations rolled in her head and started an argument: *This can't possibly be right. I'm already better this morning...I need to think if I could just be by myself for a while.*

Heading to Uncle Anthony's and the solace of "her kitchen" was what she decided she needed today. Crossing the icy pasture, Ida was determined to bake. *If I can accomplish something every day, that is enough,* she concluded.

Ida was soon elbow-deep kneading bread dough. She found it immensely satisfying to make bread, considering it almost magical how flour, starter, salt, and water stirred together transformed into a soft dough. Then later, the enticing aroma of baking filled the room and stirred the appreciation of others.

After setting the bread to rise, Ida decided to take a walk. Reaching for her coat, she buttoned it and wrapped her scarf around her head, blocking cold drafts. She intended to circle the farmyard, but she headed towards the woods, finding the walking soothed her soul. Winter had been relatively dry thus far despite all the blustering winds. In fact, the wind had driven away the snow leaving the ground mostly barren all the way to the frozen Park River.

Heading in that direction, Ida walked rapidly. At the river's edge, she sat down on a fallen log. Pulling her scarf up higher to cover her nose, she closed her eyes, raised her face, and tried to absorb the warmth of the winter sun. At that moment, she began to pray: *Oh, God, what is your plan for me? I don't understand. If I am to become sicker, help me bear it bravely.*

When she finished her appeal, she continued to sit in the stillness of the winter woods. Suddenly, she became aware of the sound of music wafting through the leafless trees. She brightened upon spotting Ernst coming towards her on the path. His lips pressed to his old harmonica, he played a cheery melody as he came up the path toward her.

"Did you come to talk to the trees?" Ernst jested as he approached. He had noticed when Ida left the kitchen, and he was not about to let her stay out in the cold and risk getting sick again. Ever since she made the trip to town with her parents, Ida had been pensive. Evasiveness replaced her usual friendly manner. He thought, Something must be wrong; if only you would tell me!

"Ida, will you come walk with me? Please tell me what puts you so deep in thought," he encouraged tenderly.

Looking up at him, she tried to stem the tears burning her eyes. But she only replied, "Let's return to the house; the bread must be ready to bake by now. Please play another tune for me."

CHAPTER 4

Ernst

*He longed for the same carefree ease
that Ida shared in conversation with Eddy.*

*Ernst was exasperated. Something is wrong with Ida,
but why won't she talk about it?* Every time he attempted to get
her to talk, she curtly cut him off. Then she'd slip away, voicing
some excuse such as, "Mama needs me at home" or "Eddy is
waiting for me." Just now, when they had returned from their
walk, she left him on the stoop, insisting, "I need to get the
bread in the oven before the dough collapses; I'm sure you
have things to get on with." Closing the kitchen door between
them, she effectively ended their conversation.

Ernst muttered as he walked away, "She is so infuriating!"
Then he recalled that Ida seemed to be on the verge of tears
at their parting. The frown on his face softening, he sought a
new perspective. Finally, it came to him. Ernst decided *Women
are "krånglight.* That Swedish term expresses when something
is complicated, messy, or awkward. *Yes,* he thought again to
himself, *that is how it is with her, "krånglight"!*

Walking along the river's edge, Ernst noticed how the month of March was giving the nod to spring. The days were warm enough to begin the snowmelt and thaw the frost line. As he continued to mull over his thoughts, a beaver shuffled into his line of vision. With its glossy, reddish-brown fur, the creature was about the size of a large dog. As the animal turned, Ernst guessed it was about three feet long from nose to the end of its black, paddle-shaped tail. While he was aware that beavers did not hibernate, it was a rare surprise to see the creature roaming about this time of year, especially during the day. Usually, the beavers retreated to their dens of sticks, bark, and mud and survived by chewing on their cache of willow twigs or other branches dutifully collected during milder seasons.

Anthony, like most men, did not tolerate the overgrown rodents on his land. Quickly disposing of any he found, Anthony had served the fatty meat and bacon-tasting tail for supper on more than one occasion. The beaver was favored for its beautiful pelts, making extremely warm coats, hats, and muffs. The problem with beavers was that they showed up unexpectedly. Working persistently, a single beaver could mess up the river's normal flow. Working quietly, the creatures carve up the countryside little by little, taking down mighty trees and stripping away bushes in their wake.

His thoughts returning to the situation with Ida, Ernst wryly concluded, *Ida is like a beaver.* It was unexpected when she arrived last summer to begin housekeeping for Anthony. Ernst remembered feeling taken aback to notice how Ida had grown into a young, slim, attractive woman.

He had first encountered Ida when he was hired to help build Arne's new home. She was a serious-minded 14-year-old girl with two golden braids framing her fair face. Running around in her bare feet, Ida was kept busy doing her parents' bidding with household chores and helping with the children. With his mind reeling in thought, Ernst suddenly thought of his mother. He always turned to her when sorting out a problem. He whispered longingly, "So much has happened, Mama. If you were here, I would ask you about Ida. I know you would like her."

Turning around, Ernst scanned the western horizon looking for the spire of the North Trinity Church. For him, the church steeple rising on the treeless prairie was an early marker of his American Adventure. He had not ended up in the Red River Valley by chance. The Mattsons, former neighbors and friends of his parents, had invited him to come. The Mattson family had moved away from Goteborg a few years ago to become part of a newly established Swedish community near Neche, North Dakota. By correspondence, they had insisted that should any member of the Svenson family make a move, they would be welcomed warmly. And while the Dakota Territory was his destination, the time of leaving home with meager resources and the journey along the way were noteworthy.

Otto Svenson, Ernst's father, was disillusioned with living in the overcrowded city of Goteborg, Sweden. An excellent woodworker, Otto was sought out by those who could pay for his skills, the higher-class society that lived in the city. Otto took on commissions working in people's homes to build or repair cabinets, shelves, chairs, bookcases, and bedstands.

Despite working long hours, he had few resources to offer his three sons and two daughters.

Ernst's parents deemed education invaluable to help their children gain a promising future. He and his siblings attended a school near their home, learning to read and write. In addition, Otto taught his sons carpentry skills, but the interest in the journeyman profession waned. Besides, despite their skills, the work was sporadic. It barely allowed the Svenson family to meet their basic food, heating, and clothing needs.

When he could manage, Otto and Ernst went to see his grandfather in the nearby countryside. Grandfather was a cotter farmer, which meant he worked for a landowner. The cottage he lived in was in a woody area adjacent to the tillable land and belonged to the owner. Beside the dwelling, Grandfather worked a little ground for a garden and kept a few farm animals that provided meat, eggs, and milk. Grandfather was the one who first introduced the idea in Otto's mind about sending his sons to "Amerika." Family friends, already settled in the new land, wrote back, "The opportunities are real and waiting. There is little to gain in remaining here."

With a heavy heart, Otto began to encourage his older boys to leave their homeland. When he was fifteen, he said to Ernst, "It is time for you to make plans. Go join your brother Herman. You will always be able to find work. If you are willing."

Practically, Ernst first had to earn the funds necessary for his trip to America. His father sometimes had Ernst assist him in his cabinetry projects. But paying Ernst drained the family resources. Therefore, Ernst discovered it was more lucrative to work down at the shipyards as a laborer. He loaded and unloaded freight and picked up rare tips for assisting emigrating passengers with their baggage. Working amongst both travelers and other shipyard workers, Ernst heard the stories of the passengers as they readied for passage across the water. Standing near the feeder ships, he imagined the thrill his brother Herman must have felt the day he left two years ago. Herman was heading to Boston, but the family had not heard of his whereabouts since his departure. That was how it was. The family said goodbye hoping to see their sons again, but the bittersweet reality was that it would not happen.

The day before Ernst left, his father presented a small canvas bundle. "Here, Ernst, take these tools with you," he said. "I have no more money to spare, but you can find work as a carpenter with these." A wooden planer, hammer, chisel, ruler, and a compactly folded square had been rolled up in the canvas apron.

Dumbstruck and gutted, Ernst understood his father was saying a final farewell. Saying goodbye to his ailing mother, Anna Sofia, and sisters Clara and Selma was even harder. The women wept, and it tore at his heart. His leaving meant his little brother Oscar, barely ten, would be the designated son to take over should something happen.

Nevertheless, his parents allowed no regret to be voiced. "Ernst," they urged generously, "you must be firm in your resolve. You have made a good plan. Be thrilled about your prospects in the new land."

On February 21, 1893, Ernst lined up with 500 other steerage travelers waiting to board the Ariosto. This feeder ship would take them to England. His possessions included a two-week food supply, his father's tools, a few articles of clothing, and a blanket. When it was his turn to register, his name was added to the passenger list. Ernst declared himself traveling alone and gave his occupation as "worker." He was directed to board the ship and join the throng of other travelers descending to the ship's lower level. Once onboard, he secured a berth, shocked to realize the six-foot-square wooden pallet was to share with three other travelers.

As the *Ariosto* began to drift out of the harbor, the third-class passengers could feel the swaying motion of the water. Up on deck, the first-class passengers lined up at the rail to wave farewell as their families and homeland faded from view. The first part of the journey took the immigrants to Hull, England. On arrival, Ernst and his fellow travelers were ushered into a holding station to wait for the next leg of the journey. When it was his turn, Ernst climbed aboard a designated train for the five-hour ride from Hull to Liverpool, England. Once in Liverpool, Ernst waited for a Wednesday departure when he would board a ship bound for Boston.

The two-week journey across the Atlantic in steerage was arduous. The Swedish folks tended to gather with their own. Still, the mix of languages and cultures grew as the trip progressed and people intermingled. Among the passengers, Ernst heard the sounds of European languages such as Italian and German, as well as many Slavic languages. The more familiar Scandinavian languages rooted in familiar Old Norse also filled his ears. Ernst, convinced it would be an advantage, began concentrating on useful English phrases, the language of the ship's crew. He thought to himself, *If English is spoken in America and is the language of business, I would learn to speak it too.*

Two weeks after leaving Goteborg, the ship arrived in Boston. Following the advice of fellow travelers, Ernst accepted the outreach hospitality of the local Swedish community offered to new arrivals. With the help of the Boston hosts and barely enough train fare in his pockets, he made his way by rail and on foot to Neche, North Dakota.

Stepping off the train, he located the home of the Mattson family. They promptly offered him temporary shelter until he found steady work, and it was not long before they directed him to see Knut Staven. Knut was the carpenter building the North Trinity Lutheran Church, located a few miles west from Nash. The church project was almost completed except for the roof. Knut hired Ernst, and the men began building the church steeple. Later painted a stark white, the spire rose from the prairie and was visible for miles around.

One day, Ernst posted a letter to his family at the general store in Sweden. Sweden was not a town or a village but a small cluster of buildings near Nash. That was the day Ernst met Arne Oihus. Arne was immediately taken by the youthful Ernst. Barely 16, he was tall with a wiry frame that was beginning to muscle out. Upon hearing his story, Arne proposed that Ernst come to help him build his home. Ernst agreed. After fulfilling his commitment at the church, Ernst gathered his tools and moved in to work with Arne and then his brother Anthony at their farms.

Ernst thought having a girl help him was entirely unnecessary, but he didn't want to cross Arne when Arne put Ida to work handing Ernst nails or holding up tar paper as the new house was built. She stood by his side, and as they worked, she began to teach him more English phrases.

Now, six years later, they had both grown up. Ernst enjoyed watching Ida at work, especially when she did not know he was around. It was a rare moment that he could catch her eyes and try to decipher what she was thinking. Scandinavians do not like to be looked at square in the eyes.

Ernst had not met many girls besides his sisters and mother, but the city girls back home were outspoken and more straightforward to talk to than Ida. Still, something about Ida struck at his heart in a manner no other girls had ever done. She was not exactly shy but calm and mild-mannered. She was also self-sufficient and never seemed to waver in getting a job done—like a beaver. But while a beaver might flap its tail on the water surface in alarm or to signal something was wrong, Ida simply withdrew. Deciphering what she was thinking was hard for him.

Ernst was unsure of how to proceed with Ida.

CHAPTER 5

Being Normal

You have clearly heard more than I said.

The doctor had insisted that Ida would benefit from more rest. When she resumed working for Uncle Anthony, she practiced taking short breaks during the day. Frustrated, she finally admitted to Uncle Anthony, "I need help. I'm having a hard time lifting the kettle and milk can." It was a plea for she wanted to keep her job.

After giving it some thought, Anthony offered, "Eddy may help you, as long as I don't need him for farm work."

When Eddy heard this news, he rolled his eyes. Grudgingly, he ensured Ida had the necessary water on hand for cooking and cleaning. But when Eddy noticed Ida struggling and so short of breath she had to sit down, he became concerned. After that, he watched for ways to assist Ida and seemed more willing to help. Soon, Eddy and Ida were enjoying their time together.

One day, Ida decided that the young man would benefit from learning basic cooking and domestic skills, and she started by teaching him how to make biscuits. Soon after, she showed her willing student how to sew on buttons. In return, Eddy amused her with his jokes and stories. On a whim, he would launch into a vivid retelling of the most recent western adventure of Buffalo Bill or a ruse solved by a Pinkerton detective. He was an engaging storyteller who enthralled Ida and the others with his tales.

Eddy's interest in adventure books happened to be the one interest he and Uncle Anthony had in common. While the actual text of the stories was never shared by reading aloud, the stack of worn dime novels, tattered and smudged, slowly grew. Eddy's keen interest in the stories reminded Ida of trading nickel novels with her schoolmates.

Growing up, Ida's parents encouraged reading as a benefit for increasing knowledge or religious fortitude. Her mother drew the line at "frivolous" reading of the so-called "penny dreadful" stories. Hannah made it loudly known she did not approve of the time and money wasted on reading those particular books. Nevertheless, Ida and her siblings contrived to obtain and read the popular adventures, being careful not to do it under Hannah's watchful eyes.

Ignoring her mother's sensibilities, as far as Ida was concerned, the stories that filled Eddy's mind were not harmful. Subtly, they cultivated the idea that adversity can strengthen a person's character. Many of the stories were about struggling, good-natured boys who got ahead or achieved success through hard work and luck.

Even in the exciting romantic exchanges that she had read, the heroine always maintained her honor, despite trouble or terrible circumstances that befell her. While Ida did not openly admit to her fascination with such novels, recently she was secretly pleased to find a dime novel lying on the kitchen table. Based on the cover that flaunted a woman in a deep pink, fashionable dress, she was convinced that Uncle Anthony had left *A Sinless Crime*, no. 194, for her enjoyment.

———∿∿∿———

As the months came and went, Ida became reluctant to talk about her health. The bouts of coughing almost disappeared, but when family members reminded her of her physical limits, she became grumpy. In fact, if a tickle stirred in her throat, she would retreat so others didn't hear her cough. Ida eventually tried to convince herself that perhaps Doctor Gamble was all wrong, thinking, *I'm not as sick as he said. Anyway, I don't want to think about it anymore.*

The spring fieldwork was underway. Along with the seasonal demands, Hannah was soon expecting another child.

Under the circumstances, Ida and Caroline took on the most demanding household chores so that their mother could rest.

After three girls in a row, Caroline, Laura, and Alma, a son arrived. Born on May 21, Clarence Oliver Oihus was welcomed into the new century of the year 1900. Arne, in good humor, began to seed his wheat under a sunny blue sky.

Ernst, ever faithful, kept watch over Ida's workload and health. The day she picked up a shovel to begin to turn the soil in the garden, he stepped up, taking the shovel from her hand, and asked, "Where do you want to start?"

Ida sighed and handed him the shovel. The same thing

happened when she tried lugging water for the washing. He came to her side and took the hot kettle from her. An outsider might perceive these actions as a chance for Ernst to flirt, but not Ida. She had the knowledge that her life was tenuous, and she was learning to accept her limitations.

As time went on, Ernst's thoughts remained fixed. He wanted to marry Ida. He brought up the subject for the first time in late summer. He and Ida were walking through the trees by the river. The turkey flock had strayed from the corral, and they went to drive the errant birds back home. Occasionally, the jingle of a bell alerted them to the location of the birds. Ida recalled the day Eddy had purchased the ten-cent bell and tied it around Henry's neck.

Ida giggled when Ernst spotted the rafter of birds perched overhead in a tree. "We will need to wait or startle them to come down. Which will it be?" asked Ernst.

"They will come when they realize there is wheat in my apron pocket," replied Ida, leaning back on a tree to watch. "Let them rest a minute before we disturb them. They think they have cleverly hidden from us."

In this intimate moment, alone in the woods, Ernst broached the subject on his mind. Coming closer, he began, "Ida, I don't know what my future will bring, but I want you to be a part of it. I want to take care of you, and I know you must have feelings for me." He paused, waiting eagerly for her response.

Ida looked up at him with sad, wistful eyes, wanting to utter aloud the bitter words on the tip of her tongue, *I have no future, but you do, and you must plan for it without me. It would be a big mistake.* Instead, she stuttered awkwardly, "I...I can't talk about this right now." With those words, she walked away, but not before reaching into her apron pocket and tossing a handful of grain into the air. The band of turkeys, suddenly roused, flew down in a flurry. The intimate moment was over, leaving Ernst confused about Ida's feelings.

—⁓—

Both Arne and Anthony suspected something was developing between Ida and Ernst. While they sometimes teased him, the brothers had considered Ernst with high regard ever since he arrived from Sweden to work for Anthony at 16. They found him honest and a hard worker, but they decided he lacked initiative and opportunity.

Hannah entered these discussions about Ernst too. She was practical and thus mystified as to why Ernst would be willing to take on the future burden of their daughter's frail health. The day Ernst came to ask Arne if he could formally court Ida, Arne was ready. He remarked, "If you have a mind to stir up her heart, you must know the doctor says it is most likely Ida's health will worsen. She will never be a strong woman. Think about what that means."

"Her condition doesn't matter to me. I want to marry her if she will have me," pleaded Ernst.

"That is not our only concern. We know you are a capable man, but you must develop a different plan for your future if you expect to support and provide a home for her."

"Then help me figure this out!" countered Ernst

"You may court her if she agrees, but I repeat, don't mislead her or promise her anything you can't deliver," grunted Arne in a final comment.

Ernst walked away in a daze. At first, the comments stung. *Arne is right…I've been here for years, and all I can call my own is Andy and Felix,* referring to his horse and mule. *So, what will I do to make my way ahead?* His next encounter with Ida only deepened his resolve to become better for her.

Arne and Anthony rallied to help Ernst explore ideas with a goal in mind. Ida, ever in the background, listened with interest. Upon hearing that a piece of land was coming up for sale, the two brothers pushed Ernst to consider the prospects. When they read the paper, they pointed out other possibilities not pinned to farming.

Leaving the area seemed more like the best option. The newspapers and advertisements boasted enticing opportunities while encouraging readers to go west. California especially drew the young man's attention. Heavily promoted as a center of rising agricultural activities, the seacoast boasted a year-round growing climate. The thought was novel and appealing. Southern California was increasing its economy with both minerals and oil industries. With these new ideas brewing, the prospect of long Dakota winters in the tiny house at Nash now seemed like fruitless effort toward his long-term goal of getting ahead.

CHAPTER 6

Cookies and Conversation

You sure keep your worries at the front of your mind
so you will not have any problems finding them.

The months continued to turn over. Anthony insisted that when a cold snap kept the temperatures close to zero, "Ida, you needn't come so often. We will manage if you will do the baking." Ida was not happy about the change in her daily schedule. She enjoyed the diverting time away from home and the younger children who demanded her attention.

One day Ida arrived to find the kitchen in grubby disarray. More than a week had passed since she had been there. After helping her out of her woolen coat, stiff with cold, Eddy went back to join Ernst in a game of checkers. Disheartened, Ida went to the stove to warm her hands and inspect the room. In one corner, she spotted a pile that made it apparent Uncle Anthony had dragged horse harnesses and bridles into the house. Nearby was a container of harness oil used for cleaning and softening leather. A large circle of grease adorned the floor.

Looking around, she spotted a sizeable furry rodent paus-ing in the shadows of the kerosene light. After picking up a bread heel, the creature scuttled along a wall to disappear into a bedroom. Ida gasped and pointed.

The men chuckled, and Eddy scoffed, "Oh, Ida, you should meet our new house guest. That is Elmer; he picks up the crumbs."

"You have given that thing a name?" Ida was dumbfounded. A *zing!* caught her attention as she saw a flying missile hurtle across the room and land in the metal bucket in the corner. Looking up, she saw Eddy using his sleeve to wipe his mouth.

"Eddy! What was that? Ida asked, squelching the rising an-ger she wanted to save and direct to Uncle Anthony.

"It is chewing tobacco, Ida," explained Ernst, realizing that her temper was rising. "Your Uncle Anthony gave him a choice—he could smoke or chew. It really isn't something to get worked up about."

Ida glared at him, and a disgusted look crept over her face. Both men felt the sting. She bit her lip and held her words as she pondered what to do. *Is it my place to say something about this vile situation? What would Mama say?*

Without another word, Ida turned her attention to the dirty dishes in the sink. The blaring silence from the usually agreeable Ida made everyone uncomfortable.

Ernst and Eddy stared at each other, willing the other to speak first. They wished Anthony would conveniently return from the barn. Finally, one of them made a move. Ernst got up, stoked the stove with some wood, then knelt to shuffle the woodbox into order. Eddy, following his lead, quietly stacked the checkers and put away the game. Then he began to pick up their coats and place them on the pegs by the door.

As Ida dried and stacked the dishes, the men continued to tidy up. When Ida had washed the last cup, she sighed and turned to face them. Now composed and calm, Ida suggested, "How about some hot biscuits and gravy for lunch?"

While the biscuits were baking, the boys bolted to the barn. Ida sipped on fresh coffee as she went to the pantry to check the food stores. *They have been eating the fruit sauce and crackers*, noting the dwindling supplies on the shelf.

"Stew," she announced, reaching for two jars of canned meat. "I'll use those and stretch it with vegetables." Ida lifted the trap door and climbed down the ladder to the earthen root cellar. She retrieved potatoes, rutabagas, carrots, and onions from the baskets and wooden crates on the floor of the barely lit room. After washing, scraping, and cutting up the vegetables, Ida added all the ingredients into a pot to simmer, creating a rich broth.

With the supper meal cooking on the stove, she decided to treat the men to cookies. After retrieving the large pottery bowl from the pantry, she flipped through her notebook, stopping when she came to the recipe for Hermit Cookies. *This will do. I think they will like these as much as Pa does.*

Just as she located a nugget of nutmeg to flavor the dough, she heard the door rattle. Looking up, she felt a blast of frigid air. She watched as one of the men, heavily bundled, quickly entered and closed the door behind him. She knew it was Ernst, even if the only visible part of his face was his frosty eyelashes.

"Sure is bitter out there. I can't feel my toes. Needed to come in to get warm," explained Ernst in a husky voice.

Ida moved to help him unwrap the tight muffler about his neck. "All right, I just put on more coffee. Are the others on their way in?"

"Not for a bit. Arne is showing Eddy how to repair a broken spoke on that wagon wheel."

Removing his coat and mittens, he went to stand in front of the stove. Ida returned to the table to continue her work. He noted with pleasure how pleasing it was to watch her with her sleeves rolled up and her hands covered in flour. When she noticed him staring, she quipped, "Now sit down and be useful. First, I need the nutmeg grated. I almost forgot to add it to the dough."

After duly obeying her request, Ernst was soon enjoying the delicious aroma of baking cookies. Ida looked at Ernst and, sensing something was amiss, asked, "You seem quiet today. Something on your mind?"

Before saying anything, Ernst added cream to his hot coffee and watched it swirl in and disappear. Heaving a deep sigh, he began to share his troubles. In Ida, Ernst had discovered a listening ear and an important confidant in trying times.

"I'm just circling thoughts in my head. I've worked for Anthony for more than six years, ever since I came to America, and I have nothing to show for it."

"What do you mean? What is it you are after?" Ida returned, although she already knew his answer.

"I'm of an age now to claim land. But as you know, around here, it is already full of farmers. When land comes available, it seems someone else snatches it up quickly."

"But you have a place here. Uncle Anthony depends on you," disputed Ida.

He looked at her and shook his head as he reminded her, "Eddy is getting bigger now. He will be able to take my place. Anthony sometimes talks like he is grooming Eddy to take over...eventually."

"Oh, I never thought about that. He has always seemed too young to me. Eddy is also restless—just like you," countered Ida. "Maybe Eddy will not want to stay here and farm."

"It is not the same, Ida. I want a place of my own. I want to walk into a barn that I built with my own hands. You don't understand what it feels like to always use another man's hammer or wagon."

"Then plan for a change, Ernst. You have always worked hard; you can do it. I want you to have all these things." Growing apprehensive, Ida reluctantly admitted to herself, *He needs to move on, even if I don't want him to. It is time for him to leave. He is ready.*

To change the subject, Ernst probed, "Ida, how long will you work for Anthony?"

Ida looked up and, making light of the question, jested, "As long as Uncle Anthony needs me!" But her heart spoke the truth, *Until someone needs me more.* Not sure if she had said that aloud, she turned away and focused on shaping more cookies.

⁓

As time went on, Ida continued to remain healthy and feel what she thought of as "normal." She convinced herself that maybe what was wrong with her had gone away. Her spirits lightened when she decided that she just might have a future after all. With this mindset, Ida finally allowed herself to give a little nod to Ernst's ongoing persistent attention.

In January, Ernst hesitantly asked, "Ida, will you come with me to the Auburn Winter Dance?"

Ida agreed.

CHAPTER 7

The Winter Dance

Ida blushed. "I came with Ernst."

Upstairs in her tiny bedroom, Ida carefully brushed out her Sunday dress. She was wearing a clean petticoat, chemise, and corset. Caroline sat nearby on her bed, waiting to help style Ida's hair. "I've got the iron wand warming on the stove. You must promise to show me some dance steps when you get back," gushed Caroline. Rarely did Ida primp in front of a glass, but she wanted to look attractive for her escort.

After Caroline helped pull the corset ribbons, Ida put on her dark blue skirt with the matching bodice. Maroon ruffles trimmed the yoke, and a black braid garnished the bell-shaped skirt. With her fringe lightly controlled in a curl, she was ready. Hannah gave her approval with a nod. "I want you to wear my coat and fur hat tonight, Ida," Hannah instructed as she handed them over. "It will be much colder before you get home."

Looking out the window, Arne announced, "I can see the lantern bobbing on the sled. Best not to keep him waiting."

As soon as Ernst pulled up outside the kitchen door and

stepped onto the porch, Arne opened the door and pulled him in. Ernst grinned sheepishly as the whole family of nine was assembled in the kitchen. When Alfred made a snickering noise, Ernst saw Ida's cheeks redden.

He assured Arne, "We best get on our way, but we will be back directly after the dance." Reaching for Ida's elbow, Ernst ushered her outside. When the kitchen door shut behind them, it was suddenly quiet.

"Are you ready?" he asked, helping her into the sleigh. Ida smiled and nodded. Ernst climbed in beside her and spread the sleigh blankets across their laps. With a snap of the reins, they set off into the night.

Ernst suddenly found himself wordless, racking his brain for *any* intelligent comment. Ida, too, felt unexpectedly shy. *What is wrong with me? I've dreamed of riding out with him. Why won't he say something? What is so different about tonight?*

Finally, Ernst blurted, "I'm glad to take Andy out tonight; he needs the exercise."

As if on cue, Andy sent up an icy clod of snow that landed directly in Ida's lap. Ida and Ernst glanced at each other and burst out laughing. The tension of the moment was broken.

"Can you see the outline of Auburn?" pointed Ernst.

Looking ahead, Ida nodded. On the horizon where the prairie and the night sky met, she saw a cluster of buildings. Drawing closer, the faint glow of oil lamps appeared around the edges of the muffled windows.

Ernst apologized as they arrived in Auburn, "It is too cold to have the horse stand outside tonight. I'll drop you off and come back straight away after taking Andy to the livery."

When Ernst stopped in front of the Auburn Village Hall, Lars Lykken, a former classmate of Ida's, stepped forward. After assisting her out of the sleigh, he offered his elbow as they walked down the slippery footpath leading to the hall. Stepping inside the building, Ida felt apprehensive. Having never been to a party like this before, she had no idea what to expect.

Then she heard someone call out her name. Turning toward the voice, she saw more friends from school, Martha and Belle. They rushed to her side and demanded, "Who brought you, Ida?"

Ida blushed. "I came with Ernst."

Giggling, the girls each took an arm before pulling Ida into a crowded little room to store her coat. Over the clamor of activity, she heard the piano and a violin begin to play. After patting her hair and adjusting her stockings, she stepped back into the hall.

Ernst came to meet her, smiling broadly. He gave her a glancing once-over, noticing her flushed cheeks, carefully arranged hair, and trim waist. Ida caught his look of admiration and smiled. When the music commenced, they danced the polka until they were breathless. Noticing that the women present outnumbered the men, Ida encouraged Ernst to dance with the wallflowers. Later, Ida chatted with her schoolmates while Ernst joined the other fellows in the back of the building to smoke and play pool.

At precisely ten o'clock, the playing of the Home Sweet Home Waltz concluded the dance. When the notes died out, Ernst stepped up to Ida's side and announced with a sense of urgency, "Ida, we must go." When he helped her into her coat, he leaned in close to whisper, "It sure is nice to see you having such fun."

Ida smiled warmly.

His urgency returned once he tucked the thick fur blankets around them in the sleigh. Upon leaving the Auburn village limits, Ernst urged the horse to pick up the pace as he guided the sleigh onto the open prairie. "Something is coming, Ida," he said apprehensively, pointing overhead in the direction they were traveling. "We should have left sooner." They watched as the starry night sky was noticeably overcome by an encroaching dark haze sweeping in from the west.

Ernst became even more alarmed when Ida began coughing on the way home. "Probably just the cold night air," she remarked lightly, insisting, "I am fine." Ernst frowned.

Halfway home, the dark outline of the tree grove along the river disappeared in a swirl of snow. By then, the winds had picked up and were howling fiercely. In an instant, the short journey home became treacherous. Without landmarks guiding them, Ernst had to rely on his instincts and the horse. The biting snow began to hammer them as they turned westward.

Ernst felt Ida stiffen. He nudged his elbow toward her, instructing, "Here, take my arm." He felt her pull closer to his side. "It is getting colder, Ida. Pull the blankets up higher to cover your face. You don't need to watch; I will get us back," Ernst reassured her.

They trotted on in silence. Still sensing Ida's unease, Ernst blurted out," Well, the nisse will be busy tonight!"

"What do you mean?" returned Ida, raising her quivering voice over the wind.

Ernst leaned closer, "I grew up with my grandmother's stories about trolls, elves, and nisse."

"I never heard of a *nisse*. What is that?"

"Oh, a *nisse*? In Sweden, it means 'dear little relative.' Usually, they live in the woods near a farm they like. They consider it their job to protect the place. They keep a vigil at night by checking on the animals and the family, making sure all is well."

"What do they look like?"

"My grandmother told me a nisse looks like a small man dressed as a farmer and wearing a red hat. People say they have cat eyes and are four-fingered. She never saw him but claimed she could feel when her nisse was about, especially when milking her goats in the barn."

Enjoying the story, Ida thought, *Some time when Mama is in the right mood, I'll ask if she ever heard of a nisse. She probably would be appalled!*

The powerful winter storm continued to press on them, driving snow into the folds of the sleigh blankets. All at once, Andy slowed. Ida felt the sleigh lurch as it rose and came down. Ernst murmured with obvious relief, "We've crossed the river." On a free rein, Andy guided them up to Ida's house. Arne was waiting and flung open the kitchen door when he heard the sleigh bells stop jingling.

Over the shriek of the storm, Arne shouted, "Ernst, get that animal under cover. I will take care of my daughter." Arne stepped up to pull Ida out of the sleigh. He faintly snarled something more, but his words were lost in the blizzard. Nevertheless, the tone in his voice left Ernst in no doubt of Arne's opinion of his carelessness in not leaving the dance in time to get Ida home before the storm descended. Quickly hustled into the house by her father, Ida was disappointed that she did not get a chance to turn around and wave goodbye to Ernst before he drove off.

Long into the night, the two sisters, Ida and Caroline, snuggled together under a quilt on Ida's narrow bed. Caroline plied Ida with questions about the evening's festivities. Ida did not share a word about the scary ride home. Later, she dreamed about being in a frightening, dark space while securely held in Ernst's arms. The thought pleased her, and the memory of dancing with him set her heart to fluttering.

SECTION 2

The Promise

CHAPTER 8

The Gifts

He fell in love with someone who needed him.

 $\mathcal{A}$ *s winter quickly* turned to spring, Ernst sometimes showed up at the kitchen door in the middle of the afternoon. Rapping at the entrance to get Ida's attention, he would call in, "Can I get a cup of coffee?" Ida would nod and do his bidding. At first, they spoke on safe and easy subjects, like the weather and family news. Before long, their conversations widened as Ida began to banter with Ernst. Ida surprised them both when she started to express opinions that she did not know she had. As time went on, they discovered in each other compatible spirits, and their friendship grew.

One day, Ernst stood with his back to the barn and peered around the corner. He watched Ida at work as she moved between the scrubbing board set inside the metal tub and the clothesline. It was a blustery day, and the sheets billowed in the wind. The washing effort left Ida's toffee-colored hair in wild disarray, with curls loosening from her woolen scarf. Against the backdrop of the white sheets, Ernst thought Ida looked captivating. He couldn't deny how he felt, and he was tired of safeguarding his feelings.

He sucked up his courage before stepping into view. "Well, you're a fair sight on this day."

Ida turned at hearing his voice. He noticed she was standing ankle-deep in cold water as she hung the bellowing bed sheets on the line. Concerned, he asked, "Why did you not wait for a more agreeable day?"

Removing the clothespins from her mouth, Ida laughed. "Yes, there will be warmer days ahead, but I didn't want to give my uncle a chance to argue with me about spring cleaning. So, I just didn't mention it."

Ernst chuckled, "You are learning how to manage Anthony." Ernst drew closer as he murmured in a softer, more serious tone, "You work so hard, Ida. How I wish those cold puddles at your feet were dandelions. I think you look like a nymph right out of a fairytale."

"Stop looking at me like that!" murmured Ida, blushing as she glanced up.

"But you look so beautiful!" returned Ernst, enjoying the exchange and trying to provoke her. "I like it when your hair blows in the breeze like it is trying to escape."

"I'm not pretty, and I certainly don't need to hear it. Now behave yourself!" Alarmed by the very personal compliment, Ida ran her fingers through her hair, twisting and tucking the loose strands back into place. "I need to check the stove," she said, turning and rushing abruptly back to the kitchen with her face flaming.

Ernst couldn't recall ever seeing a woman so spooked by

speaking with him, but it made him laugh. He gave her a minute to collect herself and then followed. Gently tapping on the kitchen door frame, he asked, "Is there any coffee left, Ida? I sure could use a drink."

Keeping her eyes lowered warily, Ida brought a steaming cup to the door and handed it through to him. As their fingers brushed, she was taken aback to feel his warmth. When she glanced up in surprise, he winked at her.

"Thank you, Ida," Ernst replied lightly, amused by her reaction. Then in a daring move, he reached up to brush her cheek. "You had a bit of flour there," he explained.

"Oh!" exclaimed Ida, flustered, stepping back as she raised a corner of her apron to wipe her face.

Ernst grinned. *How I wish I could put your nerves at ease. You have yet to learn, Ida; I am a patient man.*

A few days later, Ernst, feeling even bolder, decided to ask Ida if she would like to go for a walk.

Ida's face lit up, and she immediately responded. "Yes, after supper when I have finished my chores at home."

Later, through their respective kitchen windows, Arne, Hannah, and Uncle Anthony watched the couple stroll off. Finally, their suspicions were confirmed: something was stirring between them.

—⁓—

A few days later, after hunting for eggs, Ida returned to her uncle's house to find a narrow wooden board with a curious handle hanging from the kitchen doorknob. She picked it up to look at it more closely. One side of the object was flat, and the other side had a wooden handle. She could see the shape of a horse's head carved into the wood. Puzzled, Ida carried it into the kitchen and placed it aside.

When Hannah arrived for a visit, she noticed the familiar item lying on the table. "Where did this come from?" exclaimed Hannah.

Ida shrugged, "I am not sure."

"This is a *mangletraer*," Hannah chuckled and grinned, knowing the implication. Clarifying her amusement, she continued, "Ida, this is a courting gift. No doubt from Ernst."

"What?" sputtered the bewildered girl, her eyes widening.

"When Ernst came to us to ask about courting you, I mentioned how your father gave me one of these mangletraers long ago. With this gift, Ernst is honoring you as well as our old customs."

"But it is a mangle…for beating out wrinkles in clothes," remarked Ida flatly.

"Yes, but it is more. It is a gesture of the man's intentions."

"What…what am I to do?" asked Ida, slightly giddy.

"Well, you have already done it. If you were not interested in the man, the custom is to leave it hanging on the door for him to retrieve later. If you bring it inside your home, as you have done, it is an agreement of your interest."

"Just like that?"

"It is hard for a man to know how a woman feels about him. He can be left in misery far too long, waiting for an answer. The old customs serve well when a simple yes or no answer is needed."

Later that day, Ernst apprehensively approached the house. When Ida looked out the window, he saw her face blossom.

Relieved to see her smiling, he wondered, *What will it take for her to lose her composure?* He received his answer when Ida came flying out of the kitchen, wrapped her open arms around his neck, and surprised him with a quick kiss on his cheek.

"Yes!" she whispered. Then pulling back, she added, "Now off with you; we can walk later and talk about us."

Ernst walked away with a smile plastered on his face. He pulled out his harmonica and began to play a popular tune.

> *I hold her hand and she holds mine,*
> *And that's a very good sign.*
> *That she's my tootsy wootsy*
> *In a good old summertime."*

———

One month later, following Sunday services at the Landstad Lutheran Church, the minister announced their engagement. Ida blushed, and Ernst beamed. Afterward, the congregation gathered around to offer congratulations. Before long, the plans for the upcoming May wedding were underway.

———

A heavy spring rain came in April and lasted three days, saturating the ground and putting a hold on any thoughts of plowing. Having completed their necessary chores, including sharpening their plows, Arne and Uncle Anthony whiled away the afternoon playing checkers. Hannah and Caroline had just finished making apple pies and placing them into the oven to bake.

With a lull in the day, the women sat down at the table to watch the men at play. It was not long before the conversation drifted to the plans for the upcoming wedding. It had been decided the couple would marry in town, and then later in the afternoon, Arne and Hannah would host the wedding supper.

"Ernst asked me for a suggestion for the Morgongåva. Do you have any ideas?" Hannah asked, breaking the men's concentration on their game. The *Morgongåva* was a gift from the groom to his bride, given in the spirit of a Norwegian tradition.

"She is already getting that new dress, Mama," commented Caroline straining her eyes as she was now mending a patch on Oscar's overalls.

"We need not follow those old customs," returned Arne.

Hannah scowled at both grudging remarks from her husband and daughter. After catching the warning look, Caroline grimaced and dipped her face to concentrate on her sewing. Hannah continued, "My mother always talked about the old ways. The three gifts were given for a reason. They set the notion that the marriage was not to be taken lightly."

"What do you mean, Mama?" asked Caroline.

"When I was betrothed, my mother insisted Arne provide three gifts to the bride to secure the marriage agreement. These gifts were different than the engagement gifts. Do you remember the gifts, Arne?"

"Of course, I do. As you said, your mother insisted. Mind you, I did not come by the gifts so easily. I was just passing through the area when we met," responded Arne.

"Well then, what were the gifts?" asked Caroline impatiently.

"The first gift was a silver spoon. I brought it from home in Iowa and gave it to your mother the day I came asking for her hand."

"A spoon?"

"It was not the object. It was because of what it was made of. The silver is said to ward off the evil trolls and bad spirits that would get in the way of marriage plans!"

"Do you think it helped, Hannah?" quipped Arne.

Ignoring the remark, Hannah continued, "For the *benkegave*, or the second gift, your father brought me a goat. Where in heaven he came by that animal in this Dakota territory was a wonder. He never would tell me, either."

Arne chuckled, "Best not ask, for I will not tell!"

Hannah shook her head at their private joke. "That gift declared your father's intention to release me from my parents' home. If we weren't so poor, he would have given me a horse and saddle or a piece of jewelry."

Caroline wrinkled her brow and smirked at the image of Papa arriving, leading a goat for her mother. "Now, tell Caroline of the last gift. Your parents always thought the wedding day gift was the most useful, didn't they, Hannah?" remarked Arne, tipping back on his chair and puffing smoke circles from his pipe.

Hannah recalled how Arne presented her with a small wooden box on her wedding day. "He made it from a tree that grew beside the Red River near our home. Inside, your father placed an envelope containing some hard-earned money. In the old days, times were uncertain. The money signified I would have some resources to fall back on if I became a widow."

Arne cleared his throat, and Hannah predicted what he would say. "It was yourself that left it behind in Caledonia when I came to retrieve you."

Hannah sighed regretfully. "Yes, Arne, I know. It was a lovely thing, and you even added those carvings on the top."

"Where is it now, Mama?" asked Caroline.

"I guess my sister must have it," she mused. "You know, Arne, at the time, you promised to make me another!" reminded Hannah. Arne shrugged his shoulder as he returned his attention to the checkerboard.

Uncle Anthony, who had remained silent during the conversation, finally sounded off. "Ernst has done well so far, offering the gifts. Ida was surely surprised to receive the mangle-traer. Somehow, he also has managed to keep the other gift a secret."

A few of the family members were aware that Ernst was building a rocking chair for Ida. "The man takes the lantern out most mornings to work on it. She doesn't suspect a thing, and as he keeps it under a canvas in the granary, I think it will be a real surprise."

"He is a craftsman, that is certain," reaffirmed Arne. Caroline, meanwhile, was making a mental note. *I need to sneak over there and look when Ida is not around.*

"I think that rocker is gift enough for him to give her. We as a family should provide a wedding gift, something practical.

"What about a platter? That girl doesn't own any of her own dishes," Hannah suggested. Anthony shrugged his shoulder. As an avowed bachelor, he did not put stock in anything as trivial as "fine" dishware.

Finishing his cold coffee with a gulp, Anthony looked around the table. He announced, "I saw a fine clock at the Minneapolis Store in Grafton."

A short silence followed his comment before Hannah made her opinion known. "That is certainly too extravagant. Ida and Ernst do not have a house or shelf to put a clock on."

"Nevertheless, it would be a fine gift," Anthony insisted and then added, "We could split the cost."

"I think my brother is right on this. I have full confidence that Ernst and Ida will make a good marriage. If I did not, we would not have agreed to it in the first place," concluded Arne. *Besides,* he thought ironically, *giving them time is the most precious gift of all.*

With Arne's opinion, the decision was made. Anthony and Caroline went to town the next week and purchased a chiming clock. Arriving back home, they delivered the wooden crate into Hannah's care. The gift was stowed in her closet and covered with a blanket to await the wedding day.

Later, when Hannah finally saw the clock, she admitted how handsome it was with its oak case, musical chime, and the brass pendulum swinging back and forth. While she continued to contend it was a frivolous gift, she secretly admired the timepiece. *Maybe there will come a time when I might own such a fine clock myself!*

CHAPTER 9

The Wedding

Ernst noted that Ida's narrow worldview widened
in just a few days.

The wedding day dawned clear and bright. Inside the Oihus house, the family scurried about, managing the details of the festivities to come.

Upstairs, Ida was in her bedroom. The new olive-colored dress with pink satin trim was laid out on her bed. Looking out through her window, Ida mused, *Ernst is probably already dressed in his best suit.*

A light rap at the door brought Ida to attention. She saw Caroline standing at the bedroom door, staring at her.

Caroline was making a memory of the image of her sister sitting in a stream of sunlight. Ida looked angelic with her long, wavy blonde hair unfurled against the backdrop of a new white corset and lacey chemise. Her bare toes peeked out from under the flounced petticoat.

Looking up, Ida remarked, "Seems like a great deal of commotion downstairs."

"There certainly is! Mama is working on the sponge for your cake," Caroline informed her.

"I can smell it baking," returned Ida.

"Me, too; I can hardly wait to have some!" Caroline admitted. "It is time for you to get ready. Ma sent me up to help you."

Ida stood up and planted a kiss on her sister's cheek. "Yes, Caroline, help me get dressed and arrange my hair. I'm not sure I can pull my strings and hook my bodice straight today."

Caroline fussed over Ida, carefully assisting her into her new outfit. "How lovely this dress fits you," she commented with admiration. "Minnie did a wonderful job."

"Show me in the mirror."

Holding up a mirror, Caroline stepped away, moving it up and down, so Ida could get a sense of the full effect of her new dress.

When Ida sat down to pull on her stockings, Caroline reached over to drop a coin into her shoe. "Father sent up the silver piece. Mother wanted me to remind you to put it into your left shoe for luck and said you should remember it is for a prosperous and happy marriage."

When Ida was ready, Caroline led the way down the ladder steps. Emerging from the stairwell, Ida saw the sitting room had been transformed. The boys had extended the family dining table with wood planks, which Hannah covered with her best tablecloths and sheets. Early spring flowers of tulips and bright yellow forsythia were placed strategically around the room for decoration. Clean napkins and the best dishware were arranged on the table, ready to be filled with cookies, jelly, and pickles.

In addition to the delicious odor of baking cake, the smell of roasting meat wafted through the air. Nine-year-old Laura appeared in front of Ida and presented her with a bridal wreath of smilax vines. "Mama helped me make this for you."

Ida bent low for the young girl to place it on her head. When Hannah came into the room, she stopped upon seeing her daughter. *Our first to marry...are you ready for this?* she wondered.

Pulling Ida in the direction of the parlor, Caroline insisted, "Go see yourself in the looking glass. Our little mirror isn't good enough on this day."

Ida stood still in front of the mirror and stared. No longer did she look like a schoolgirl or her father's tomboy. With her unruly hair pulled back and pinned high under the traditional wedding wreath, she suddenly felt different. *I look older, taller, polished...pretty. What will Ernst think?* With that thought, the transition moment had arrived. All the panicky feelings of doubt about being "good enough" to become Ernst's wife disappeared.

Ida turned when she felt the weight of a hand on her shoulder. Her father had quietly slid next to her and put his arm about her waist. Together they turned back to the image in the mirror. With eyes watering, Pa whispered with pride, "You have always been a fine daughter, and now you will become a wonderful wife for Ernst."

Ida waited nervously in the parlor with her mother and sisters until they heard the noise of Ernst's arrival. Arne murmured as he looked out the window, "Looks like Ernst had a busy night." He noted the boy had scrubbed the mud from the buggy and had curried away the last of Andy's thick coat of winter hair.

After greeting Ernst with a handshake, Arne pointed toward the parlor saying, "Ida is waiting for you."

Laura and Alma were standing ready in front of the closed doors. Ernst grinned as he entered the dining room, and the young girls started to giggle. After giving a three-knock signal, they slowly opened the parlor doors. Caroline began playing a jolly wedding march on the piano. Ernst saw Ida standing in front of him, radiant and regal. His heart throbbed.

—◦◦◦—

The happy couple was soon on their way to town for the ceremony. As they drove out of the farmyard, Ernst turned to Ida, "I just want to look at you. Do you know how beautiful you are? Knowing we are to marry makes me happy."

Ida put her hand on Ernst's arm and gently squeezed.

Arriving in Grafton, eight miles to the southeast, Ernst and Ida went directly to the livery. After assisting Ida down from the buggy, he guided her across the muddy yard scattered with water-filled hoof and wheel impressions. The couple walked the short block to Hill Avenue. Over his arms, Ernst carried Ida's wreath of leaves. Some passersby on the street greeted them warmly as they recognized the Scandinavian nuptial symbol.

Ida's parents had arranged to have their wedding portrait taken at Ball and Rindahl's Studio. The photographer snapped their image with Ida standing behind a table. The photographer posed Ida with one arm tucked behind her waist and her left hand resting lightly on the edge of a table. Ernst was seated in a wicker chair turned toward his bride. They were dressed in their best clothes, and with the impending marriage just an hour away, they stood serious and still. Mr. Rindahl took two photographic plates and informed them, "I will make copies of the best one."

When the couple stepped out onto Hill Avenue, Ida and Ernst looked at each other and laughed. "Why should we be so stern-looking on our special day?" asked a grinning Ernst.

When they reached Fifth Street, they turned and continued to walk toward the courthouse. Ernst commented, "Herman is to meet us at the military statue." The statue he referred to was the Spanish-American War monument, placed just six months earlier on the grounds of the county building.

Reaching their destination, they paused at the monument's base to soberly read the inscriptions. One of the soldier's names was particularly familiar to Ernst as the man was a fellow Swede. They admired the bronze replica of the uniformed soldier standing tall. The day the contingent of uniformed men was sent off to the West Coast of California, the train depot filled with hundreds of cheering citizens. The war was brief, and while the idea of death was unimaginable, the Grafton area lost eight young men.

"Are you ready, brother?" came a question that startled them out of their musing. Ernst turned to see his brother grinning at him. Just behind Herman, Ida's friend, Hilda, had also just arrived. After exchanging greetings, they entered the courthouse.

Ernst turned and handed the bridal wreath to Hilda. The ladies went down the hall, searching for facilities to tidy up while Ernst and Herman waited nearby. The wedding was scheduled for ten o'clock that morning; however, they first were required to apply for a marriage license.

During the brief ceremony held in the courtroom, Ida was startled when Ernst produced a narrow golden wedding band to slip on her slim finger. Ida had entirely forgotten about a ring. Her gasp of surprise made him smile. Afterward, the couple and their witnesses signed the court documents. Ida felt a thrill run through her when Judge Shepard declared her as Mrs. Ernst Ottoson for the first time.

The friendly group then proceeded to the Exchange House. After they were seated, Herman raised his glass and offered the first congratulations of the day to the new couple. The foursome leisurely dined on oysters and sandwiches before returning home.

—⁓—

At home, the Oihus family and friends continued preparing a sumptuous wedding feast in honor of the newlyweds to be served later that afternoon. The menu included turkey and dressing, Swedish meatballs, mashed potatoes, gravy, cranberries, vegetables, pickles, rolls, and coffee. Hannah had requested help from two women friends from church. While they put the finishing touches on the food, Hannah finished layering the wedding cake. The fancy cake was a family favorite. It consisted of a vanilla sponge layered with rich custard and fruit, then lightly frosted.

About four o'clock, the happy couple returned home to warm greetings from all. When the guests assembled around the table, Arne stood to offer a toast, officially welcoming

Ernst to the family. His words were followed by Hannah's as she began to recite a Norwegian blessing, and the rest of those present joined in:

> Lord, Your earth carries enough food for everyone. Thank You for the part You want us to have. Teach us how to set a long table in the world so that everyone can come and feel welcome.

After the meal, they opened wedding gifts, including the oak clock and some china dishes. Finally, Ernst summoned Ida to the porch, where he revealed the rocker hidden beneath a quilt. Sitting in the polished rocking chair, Ida glowed with delight as she listened to the story of how long Ernst had worked in secret to build it just for her.

—⁓—

At Uncle Anthony's insistence, Ernst planned to take Ida away for a short honeymoon. The day after their wedding, she put on her olive-green dress again and packed a few things in a small suitcase to prepare for a weekend in Grand Forks. She had heard people talking about Grand Forks, but she was unsure what to expect, having never been there.

Ida's parents and siblings showered the couple with barley as they climbed into the buggy to leave for Grafton's Great Northern train station. Ida knew she was to open her hands and try to catch the kernels as they rained down. The more she caught, the brighter the future it signified for the marriage. Once they were off, Ida nudged her husband to show him the great number of barley seeds that she had collected in her hands.

After purchasing the train tickets and climbing aboard, Ida

rushed ahead to sit on the depot side of the compartment. She promptly pressed her nose to the window to peer out excitedly. As the train lurched forward, Ida admitted she had never traveled farther than Grafton. "Of course, I have taken the short line to Grafton, but my father always says it is better to save the fare and use a horse or walk. It is only a few miles."

As the train rolled out of town, the view opened to the flat Dakota prairie. Eagerly Ida elbowed Ernst to look out the window every time she spied something new or curious that caught her attention. Ernst just grinned. He now understood why Anthony suggested, "Take in the town. It will be fun to show Ida something different."

When they neared the Minto, Ardoch, and Manvel depots, the train's shrill whistle sounded off as the engine slowed to a stop. At Manvel, there was a flurry of platform activity. "Watch, Ida," urged Ernst, pointing down the platform and sticking his head partway out of the open window. They watched as men pushed a wide ramp up to the last boxcar. When the door slid partly open, a commotion followed. The observant bystanders nearby cautiously backed off on cue to the racket of yelling and snorting that erupted from the boxcar.

"Looks like there will be a horse auction," remarked Ernst. They watched as men led the anxious horses down the ramp. Once on solid ground, some of the uncooperative animals began sidestepping and circling the handlers. In turn, the men jerked back on the lead lines.

"They sure don't like the train," observed Ida, sitting back down on the bench and feeling sorrow for the plight of the horses standing so near the idling steam engine.

Ten miles farther south, Ida and Ernst arrived at their destination of Grand Forks in the middle of the afternoon. On stepping down from the train, Ida staggered a little, reaching for Ernst's elbow. He smiled, saying, "It is just a leftover sensation you feel from riding the train. It will go away in a few minutes after you've walked." Picking up Ida's bag, Ernst led the way toward the town center. Turning onto Third Street, Ida was astonished to take in the seemingly endless storefronts and the wide streets busy with traffic.

Famished, the couple stepped into the first café they saw. As Ida perused the menu, she was amazed at how a cook could provide the bewildering array of different choices. Finally, after selecting what she wanted, Ernst helped her order.

Before long, Ida spotted their waitress coming toward their table carrying two fully loaded plates of food. Ida leaned back as the woman placed sizzling ham and steaming hotcakes in front of her. Ernst looked at Ida and quietly chuckled as he picked up his fork. *Maybe this is the first time she has been served a meal that she did not need to help prepare.*

As they dug into their satisfying meal, Ernst commented. "When I was in Grand Forks a few years ago, I don't remember it being so busy. This place is growing."

"Why do you think it is?" questioned Ida.

"Well," Ernst paused. "I suppose the biggest draw is that time has proven people can make a successful living here. Grand Forks was only a small settlement on the end of the train line. When the land was opening for settlement, only men who intended to farm came. Now, more women, families, and business ventures are attaching themselves to the way of life out here."

"And with more people, that means more of everything. Is that right?" asked Ida.

"Yes, folks aren't needing to be so self-sufficient anymore, especially if they don't have to be. With a little prosperity and spare change in your pocket, you can buy convenient or more efficient things. That is what drives business. That is why the mercantile stocks canned peaches, ready-made clothes, and tools."

"Spare money? Doesn't seem like there is ever any of that at home," remarked Ida.

"Probably the wheat crops drive the economy around here. Still, I think both you and I were raised to be frugal."

Changing the topic, Ida questioned, "I wonder how many more people live here than in Grafton?"

"I overheard someone say more than 10,000 when we were on the train."

Back on the boardwalk, strolling arm in arm, the couple found many things to admire and marvel at. Ida slowed and came to a stop. "Look at those dresses, hats, and shoes," she commented, admiring the window display of a women's dress shop.

Weary of window shopping, Ernst pulled Ida in the direction of the river. Standing on the riverbank, she observed with obvious admiration, "I never imagined the Red River looked like this!" They quietly watched as several boats drifted past them. One larger boat had to push against the muddy current. "Is Grand Forks like your city in Sweden?"

"Oh, no, Goteborg is much, much larger and older. It is a seaport town, and the city begins at the edge of the water and goes inland a long way."

Ernst and Ida turned when they heard a comment from a man passing by, "So this is the Mighty Red." The man paused to explain himself when he realized he had the couple's attention. After tipping his hat in Ida's direction, he said, "Please excuse me. I sometimes talk to myself. Did you know that 40 rivers run north in our country?"

"That is curious. Seems the water should always run south, toward the equator," puzzled Ernst.

"Yes, many think that, but it simply depends on elevation, where the headwaters begin and where the river ends," explained the man in a shabby brown suit. They watched as he tucked a tattered book under one arm and cupped his hands around his eyes as he scanned the river.

"The river runs all the way to Canada," offered Ernst.

"Actually, it is about 500 miles from the headwaters to Lake Winnipeg," added the man. Turning to Ernst, he extended his hand and introduced himself. "I'm Professor Randall. I will soon begin teaching American history at the university here in town. Do you folks live around here?" Struggling to understand the older man's German accent, Ernst finally explained they were visiting but lived nearby.

Upon learning they were from Grafton, the man surprised them by launching into an engaging history lesson, explaining how the railroad's arrival had influenced the development of the local economies. "Every time a railway comes to an area, a community has great potential to develop and flourish. For instance, many years ago, the Red River was a valuable way to transport goods for the Indians, fur traders, and settlers. It's a wonder the railroad didn't run the tracks along the river."

"But that would have changed everything for the place where we live," commented Ernst.

"Ever hear about the town of Acton?" queried the professor.

Ernst and Ida gave him an affirmative nod. "My father used to go there for supplies when he first came to this area," Ida commented. "It took days for him to make the trip."

"The town of Acton, or Kelly's Point as you probably know it, is directly west of Grafton. It was a significant trading post located on the river in the day. Everything changed when the Great Northern Railroad decided to lay tracks in Grand Forks and then divert the route westward."

"So, while Grand Forks and Grafton thrived, Acton did not," concluded Ernst.

"That is exactly what happened. Train travel is easier and faster than horse and carriage on paths and rutted roads." Building in enthusiasm, the man went on. "Transportation is a growing industry. Just you wait. The time will come when horses will be obsolete, their place taken over by horseless carriages."

"Horseless carriages?" repeated Ida timidly, trying to envision what that would be.

"I lived in Detroit a couple of years ago and got to see something called a Quadricycle. The contraption, powered by a gas engine, moved along on four bicycle tires."

"How could you steer such a thing?" questioned Ernst.

"It has a handle like a tiller. The man driving it pushed the control side to side. It was a wonder."

"I'd like to see that sometime," replied Ernst, impressed.

"There are a few around on the streets in the bigger cities. Folks say they are a rich man's toy, but maybe not for long. That

Ford fellow is clever. I heard he was born a poor farmer boy, but he keeps overcoming problems by tinkering with ideas already out there. I read that he thinks the runabouts eventually should be affordable for anyone who wants to drive one in the future.

"That is hard to believe," responded Ernst.

"This is an age of technology with all manner of possibilities on the horizon." With that comment, the professor pulled out his watch. Noting the time, he looked up, saying, "I must be on my way." They watched as he turned and walked rapidly away, leaving Ida and Ernst with something to discuss.

The pleasant and carefree weekend passed quickly. Ernst noted with satisfaction that he had widened Ida's narrow worldview in just a few days.

—∿∿—

For a time, all seemed well as the seasonal farm routine set the motion of the days. Ida resumed her duties as housekeeper and cook while Ernst worked with Anthony on the fieldwork demands. It was clear that Ernst was "over the top" in love with Ida and married life. On their day off, Ida and Ernst often hitched up the horse, Andy, and ambled out of the yard to spend time exploring the area. They talked of their future and dreams of owning their own farm as they admired farmsteads and crops along the way. Sometimes they went to Grafton to enjoy some ice cream or the opera house to see a show, hear a guest speaker, or listen to a political debate. When the word went out that the Ringling Brothers Circus was coming to town, they planned to take in all the excitement.

CHAPTER 10

Bloody Rags

...her foot caught the handle of the hidden metal bucket

"*Not now!*" *exclaimed* Ida in frustration, looking out the kitchen window. She had just noticed her mother, Hannah, coming toward her following the worn path linking her parents' home with Uncle Anthony's farm. Hannah moved along leisurely, pacing herself to the two-year-old Clarence waddling behind her. The cool breeze played with her apron, causing it to billow up as Hannah walked.

Hurriedly, Ida gathered all the troublesome rags into a bucket before covering it with a dirty shirt. Then shoving the bucket under the table, she prayed it would remain hidden. She glanced around her uncle's kitchen quarters just as Hannah stepped onto the porch and lightly knocked on the door.

"Good morning, Ida," greeted Hannah cheerfully as she pulled open the screen door and ducked inside. She was now carrying the little boy tucked on her hip. "Are your new fly rags ready yet?"

"Almost. I'll get the string up this week," replied Ida. Every year during spring cleaning, her mother placed a new row of torn rag pieces attached to a length of twine to hang over the door frame. While the fly rags were to keep flies out of the house, living on a farm with livestock near the home made it seem like a useless effort. Along with the flies, bugs, grasshoppers, and mosquitoes were also daily nuisances during the summertime.

Ida went to the stove to drag the coffee pot closer to the heat. "Would you like a cup, Mama?" asked Ida, reaching up to an overhead shelf.

"Yes, please," Hannah replied. Hannah's eyes began to rove critically around the room when Ida turned her back. She noted the pile of undone washing and pot of water on the stove just beginning to steam. "Isn't it getting a bit late to begin your washing?"

Ida shrugged. She had expected her mother's judgmental remark, and even though she was on edge, Ida tried not to sound irritated. "I'm just feeling down today. Come and sit with me," she invited. "Rest after your walk."

Hannah moved to sit at the table, and Ida slid her coffee cup closer. Upon noticing Clarence standing at her knee, Ida said, "Here, have a biscuit." She reached for a bowl of the sugar sprinkled golden-colored biscuits she had made for breakfast and handed it to the boy.

"These look tasty, Ida," replied Hannah as she also reached for one to dunk in her coffee.

"Yes, Uncle Anthony says he will keep buying sugar as long as I am willing to bake his cookies and biscuits!" brightened Ida.

Standing up and taking the corner of her apron in hand,

Ida reached for the hot coffee pot to carry to the waiting cups on the table. As she gingerly poured out the steaming liquid, Ida coughed. The coffee bounced and splashed a large brown stain on the clean tablecloth. *"Uff da,"* Ida exclaimed. As Hannah blotted the spill, Ida sat slouched and quiet.

The conversation seemed to have run its course as they quietly sipped the hot coffee. Hannah's eyebrows furrowed as she looked Ida over, noticing how pale she appeared as she sat limply across the table from her with downcast eyes. *I wonder what is wrong with her. Something is on her mind,* thought Hannah with a mother's intuition.

Hannah reached out to touch Ida's hand. Finding she needed to move in closer, she adjusted her chair. The movement caused her foot to catch the handle of the hidden metal bucket. When she pulled back, the bucket overturned, spilling the contents at her feet. Leaning over to see what she had disturbed, Hannah gasped.

Ida stiffened and stared straight ahead, waiting for her mother to speak first.

"What is this, Ida?" whispered Hannah, her eyes round with disbelief.

"Oh, Mama, I did not want you to see this," sniffed Ida in distress as she slid to her knees on the floor. Gathering up blood-tinged rags, Ida confessed, "The coughing came back, and this time there has been a little blood. You know Dr. Gamble told us my lungs were bad," sobbed Ida, realizing how shocked her mother must be.

"Does Ernst know about this?" Hannah calmly asked.

"I think he suspects, but he is working many hours right

now, so maybe he doesn't see. He always is saying that I need rest. There is more, Mama. I think I am pregnant."

—∞—

A week of unrelenting turmoil for Ida had passed since Hannah's visit. That day her mother stayed until her chores were complete. Together they worked away in a daze, washing clothes and bedding before hanging them out on the line to dry in the cold wind. Hannah insisted on scrubbing the blood-stained rags until only faint brown outlines remained. The silence hung as gloomy as the gray clouds gathering on the western horizon.

When the hungry men came for lunch, Anthony, Ernst, and Eddy were handed simple ham sandwiches on thick slices of bread. Sensing something was amiss, they took the proffered food and hastily retreated to eat.

Hannah refused, despite Ida's pleas, to go home and take care of the others. She sent Clarence off with Eddy, saying, "Tell Caroline to prepare supper. I will be home later." She didn't prepare to leave until the laundry was folded, and the ham hock and beans were simmering on the stove. And before she left, Hannah advised, "Talk to Ernst about this. Tell him everything. He needs to know you need help. The others should know too, but it can wait until after seeing the doctor. You are not meant to bear this burden alone."

"Pa…what about Pa?" asked Ida wearily. The thought of the grief she would cause her father was too much to bear.

"I will tell your father of this. It serves no purpose not to let him know." Those were Hannah's last words as she positioned her scarf on her head and stepped out the door. Hannah would wait until later that night before allowing herself to feel the anguish about what was ahead for her young daughter.

Ida needed to think. Wrapping a shawl about her shoulders, she left the small wood-frame house and headed towards the solitude of the river. Settling on a tree stump, she barely noticed the dropping temperature until sleeting raindrops began to fall. The cool water on her face felt soothing. *Give me the strength to bear what I must,* she prayed.

The day they returned to see Dr. Gamble, the eight-mile trek over dirt roads seemed unbearably long, though Ernst tried to avoid the worst of the deep ruts and mudholes. Once they arrived, there was a long delay in the doctor's office. His waiting room was full of patients, including a crying baby and a man with his foot wrapped in a bloody bandage.

Finally, when it was Ida's turn to be seen, she stood, giving Ernst a final glance with worried eyes as she headed to the exam room.

When Ida returned to the waiting room after her exam, she was told her family was waiting in the parlor. Upon entering there, she immediately noticed the grim faces of her mother and Dr. Gamble. They both looked up when she entered, falling silent mid-sentence.

"Where is Ernst?" she asked pensively.

"He is outside. I will call him in," replied the doctor, rising from his chair.

Seeing the forlorn look on Ida's face, Hannah came to stand beside her daughter, who was now leaning into the door frame for support.

"Mama, I am afraid," Ida whispered.

"Let's listen to what the doctor says," soothed Hannah.

After Ernst returned, the doctor directed the women to sit. Ernst chose to remain standing. He was nervously clutching his hat as his eyes lay on Ida. After taking a seat behind his large desk, Dr. Gamble took off his spectacles. They watched as he slowly polished the lenses, giving the sense that he was carefully gathering his words.

Clearing his throat, he began to speak very formally. "Upon evaluation, your lungs are worse. Your symptoms—the fevers, coughing fits, productive congestion, and now the show of blood—continue to confirm you have consumption."

"What about the baby?" asked Ida numbly.

"The pregnancy will only add to the aggravation of your lungs. These months ahead will not be easy. I believe they will take a toll on your health."

Stunned, Ernst interrupted, "But, what can be done? She will be able to carry the child…right?"

"I believe the baby will come mid-October. In the meantime, it is critical you rest and no heavy lifting. I mean it, Ida. No heavy armloads of laundry or buckets of milk. Even your mother's baby is too heavy for you to carry." The doctor included Ernst and Hannah in his gaze.

"Will the baby be healthy?" asked Hannah, trying to gauge if the doctor was implying the worst.

"Ida, you told me you've lost weight. That cannot continue. You must fortify yourself with food for this child to grow—even if you have to force yourself to eat."

"She tries to eat, Dr. Gamble, but she has a lot of morning sickness. She usually just ends up picking at the food," responded Ernst, his voice trailing off worriedly.

"The morning sickness will pass, but only time will tell how this will play out. That is about all I can tell you," concluded the doctor. "In these cases, the mother's pregnancy is often difficult. I must stress it is imperative for you to rest and eat. As I told you before, this disease is contagious. Cough into clean handkerchiefs and wash them often. I expect the episodes to increase."

"You must know, and I am sorry to say this, but it may be that Ida will not be able to carry this child. Or she may deliver early, and the baby will be small. Only God knows what the outcome will be," stressed Dr. Gamble.

Hannah agonized in her mind, *This time should be filled with joy, and this illness steals it from her.*

Ernst took Ida's hand as he handed her his handkerchief and exchanged another worried look with Hannah.

Dr. Gamble went on, "Ida, you must find courage. Although you feel poorly, you are a strong woman, which is an advantage."

"I know how to help her during confinement, but tell us what to do about the sickness," begged Hannah, frustrated.

"Ease her symptoms. I can suggest some remedies—a cough elixir and something for the fever," replied the doctor. "Many patients are lured by cures in a bottle, but I warn you, there is not one. Treating her normally as much as possible is the best. So, unfortunately, Ida, you must endure what comes. I'm sorry to say this. I truly am."

"Nothing?" uttered Ernst, recoiling in shock. "That is it?"

"This is a brutal climate for consumption. You know the wild swings of temperatures all year long. Some medical doctors propose milder weather might be helpful. The other thing is to pray that the tuberculosis will progress slowly," explained Dr. Gamble.

Addressing his patient, Dr. Gamble offered, "Ida, I promise I will follow you closely, but you must do as I say. The morning sickness will soon pass. You must try to gain a little weight for your baby's sake."

Ida gave a weak nod but said nothing. She was frightened by the realization of just how sick she was.

When the office visit concluded, the group rose to leave. As Hannah paid the bill, Ernst tenderly helped Ida into her coat. After he wrapped her woolen scarf around her neck, he gently embraced her and placed a reassuring kiss on her forehead. The three of them left the building and somberly walked down Hill Avenue until they reached the corner of the buggy lot. Ernst assisted the women into their seats, shook out the dust blanket, then resettled it in their laps. With heavy hearts, they drove back to the farm. The bitter northwest winds blew at them all the way home.

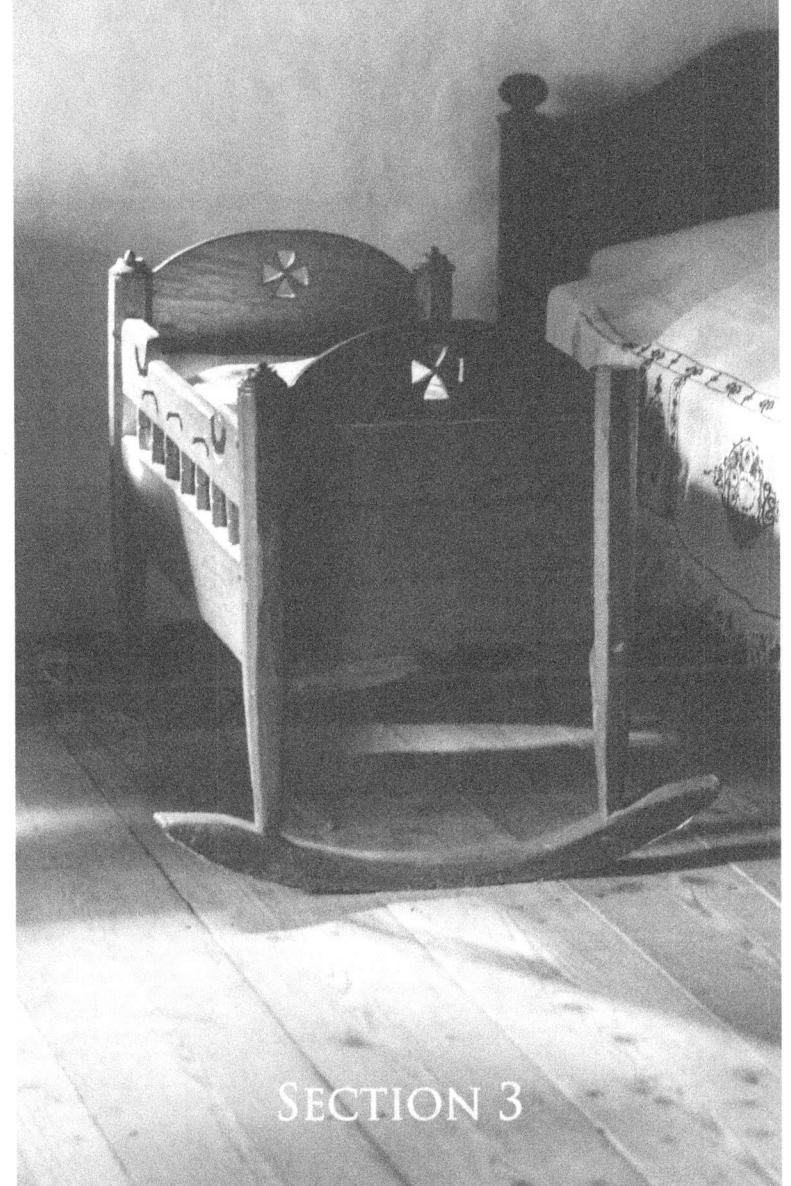

SECTION 3

Tender Moments

CHAPTER 11

A September Baby

The danger of this all…why did I not see this before?

The days of that spring and summer seemed to move slowly forward for Ida. At one point, Hannah instructed Ida to come spend her days back home. With the hectic threshing season underway, her mother wanted to keep Ida nearby. So, every morning, Ida trudged across the meadow to her parents' house. When she had finished helping Hannah with kitchen tasks or watching Clarence and Alma, Ida retreated from the hot home to the porch. She sat for hours at a time, trying to mend or read. With the summer heat and rains, necessary for growing crops, came hatches of insects. Using a lilac switch, Ida batted at the biting flies and mosquitos. By the time Ernst came to take her home, she was often cranky.

In August, Arne set up a resting bed for Ida in the parlor. Despite Ida's protest, Hannah finally decided it would be best for Ida to move back home entirely with the approaching wheat harvest. The shocks were already standing in the field to cure. Caroline helped Ida move a few of her things from her bedroom into the parlor, making it more comfortable. Besides, her father warned that she was not to climb the steep ladder-like steps to her old bedroom in her present condition.

Ida missed her privacy and her place beside her husband. However, as the days marched on and Ida continued to feel unwell, she became resigned to her situation. The family also had to adjust to her presence in the home again.

Every evening, Ernst came to sit with her. They talked of tender things, held hands, and sometimes took short walks around the barnyard. As they worked on their dreams for the future, Ernst would often repeat, "We are saving a little at a time. I want you to have a house of your own. I will work hard to care for you always." His talk warmed Ida's heart, but it was hard to imagine anything would change for the better.

When Ida grew weary and sleepy, Ernst would slip out and cross the field to return to Anthony's home. Her loneliness for her husband often came, especially at night, if she woke to find his chair empty. In those dark hours, Ida's only solace was feeling the quickening of their baby as it kicked and twisted inside her growing belly.

The threshing team had arrived the day before, and the various rigs were gathering in the field nearest the house. She could hear the roar of the steam engine as it warmed up. Ida sighed. Her time was getting near, and she could often feel the baby stirring. Resigned to staying near the house, Ida was forbidden to help in the kitchen. She was often restless and constantly tired.

Rising from a chair in the shade, Ida set out to cross the

farmyard, wanting to get a closer look at the men at work in the field. By the time she reached the granary at the edge of the yard, her thighs burned, her feet ached, and she was out of breath. Impeded by her changing body, Ida unconsciously patted her rounded belly, aching with heaviness. As she leaned against the granary, she grumbled, "I just wanted to see what was going on."

A sudden fear gripped her chest as she watched the commotion of manpower at work in the field. Other years, the harvest time brought a sense of excitement, but this time it gave her a feeling of dread. *The danger of it all. Why didn't I see this before?* Watching from her shadowy shelter, the threshing team was suddenly operational. The men were stationed about the field in shabby work clothes and wearing hats of all kinds. Those on the ground and in the back of the wagons held pitchforks. Others were maneuvering teams of horses, coming and going as they brought the wheat shocks to the combine.

The men on and near the equipment were the ones Ida was scrutinizing for safety. When she located Ernst, she gulped. He was standing close, way too close, to the shaft of the rotating belt of the engine. The long straps between the engine and the combine flapped dangerously.

Near where he stood, the wheat bundles were pitched onto the conveyer belt and fed to the combine. Inside, the machine stripped the wheat of its husks and separated the kernels from the chaff. The precious wheat kernels then spilled out from a chute into a waiting bag. When the bag reached a certain weight, it was handed over to a "sewer." The sewers quickly whipstitched the bags firmly closed and moved on to the next.

Others were loading the wheat into wagons to be taken away for storage. At the opposite end of the thresher, the dirty chaff moved along to the rear of the machine, where it fell to the ground in growing straw piles.

The work was grueling, repetitious, dangerous, relentless, and only one wrong step away from disaster. Ida admitted to herself that the thrill of the harvest was gone this year. The influx of hired men and the neighbors who worked on the line and the perpetual rush to feed a crew of 30 multiple times a day added to the frenzy of activity. All of it just made her feel left out and exhausted.

Ida could understand why her Pa became so difficult this time of year. *He and Uncle Anthony bear all this responsibility and depend on many to do their jobs right.* All efforts were focused on the fields until the wheat was safely stored.

Confined to the house per Hannah's order, Ida could see how quickly the structure her mother maintained could fall apart during threshing time. The younger children had to manage on their own. Leaving Ida in charge, Hannah repeated her instructions that the children were to be fed only gruel or sandwiches. In addition, any baked goods or other prepared dishes were to be left alone until she said otherwise.

Ida remembered that she always looked forward to threshing time as a little girl, considering it as thrilling as Christmas. Her parents knew the serious potential for harm would keep her out of the fields. They also insisted she stay away from and never speak to the working men. When Ida turned 12, she was sent to help at the cook car during lunch and then back to the house to watch the younger children at home. At the same time, her mother continued to work long, demanding hours to provide food for the crew.

Ida, still watching from the granary, noticed Ernst had moved and was now tossing bundled shocks into the combine with a pitchfork. Those belts, the belching smoke, the yelling, the heat of the day, worry for her husband's and father's safety— it all made her feel faint. Suddenly, a breeze lifted her bonnet. As she raised her hand to clamp it back down on her head, she noticed Ernst waving at her. Somehow, she wasn't reassured.

An hour later, back in the house, Ida heard the whistle on the steam engine sound off in a short sequence of tooting. When the engine stopped, a momentary silence ensued, followed by the yelling of a man taking charge. Ida got up and walked outside to see what was up. The men were gathering around the steam engine. *Something is terribly wrong.*

She watched as an empty wagon was moved to the circle of attention. Then, horrified, she saw the a body being lifted and settled into the wagon bed before the wagon eased through the throng of onlookers and made its way toward Anthony's place. Ida paused, considering what to do. *What if it was him? Should I go check? Where is Mother?* She saw Oscar heading toward the house at a gallop on one of the horses and felt both relieved that she could ask her questions and afraid of what the answers might be.

"Pa sent me for bandages and alcohol."

Seeing the worry in her eyes, he went on to explain. "The fireman caught his jacket on the shaft. He was oiling the engine. Cut bad. We need the bandages, and then I need to get the doctor."

"So, it wasn't Ernst?" confirmed Ida, gasping as she coughed.

"No, but Ernst got to the fireman first and shut off the engine. Ernst is fine, Ida."

Though visibly shaken, Ida turned away and headed into the house for the supplies. When she returned, she asked as she handed over what he needed, "Do you need help over at Anthony's?"

"No, Pa said you are to stay put. Someone will bring Ma from the cook car to help Halvor."

The doctor could not come out to the farm for several hours. When Dr. Gamble did arrive, he found his patient pale and shaken. He asked, "How did this happen, young man?"

Halvor stammered, "The most I remember was being up on the engine. I was oiling the rig, and I guess my jacket caught the shaft, then I fell."

"It sounds like you caused a lot of excitement. When Oscar came for me, they said you lost a lot of blood."

"Yeah, but as you see, Mrs. Oihus took care of the stitches on my face already."

"Yes, but those other gashes will require stitching too. Don't expect my work to be as neat as hers," said Doc Gamble, nodding to Hannah, who had just arrived.

After Halvor's accident, Ida admitted to Ernst how worried she was to have him on the machines. He shrugged off her concerns. Then two days later, while Ida was washing dishes, Ernst came to her with an injury. "I was stuffing the shocks in and caught one of the belts." The burn ran the length of his arm. Ida tenderly covered the injury with petroleum jelly and brewed willow tea to soothe the pain. The next day, Ernst got up and went back to work. Ida sighed. She knew this was the life of a farmer. Everything was tied to the land, the horses, the weather, and the men worked through it all year long, year after year.

—∿∿—

In September, Hannah insisted Ida remain near the house. She was worried that Ida might wander off on one of her walks and stumble. Hannah wanted her daughter close enough to watch her out the window, just like when she was a toddler. In addition, Hannah was concerned that Ida appeared sickly despite being so heavy-bellied and had gained almost no weight.

At night, Ida would sometimes suffer a fit of coughing. She would try to shield the sound the best she could, hacking into her pillow, but the thin walls of the house and the floor grates overhead amplified any noises. Ever aware, Hannah would rise, wrap herself in a shawl and attend to her daughter. Sometimes soothing tea helped or the application of a stringent poultice. If Ida's night fever flared, she brought a cooling cloth for her forehead and helped her into a dry nightgown.

In those quiet times, Ida drew comfort from her mother's care. Though Hannah's hands were so strong from milking that she could break an apple in two, her tender side came out when her children were most vulnerable. At those times, the brisk, short-tempered, busy woman of the daylight hours became compassionate and attentive.

Finally, on September 30, 1902, a few weeks earlier than expected, Ida began to feel twisting labor pains. A tiny baby girl finally arrived with Ida's last bit of energy. When Ernst saw his wife after the delivery, he was shocked by Ida's frail and disheveled appearance.

"Here is your daughter, Ernst," announced Hannah, triumphantly presenting him with a small bundle wrapped in a flannel blanket. At first look, the child had a reddened bald head with a wrinkled forehead.

He turned to Hannah with a questioning look. "Is she all right?"

"All newborns look like that when they arrive. Give the child a few days, and you will see what a pretty baby she is," Hannah reassured.

When Ernst pulled back the blanket to inspect his new daughter, the infant stretched her arm upward, unfurled her tiny fist, and wiggled five fingers. "She is perfect, Ida! It is a wonder to see how small she is."

Ida looked up and beamed when he dropped a kiss on her forehead. "So shall we be calling her Hazel?"

"Yes, Hazel Sophia is a good name for her, don't you think, Ernst?"

"Yes, it pleases me to remember my mother's name too.

Ida asked, "Will you sit with me a while?"

Hannah grunted in disapproval. "Leave her, for now. She needs her rest. The poor girl did not have an easy time of it." Hannah then ushered Ernst out, but not before saying quietly, "Come back later. We need to talk." A worried Ernst closed the parlor door as he left.

———

Two months later, Ida was still living at her parents' home. Ernst, increasingly frustrated, wanted Ida to return to Anthony's with their child. He ranted to himself. *I should be taking care of my own family.*

Every time he broached the subject, Hannah asserted, "She is better with us. You don't understand what a young mother in Ida's situation needs. Maybe when she is stronger. Besides, that baby is not easy to care for."

Ernst acquiesced, but inside he was in turmoil. More than anything, he wanted his darling wife to regain her cheerful disposition and return to health. *Surely there is something I can do about this situation.* But as the winter settled in, Ida did not rebound from the toll her pregnancy had taken on her frail body. Hannah was worried. Moreover, Ida was discouraged as her ever-present cough worsened. The constant burning of wood and oil necessary to heat the house aggravated her condition.

———

Ida lay in bed, dozing under a cozy, thick quilt. She perked up when her newborn began to stir, letting out a sleeping whimper. *How long has it been? Is it time to feed her again?* she wondered as she reached out in the dark to touch Hazel, who was sleeping in the wooden cradle on the floor next to her.

Then she heard the clock strike the hour. *One, two,* she counted. Thoughts whirled in her head, as they frequently did at this late hour. She lay still. She had learned to do this as her mother was quick to rise and come to her side. She missed her "alone-and-thinking" time. She listened, picking out the night sounds: the ticking of her wedding clock, Pa snoring next door, her baby breathing with a congested nose, and her own wheezing. Most of all, she missed her husband's snoring.

Ida knew that her mother would come to manage Hazel's

needs if the baby started to fuss. Hannah had ordered her to stay in bed earlier that evening, even if she had to sit up to overcome a coughing fit gripping her lungs. *"Try to rest; we'll take care of the baby,"* recalled Ida, discouraged. *How can I call myself a mother if Mama and Caroline are always taking over?* With a growing baby demanding attention, times were not all peaceful under Arne's roof.

CHAPTER 12

A Wailing Baby

"Do you have a better idea?" Hannah snarled.

"I'll be in the barn," Arne grunted as he rose to put on his coat.

"I'll go with you, Pa!" Alfred responded, rising from the table where he was trying to read. "I'd rather listen to the cows than this," he added callously.

Hazel had been crying for hours, and the family was tired of listening to her. Even cheery two-year-old Clarence was grumpy.

"Ida, what's the matter with her?" moaned Laura in complaint as she glared at her sister holding the wailing baby.

From the day Hazel was born, Ida struggled to feed the baby. *How could a mere few pounds of wailing baby disturb an entire household?* Ida wondered. She had tried to nurse, but the growing baby could not be satisfied. Finally, in desperation, Hannah took charge. Going to the pantry, she climbed up on a chair to retrieve an object from the highest shelf.

When Arne saw it in her hands, he raised his eyebrows. "I

thought you swore you would never use that again. I recall you saying it made the babies sicker?"

Hannah stiffened and scowled. "Do you have a better idea? Clarence is weaned, so I cannot help, and Ida cannot feed the baby enough. A wet nurse is not easy to find. Don't you think I've thought about it? The child squalls because she is growing and hungry."

Feeling the sting in her voice and knowing better than to comment further, Arne turned to the paper he was reading.

When she brought it to Ida, Hannah began by saying, "I thought we could give the old bottle a try, Ida. Sometimes, it just does not work to nurse your baby."

"I've tried everything you suggested. Am I supposed to give up entirely?" Ida countered dejectedly.

"Come with me to the kitchen, and I will show you how this works. If we can get some food into the baby's belly, mothering Hazel won't be so hard." As Hazel squalled at a fevered pitch, Ida watched her mother pour out a measure of milk into a pan to warm.

"You must boil the milk before you give it to her." Hannah cautioned. "It is too strong for the baby if you don't."

Hannah pulled it from the heat when the milk began to steam, stirring it until it cooled. Filling the nursing flask half full of milk, she inserted a nipple stopper, cautioning, "This rubber nipple is old and hard. Watch her close when you are feeding her. If the pieces break off, she can choke."

Ida began to play gently with the bottle top, putting it to the baby's mouth. Hazel finally paid attention and began to suck the milk successfully.

Ida was thrilled. Once Hazel mastered the knack of feeding, that immediately resolved the other issues like lack of sleep for the household. The baby began to thrive and seemed to grow heavier almost overnight. She also slept soundly, and when she stirred, Ida was ready to feed her.

One exciting day, Ida realized that Hazel was listening to her voice. She watched as the baby began to smile and bat her eyes. "Yes, little one," she murmured gently, "I am your mother! I can take care of you. All will be fine now."

—⁓—

A week passed, and it seemed as if the family routine was finally on track again. Then the unexpected happened. Ida heard her sister sound out in frustration, *"Uff da, uff da, uff da!"* after the sound of shattering glass echoed from the kitchen.

Ida called out from where she sat, playing with Hazel in the dining room, "Whatever is the matter, Laura?"

Laura entered the living room, wiping her hands on her apron. Ida could see she was in distress as her eyes were brimming with tears. She groaned, "I broke the bottle, Ida. I was just trying to wash it, and it slipped and smacked the sink. Mama will be furious. She told me before that the bottle did not need to be washed every day." Ida watched as Laura grabbed her coat and stomped outside, saying, "Maybe Pa will help."

It was midday when Arne pushed through the door of the Grafton Drug Company and paused to survey the store. Recognizing Arne, Mr. Fleming stepped forward in greeting. "Good to see you, Arne. Have you finished your harvest yet?"

"No, it is going kind of slow this year. The rain sets me back.

I'm in town to get a harness repaired and thought I would look around," said Arne, his eyes roaming the store shelves.

"Can I help you find something?" Fleming offered.

"I'm wondering what you have for a bottle. Got a young'un who is having a hard time."

"Come this way. We have a couple of choices in stock."

Toward the back of the store, Mr. Fleming stopped to point out a display of infant items laid out in a glass case. Besides bottles, there were rattles, silver cups, and toys.

"Let me see that one," indicated Arne, pointing to a box containing a shaped bottle. Arne could easily visualize how the gadget would operate with his years of milking a cow. "How much is it?"

"That nursing bottle is the best one I carry. My niece tried it. She said it worked swell, mostly because it did not leak. A dollar for all. If the glass breaks, I carry the replacement for 50¢."

"Isn't that kind of steep?" replied Arne, looking to thriftier versions.

"It is a fair price if it does the job!" Mr. Fleming countered as he turned away to let Arne consider his options.

Arne then noticed a display of pharmaceuticals lined up neatly in their bottles with colorful advertising labels. Among the tonics, signs pointed to the new products on display. One bottle claiming to be a "pure source" of Norwegian cod liver oil drew Arne's attention. Maybe Ida should try this one, he thought, remembering his daughter had been complaining that the bottle she was taking already smelled rancid.

"Well, did you decide?" asked Mr. Fleming, circling back.

"Maybe I'll just get a nipple and an ordinary glass bottle. I'll also take this oil and a bar of this baby soap," Arne replied, pointing to the items. "I also need some stomach bitters."

"That will be 50¢ for the cod oil, 20¢ for the small nursing bottle and nipple, 5¢ for the soap, and 60¢ for the bottle of Dr. Hostetter's. That's a $1.35 altogether, Arne."

Arne paid the bill, and with the precious baby bottle firmly in his hands, he strode out the door, thinking his money was well spent.

Arriving back home, Arne leaned through the kitchen door and beckoned Ida. When she appeared, he handed her the brown paper-wrapped package. "These are for you. Don't tell your mother I bought that special soap. I thought it might help with the diaper rash."

Ida laughed in agreement.

"Thank you, Pa, for making the trip into town. Hazel has been cranky. Maybe Laura will stop moping around cause she feels responsible." Pa smiled and headed back to the quiet of the barn.

Ida untied the string-bound package and frowned upon seeing the fancy label of the bottle of cod liver oil. Ida knew her mother would approve as Hannah often insisted, "You must take this medicinal every day to loosen the phlegm in your lungs."

Obediently, Ida complied, taking a large spoonful daily, but nothing could get rid of the foul taste it left in the back of her throat. Moving on, Ida slipped the soap bar into her pocket and then unwrapped the precious new baby bottle.

Retrieving a pan, she set a portion of cow's milk to boil on the stove, stirring so it would not scorch. When it cooled, she gratefully filled the new precious bottle. When Hazel began to stir from her nap, Ida took the hungry baby into her arms. Ida softly addressed Hazel, "My little one, you think this is lunch. To the rest of the family, it is so much more!"

CHAPTER 13

California Dreams

They did all the planning. She just nodded in agreement.

One dark and bitterly cold night, Ernst came for supper. Afterward, he stayed late into the night, sitting with Ida and holding his baby girl. Hazel had begun to smile in recognition of the different family voices. Tonight, she laughed. It was the first time he had heard the charming chortling sound, and Ernst beamed. Then in delight, Ida giggled too, and for a moment, all felt exceedingly joyful and normal. But it didn't last. When Ida got up to refill coffee cups, the exertion caused a fit of coughing.

"Alma, go get your sister one of her rags," instructed Hannah.

Concentrating as she played with some jacks on the floor, six-year-old Alma replied, "I'm almost done." Hannah grunted. Looking up and seeing the displeasure in her mother's eyes, Alma immediately left her game to do as she was told.

Arne closed his eyes and held his breath, trying to will Ida's coughing to still. Ida, in a panic, looked around the room, hoping for some relief. Her glance took in the image of one of her brothers, with disgust painted over his face. When she finally overcame the fit of coughing, she excused herself and, in a harsh voice, said, "I'm going to put Hazel to bed now. Good night."

After the children were sent to bed, Ernst, Arne, and Hannah remained at the kitchen table, making idle conversation until Arne cleared his throat and began to speak. "I read about this place out in California. They say the climate is just right to help people with consumption. A man there, Dr. Duclane, is building a place for people to live. He claims that his patients improve with proper rest and breathing the better air."

Hannah huffed. "The doctor here knows different. He says Ida will only get worse. She can rest here. At least if she's here, the family can help her with the baby. The birth took a lot out of Ida. She just needs more time to recover."

"California? That is a long way from here," mused Ernst.

"Yes, it is. But it is now possible to ride the trains all the way to the water," encouraged Arne.

Hannah snapped, "What are you saying, Arne? Surely you are not suggesting we put that sick girl on a train to travel away from here. And what about the child? There is no way she can manage without help."

"Hush, Hannah! You are not being practical and thinking about the best thing for Ida. She is not getting better. If we don't consider these ideas with our heads, we will not do all we can for her. I do not say this to rile you, Hannah, but I remind you that Ida is a married woman. Any decisions about these kinds of things are up to Ernst."

Ernst spoke up, "This is not a new idea, Hannah. Ida and I have already entertained the idea of leaving the area."

"I know, I know, but things have changed. Surely you cannot think this will go well. Turning to Arne, she growled, "You are always coming up with ideas from all those papers you read."

"Be reasonable, woman. Don't you see that this could help Ida?" Arne responded.

"It's just not practical. This is your daughter we are talking about, Arne!"

Ernst slid his chair into the shadows and grew quiet. The fiery exchange between the husband and wife had become intimate, edged in anger and heartbreak. Considering Hannah's previous comments about keeping Ida at the house, Ernst began to understand her fears.

Is Ida so ill that her death is inevitable? He pulled on his coat and wrapped his muffler around his neck. Pausing briefly, he looked at his in-laws and bolted out the door with his eyes full of hurt. Numb of heart and lonely, Ernst headed south across the field toward Anthony's, leaving footprints in the light covering of snow. He paused before ducking under the fence. He inhaled deeply of the night air. The sharp bite of the cold startled him, taking his breath. Looking up, he noticed a half-moon overhead. *Winter is only beginning. Will Ida worsen as the season goes on?*

Ida heard most of the conversation going on in the kitchen. Through the thin walls of the house, the tone of her parents' voices was disturbing. She also remembered the irritated looks on the faces of her family earlier that night when she started to cough. Hearing the door close, she knew that Ernst had left. Disparaging self-talk rolled around in her head. *Will I ever get better? I'm a burden to my family. Maybe Ernst wishes he never married me.* And with that thought, she pulled the blanket over her head and murmured, "I am so afraid."

Ida cornered her father near the barn the next morning, asking bluntly, "I heard you talking last night. Would there be a future for Ernst if we went to California?"

Arne looked up from where he was pitching hay. "Come, Ida, sit here out of the wind," indicating a stool nearby. Leaning against a post, he sighed. "So, you heard us talking. First, let me say that we are worried about you and the baby."

"I'm getting stronger again," interrupted Ida emphatically.

"Your ma and I don't see it. I went around to see Dr. Gamble about you. He said there isn't anything new he knows to give you. But he did point out an article in one of his magazines. It sounds nice, this place where people with consumption can go. The man, Duclane, claims to take anyone who comes—even if you can't pay."

"But you did not answer my question. What about Ernst?" insisted Ida.

"He has traveled before, and I think you would do well to go there with him. Ernst is looking for opportunities like he should be. This place around here is growing—the schools, the roads, and Grafton. But if he wants to farm around here, there isn't land left unless someone gives up."

"Do you know if there is any land to farm in California?" asked Ida.

"Probably, but California is a big place. Ernst could sort

out a job later. A big city like Los Angeles will probably have more work. Maybe he would find something better…farming is not for everyone."

Ida frowned. "So, you don't think Ernst can make a living here?"

"Well," Arne drawled, "he can try; he knows what it takes. It has been six years since Ernst came as a teenager to work for your uncle. He was too young to claim the land back then, but now he can. Ida, your uncle and I have full confidence that he will make something of himself if given a chance."

"And you don't think there is a place for him here?" repeated Ida, sweeping her arm outward.

"You know that I work this land for your brothers' future."

"Ma doesn't think it's a good idea, us leaving. She also says it would cost too much money," declared Ida, looking at her pa to take in his reaction.

"Give your mother time to get used to the idea. I know Ernst will take care of you, no matter what. You need to talk to Ernst about it. There is a lot to consider," advised Arne.

"I wish I weren't such a burden; I get so tired of being sick," murmured Ida as she rose to return to the house.

Arne stepped up. In a rare moment of comfort, he wrapped his arm around Ida's shoulders. Ida trembled as a tear rolled down her face.

"Ida, we are ordinary people, but we must always strive for more. You must remain hopeful."

———

They made the agonizing decision to leave the Red River Valley and move to California during the wintertime. Arne reminded them that travel could be tough if they left before the last winter storm. Ernst finally agreed they would stay until the spring fieldwork was complete and the wheat was planted. With that goal in mind, Arne, Anthony, and Hannah sat around the kitchen table and helped the young couple plan for the move. As the men smoked their pipes, Ida scribbled notes from their conversations on a brown paper wrapper with a stubby pencil. The day Arne produced a printed schedule of the train routes and Caroline brought a picture map of the states from her school books, the idea of leaving suddenly became real.

During the discussions, Ida cornered her husband and made an adamant request. "If we are to do this," Ida said sternly, "you must promise me you will not ask me all the time how I am. I am tired of answering that question. I want to leave here and become well. But the looks and the judgment others give me is too much."

"I promise," returned Ernst. *I don't need to ask; I can tell how you are doing by the look in your eyes.*

As March turned to April and the day of the last frost seemed imminent, time seemed to quicken, drawing them nearer to their departure for a land unknown. Ida made several genuine attempts to pack her things, but her heart wasn't in it. One afternoon, Hannah found her daughter lying on her bed with Hazel next to her, surrounded by a disarray of clothing, books, and sewing kit.

"Are you feeling all right, Ida?" her mother questioned.

Ida sat up. "I keep thinking about leaving, and I am already homesick."

"It has been decided, Ida," Hannah responded in irritation. "That is how it is. You must do what your husband tells you to do. Ernst did not make this decision lightly, and you know it. He has been talking with your father and Uncle Anthony about this for weeks now."

"I know that, Mama. Ernst tells me everything!" replied Ida defensively. "I just don't feel it is right to leave my baby."

"Ida, we have tried to help you get better, but it is not working. You have been raised to be a Christian woman, and now you must respect and follow your husband's wishes. This you must do. I will leave you to think on my words. I advise you to check your attitude, especially around Ernst. He needs to be confident about this plan."

After her mother left, Ida dropped her head to her pillow, held Hazel to her chest, and closed her eyes. Her head reeled in a protesting argument at her mother's coldhearted words. *Of course, I'll do as Ernst says. Mama is right. It is my duty, but don't my feelings matter?* Ida sought consolation reminding herself, *I have married a good man. He works hard. He came all the way from Sweden to find me, and he deserves to get ahead.*

CHAPTER 14

The Sears Catalog

"Try to enjoy picking out some new things;
most girls would."

Ida pulled the front porch rocker into the shade and sat down. The younger children were in school, Hannah was inspecting the garden, and the men were at work in the field with the horses hitched to the plow. Hazel was sleeping near the open window, but she was close enough that Ida would hear when she started to stir.

From under her arm, Ida withdrew a new copy of the *Sears and Roebuck* 1902 catalog. Her mother had been pushing her to look through the pictures for ideas of clothing articles she would need for the trip.

After breakfast, Hannah insisted, "Caroline will be going to town with your father soon. Make a list, and she can get some similar things for you. I am giving you some of the egg money, eight and a half dollars." When Ida raised questioning eyes, her mother continued in a softer tone. "I want to do this for you."

Ida began to stammer, "It costs too much; I can get along with what I have."

Hannah shushed her. "Don't question this, Ida. You should enjoy thinking about getting some new things; most girls would. This is a big trip, and you must arrive prepared. Look at dresses, nightgowns, and the like, Caroline can fit some smart shoes for you, too, but you can decide what you like. For once, try to enjoy yourself!"

Resigned, Ida gingerly opened the thick catalog. She found the women's clothing and scanned the prices before looking at the items. *I wish I could go along and do this with Caroline,* sighed Ida. However, she knew it was wiser to stay home and regain her energy after her latest coughing episode.

Last night, Ernst and Ida learned that Uncle Anthony insisted on providing enough money to cover the traveling expenses to get them to California. They hoped those funds and the money Ernst had saved would be enough for a new start out west. Unfortunately, Ernst would have to sell Andy, the horse he had trained from a colt, and a mule named Felix.

$8.50 seemed like a great deal of money to Ida. She had never held such a sum in her hands or been instructed to spend it on herself. Flipping through the pages of the book, she came to the children's department. Unable to keep her thoughts at bay, her eyes began to water. The thought of leaving Hazel behind with her parents filled her with anguish. *My parents already have a full house. They should not have to add the care of another youngster. Clarence is still a baby.*

As Ida continued to turn the pages, pictures of children's shoes, coats, medicine, a child's silver cup, and a pretty doll filled her eyes. One doll at the top of a page caught her attention. It was a china doll in a lovely dress with a bonnet. The details indicated the doll's body was of kid leather. *I never had a doll like that,* thought Ida longingly. *Uncle Anthony carved one for me when I was little. It did not have hair, and the face was drawn with a pencil. Mama made the overalls from Papa's old denim one. It looked like a homely little boy.*

Overwhelmed, Ida slammed the book shut. Sniffing back the threatening tears, she thought to herself, *And the greatest price of all was yet to be paid. How can I do such a thing as leaving Hazel behind? They say it is for the best; even Ernst agrees. But how can I do that?* Feeling for her handkerchief, Ida was startled when the catalog slipped from her lap, thudding as it hit the ground.

Caught between feelings of anger and sadness, Ida burst out, "Enough of this self-pity!" After retrieving the catalog, she put pencil to paper and resolutely wrote out a list. She took no pleasure in the task but, yet again, did what she was told. After adding up the prices beside each item on her list, she had spent $8.00:

1) Skirt, every day 1.50
2) Stockings, two pairs 25
3) Shoes 2.50
4) Shirtwaist 75
5) Hat (for Ernst) 2.00
6) Nightgown 1.00

Later that day, Caroline came to Ida, and they reviewed her list. Caroline also pointed out some goods listed in the advertisements in the *Grafton News*. "I see the mercantile has a shoe sale," noticed Caroline. "I will go in and look. Show me what style to get, and I can try some on."

"Your foot is a little bigger than mine, so get them snug," Ida reminded her sister as she pointed to a sturdy pair of black leather oxfords. "Like this kind with the heels."

"Is there anything else you want me to look for?"

"Well," Ida hesitated. "I would like to get a doll for Hazel."

"She's too young, Ida. Hazel won't be playing with a doll for years!" joked Caroline.

"You know when we leave, I will not be back for a long time. I would like to think I could leave a doll for her, one that she will always know is from me."

"I wish we could go together to look," pouted Caroline, growing emotional.

Ida responded firmly, "I have money from my job. Maybe you could look and tell me if you find a nice doll in town. Please do this for me. Of course, I would like to do it myself, but Mama says I must rest."

"I don't want to think about any of this. I cannot believe you will leave us," choked Caroline.

"We can write; that will help. Come now, let's not be sad. It is decided, and I must get ready to go. Anyway, now you can look forward to spending *my* money!" said Ida, bravely trying to lighten the mood.

Her father and Caroline returned from town a few days later with assorted bundles wrapped in brown paper and tied with string. Arne returned to the wagon to fetch one more item. "I saw this and realized you will need a traveling bag."

From behind his back, he produced and presented Ida with a new canvas valise.

"Oh, Papa!" she exclaimed, bending down to examine the new bag with shiny buckles.

Then, opening the latches, she peered inside. It looked like a bottomless black hole. *What did you expect?* she wondered bleakly.

Ida turned to look at her father, trying to look pleased, all the while holding back the dejected feelings that held her heart in an iron fist. It would not be long before her things would fill the bag, but she could not stop thinking that the most important things would not fit.

Later, the girls began to unwrap the packages with their mother looking on. Ida tried very hard to show interest in Caroline's carefully chosen purchases. When her sister held up the newly polished leather shoes, Caroline exclaimed enthusiastically, "These should be about right for your feet, Ida. They were on sale at the Chicago Store. I think they are the closest to what you said you wanted."

Knowing she needed to conjure up more gratitude for Caroline's efforts, Ida slipped on the shoes. After tying the laces, she proceeded to parade around the room. Caroline and Hannah smiled when Ida finally twirled once on her toes. "These are perfect! Thank you, Caroline."

"You made some wise purchases, Caroline," complimented Hannah as she exited the room to return to the kitchen. Before she left, Hannah addressed Ida. "You will make good use of all these things."

Caroline, rising from her seat, came over to where Ida

stood. Smiling mysteriously, she whispered as she took Ida's hand. "There is one more package, Ida. Come with me."

Ida followed Caroline into the parlor. After they shut the doors, Caroline went to Ida's bed and pulled back a blanket to reveal a box. "I thought you would like to open this package in private. I know you wanted to go yourself, but I knew she was the one."

Ida looked up with genuine interest. Speaking softly, she asked, "The doll?"

Caroline nodded.

—*∿*—

"What hangs on your mind to set you to worry so, Ida?" asked Ernst later when they were out for a walk. He was concerned, trying to understand the source of her melancholy mood.

"Oh, Ernst, everything! I am a burden to everyone. Now with the baby. How can we think of leaving her with my parents? How can this all possibly work out? There is not enough money, even with Uncle Anthony's help. What if I get sick while we are traveling?" Ida worried. "You don't know what it feels like to have people stare at you with disgust."

"Hush! Stop talking like that, Ida. There are many unknowns in our lives. Things may happen, but we will face them bravely. If we can get the funds, we will plan to go. But we cannot be fearful of what we cannot control. And about Hazel, you know your mother loves her as her own. You must stop these harmful judgments," he reprimanded. "I want to love you for a long time, and therefore we must focus on getting you better."

"I don't want to create problems for others," repeated Ida with a heavy sigh.

"You always try to please everyone else, Ida. For once, you must listen to a different voice." He gently pushed his finger to her lips when he could see her trying to protest.

—⁓—

As the time to leave drew closer, Ida began to pack. She quickly grew tired of being reminded of how few things she could take with her on the move to California. As Ernst looked on, he became almost grumpy, repeating, "Space is limited. We will take what can fit into a suitcase and your new bag, nothing more."

Ida quietly nodded, hating to be admonished but also hating to leave behind her trunk.

Ernst reminded her, "There are too many train transfers along the way. Taking a trunk is not practical."

Later, her father promised, "Ida, more things can be sent out once you are settled."

Today, the item of contention was an unfinished quilt. Hannah had suggested, "Ida, why don't you pack the rag quilt top you are working on? It will fold down well and will not add much weight."

"It looks bulky," said Ida flatly.

"You need a project to keep your hands busy." When Ida finally relented, Hannah was pleased. She had been wracking her brain for something practical to send along on their journey. *Ida needs something that will sing out with memories. This has fabric bits from our old dresses and aprons, even Arne's wool vest.*

Finally, tired of packing, eliminating, and repacking, Ida stepped outside to clear her head. The perfume of blooming lilacs drifted through in the air. Walking east by way of the perimeter of the cow pasture, she shortly arrived at the heavy tree line growing alongside the river.

Turning back around to face her parents' home, Ida thought, *It still looks new.* First, she studied the gray house sitting snuggly between two fir trees. Her eyes roved, taking in the barn and counting the horses and cows. Near the animals, she saw the slim figure of her father in his weather-beaten hat. *He works so hard every day.* In the months ahead, when homesickness came, Ida knew she would return to this memory of what home looked it. *How will I ever bear it if something happens to Mama, Pa, or Hazel?*

Ida, feeling compelled to pray, began, *Please, God, take care of my family. Maybe I will come back someday, but give me the courage I need to leave.*

Then, feeling her spirit a little bit soothed, she turned back to the woods. Making a gesture of putting her hands up to the sides of her mouth, she called out boldly, "I know you are not real, little nisse, but if you are, keep watch over my family!"

Somehow, the endearing picture of the little man, a guardian of the farm, making his rounds to check on the animals and people comforted Ida.

SECTION 4

The Journey

CHAPTER 15

Leaving Home

The miles began to separate her
from the home she loved.

Two days after Hannah and Arne left Ida and Ernst at the depot in Grafton, their train pulled into the Minneapolis station. The farewell back in Grafton had been a somber exchange of a few forced encouraging words. Ida waited in the buggy with her parents while Ernst purchased the tickets through to Fargo. She sat stiffly and said few words as she fought to keep her composure.

Her parents, too, were unusually silent. For the first time, Ida observed that her parents seemed older. She noticed their gnarled and wrinkled hands at rest. All those years of difficult farm life have taken a toll. *What will they look like next time I see them? Pa has such stomach problems all the time. How will he get along if I am not there to remind him about his food?*

"Your traveling suit looks smart," offered Arne, breaking the silence.

"Yes," agreed Hannah. "And it is sensible for traveling."

Ida smiled. She was wearing her favorite navy-blue dress trimmed with pink ruffling and dark braid. The matching ground-sweeping skirt was heavily reinforced with sturdy corduroy at the hemline. It would be durable and warm on the drafy, dirty trains. Under her skirt, her new shoes were already pinching her toes.

"Is the wallet in a safe place? Best not to have it in the luggage," reminded Hannah.

"Yes, I have some of the money in my purse, and Ernst carries the balance of what you did not sew into my skirt. I will be watchful," added Ida reassuringly.

When it was time to go, Arne assisted Ida down from the buggy. He gruffly enveloped her in his arms and pressed a small sack of her favorite candy into her hands. Arne felt numb and had few words to offer. Kissing her on the forehead, he turned to shake Ernst's hand. Ida turned to her mother. Hannah could see the tears beginning to well in her daughter's eyes.

"We will wait for word of your arrival," Hannah asserted, "Send a letter as soon as possible."

Two years had passed since Ida and Ernst had taken the train to Grand Forks for their honeymoon. At the time, they could not have foreseen how brief their time of carefree canoodling would last. Now, every day had elements of apprehension, making it hard to look forward to a hopeful future.

Ernst picked up their luggage, consisting of one suitcase and a valise. Ida stoically followed him, refusing to look back, holding her emotions in check. Once they boarded the train, Ernst directed Ida to an empty window seat on the east side of the car, from which she could wave goodbye. Soon after, they heard a loud signal whistle, and the train moved out of the station. Unable to hold them back any longer, silent tears started to roll down Ida's cheeks. Turning to Ernst, she leaned into his shoulder, and he reached out to take her hand.

"I just need a little cry," she whispered.

"It's all right. We knew it would be hard to say goodbye. I could hardly bear to give Hazel over to Caroline when we left."

"Do you still think it is the right thing? To leave her behind?" asked Ida timidly. She knew the answer but felt compelled to ask anyway.

"When you get better and stronger, I promise we will see her again." Ida found comfort in Ernst's desperate tone of response. *He is not as indifferent about this move as I thought. His heart is also troubled.*

At the crossroads of their life, they made a decision. The unknown way ahead was uncertain, and it demanded much of them to continue onward. Outside her window, the scenery of farm fields rushed past. Ida whispered, "We must be fearless now. It is decided and planned. Moving forward begins this day."

The stop in Grand Forks was brief. Just long enough for them to descend and stroll on the walkway. The smell of burning coal hung heavy in the air. Ernst thought with a sigh. *It will be a long time before we smell fresh air again.*

Four hours after leaving Grand Forks, the train horn sounded off as they slowly rumbled to a stop at the Fargo station. When the conductor came by, they asked about lodging. The kindly man suggested, "The Dakota Inn is right beside the train station, but walk on if you want food. I suggest eating at the café a couple of blocks farther down."

After stepping down from the train, Ida and Ernst followed the other passengers into the Great Northern building. They joined the line to talk to the station master. When it was their turn, the man told them, "You can purchase a ticket from Fargo through to Chicago, but I suggest spending the night in Minneapolis before traveling on. The connection can be unpredictable."

The informative agent then suggested taking a train with a southern route heading out of Minneapolis to Kansas City. When the station master finally issued their tickets, Ernst and Ida were reeling. All the planning they had done now seemed to be in question. Ernst was no longer certain of what he should do once they reached Minneapolis.

"Two tickets to Minneapolis will be $9.50. Leaves at 10 a.m. I calculated at the standard rate of two cents a mile," informed the agent.

Ida and Ernst looked at each other, wincing at this announcement. Gingerly, Ernst opened his billfold and carefully counted dollars and change for the one-way tickets. Then, gathering their possessions, they headed out silently through the door marked "Fargo." It was a relief to step away from the train station after completing their first day's journey. As they had been told, the hotel was easy to locate exactly one block from the station.

The reality of the day's journey moving away from home came with a jolt as they left the train station. The city was unfamiliar, the tickets took their hard-earned cash, and the young couple was tired, hungry, and emotionally drained from leaving behind all they knew for an unknown future.

Ernst looked at his wife and urged, "Let's go find the hotel and get some supper. I guess I should study the train maps again."

Entering the Fargo Inn, they were greeted cheerfully by a tall thin man with wire-rimmed glasses. After they signed the register, he assigned them a room on the second floor. They handed over a dollar and picked up their luggage. As they started to walk away, he suggested, "If you are hungry, you can still get food in the restaurant. My wife's mutton stew is memorable."

The room was faintly light and smelled of cigar smoke. The two narrow beds appeared lumpy under the shabby and yellowed bedspreads. Drawing back the curtains, the young couple stood at the window and surveyed the rising buildings of the city of Fargo. "I saw a sign at the train station that said Fargo has a population of 9,000 people," announced Ida. "That's four times bigger than Grafton."

"Just you wait, Ida. I think the cities ahead will be far bigger than what we are used to. Now, I'm hungry. Shall we try the mutton stew?"

"Yes, and then maybe we can take a walk before we turn in," suggested Ida.

Much later, when they were settling into their beds for the night, Ida started to giggle. "I do agree that was indeed memorable stew!"

Ernst chuckled, "Yes, that was probably the chewiest meat I've ever tackled. We should have listened to the conductor's warning. But the pie was tasty, and we shan't spend any more money this day!"

That night in the hotel, Ida woke up feeling chilled. The

floorboard in the hallway creaked as a late-night guest passed outside the room. From the street below came the sound of passing wagons. The disquiet seemed to steal her sleep as much as her runaway thoughts. She blinked and winced as she twisted on the lumpy mattress, trying to get comfortable.

By the dim light coming in underneath the door, Ida was relieved to see and hear Ernst snoring nearby. Her first thought was that she was hungry, but she knew there wasn't any food in the room. Ida sighed and lay quietly staring at the ceiling until dawn. All the while, her mind raced with thoughts of what the future might bring and the faces of her family that she would no longer be able to talk to, except in her imagination.

Chapter 16

Riding the Rails to Chicago

Ernst opened his wallet and doled out the ticket money,
two cents per mile.

After a leisurely breakfast of coffee and toast, Ernst and Ida returned to the train station to ride the "Great Northern" to Minneapolis. Consulting the schedule printed in a pamphlet, Ernst confirmed, "The train leaves at 10 a.m. It will be a long day…245 miles."

"I guess we won't get in until late again. That means another night in a hotel," noted Ida. "It seems like a waste. I spent all night staring at the ceiling, unable to sleep. I would have slept just as well on a bench in the train."

"It will be easier when we finally turn south; then we will not need to change trains so often. I can ask how much a Pullman sleeping car would cost. Would you like that?"

At the time, Ida was looking out the window, watching the passing fields and homes. She answered his question with a noncommittal "Hmm."

Waking up that morning then having to board another

train was a stinging reminder of the increasing distance from home. *I suppose Hazel has been fed and maybe is down for her nap. I wonder if she slept through the night. How I miss you, little one.*

While Ida was feeling homesick, Ernst was mulling over the issue of money. *I knew this trip would be costly. How much less painful it would have been to purchase the tickets all at once. There are so many stops along the way yet to come.* Restless and fidgety, he leaned over to Ida, remarking, "I'll return in a while."

Exploring the train, he located the dining and lounge car. All the time, he was hoping to catch a conversation with fellow travelers familiar with the train routes. Finally, he spotted an older-looking porter who seemed to be on a break in the smoking car. Approaching him, Ernst said, "I have a question. I wonder if you can advise me."

The man nodded agreeably and informed Ernst he had to talk fast, as he only had a few minutes before he needed to return to work.

Ernst quickly launched into his dilemma about the rail options to get to Kanas City.

"You can take those short lines south from Minneapolis, and you'll get to Kansas City eventually. But when you factor in the stops, transfers, and waiting time for the next train, it is better to stay on the main line."

"But the station master yesterday indicated that Chicago was too far out of our way, as we are heading to California."

"You do have a long ride ahead of you, and the Chicago route adds some miles," reminded the porter. "Still, it is more prudent to continue on this line unless you have some business or need to visit family along that southern route from Minneapolis."

"I guess you are right," agreed Ernst as he silently fumed. *After all those hours at home planning our way, it irritates me that I let a stranger make me question our route.* But logically, he knew if a more prudent route existed, he should find out about it so they could take it for Ida's sake.

Finally, they steamed up to the famed Chicago Railroad Station, a hub for the entire nation. Beginning to gather their belongings, Ernst announced, "We change trains here, Ida."

Ida nodded. Looking out the window, she saw in the distance a platform, the colossal depot building, a milling crowd of passengers, and billowing steam clouds drifting into the air. In addition, she felt the rattling of converging train tracks through her shoes. It was more commotion than Ida had seen, heard, or felt in her entire life. *How are we ever going to find our way?* she groaned inwardly.

Ernst, too, seemed overwhelmed but managed to ask, "Are you hungry?"

She turned to give him her attention, "Yes, I'm famished."

"Me, too. Once we get off, we'll get our bearings and then look for a lunch counter. I expect we have a long day ahead."

When the engineer blasted the train whistle, signaling that their train was slowing down, Ida put her fingers in her ears and cringed.

Ernst smiled. "It must make that racket so people can hear it from a long way off. It takes a long time for a train to slow down, and people have time to get out of its way."

She watched as passengers around her seemed to come to life. Men wiggled into their jackets, and women straightened their hair. Seeing a woman bend down to tie her child's shoelaces reminded her that her own laces needed tightening. Finally, the train came to a stop, and everyone rose simultaneously in a rush to leave.

Ernst motioned for Ida to stay seated and wait. Ernst leaned out the window to study the flow of people. Finally, he straightened up and beckoned Ida to follow him. He picked up their two suitcases, and Ida carried a small bag and her purse. When she got to the steps of the train car, a steward reached out to take her hand. Gathering her skirt, she stepped down to the platform.

"There should be a map posted on the wall," repeated Ernst distractedly. "It would be best to get an idea of what we want before getting to the ticket counter."

Nearby, a train employee stood on a box above the crowd. He kept everyone moving by shouting and pointing in different directions. Ida walked behind Ernst, wanting to tell him to slow down. Still, he kept weaving and darting around people, making his way to the terminal entrance.

When he reached the fancy glass door, Ernst stopped to look for her. Ida's heart was beating furiously out of worry over being separated from him by then. The ground beneath her was solid, but she still felt the train vibrations in her legs. When Ida spotted a sign for a washroom that pointed down a side hall, she finally insisted. "Please, can we stop a moment? I would like to go in there; I won't be long."

Ernst grimaced when he realized he had been rushing, and

Ida was out of breath. In apology, he offered, "I'm sorry, Ida. But, of course. Go ahead. I will be right here when you are done."

In the washroom, Ida splashed her grimy face and hands with water. Stepping over to investigate the mirror, she was appalled by the reflection of her disheveled appearance. Retrieving a comb from her handbag, she attempted to fix her hair by twisting and re-pinning the free strands back into place. *I never thought train travel would be so dirty!*

Refreshed, she rejoined Ernst. He, too, looked slightly restored. "Feeling better now?" he said.

"Yes, let's go figure this out," asserted Ida with feigned enthusiasm.

Ida looked over their fellow passengers with curiosity when they reentered the main hall. Several salesmen carrying heavy demonstration cases passed them at a brisk trot. These sellers of goods wore colorful lounge suits that Ida could not begin to imagine her father or Ernst wearing, as they looked clownish in her view.

Passing a large family, Ida could read the stress painted across the mother's face as her eyes darted frantically between her husband and children, trying to keep pace. Two of her small children were kept in check by a leather tether attached to their waists. Ida wanted to rush over and help her manage the brood, but she was having trouble again keeping up with Ernst's long stride. And, at that point, nothing could quell her fear of losing him in the expansive building.

A few couples passed by who were headed in the other direction. They strolled along deep in conversation. *They don't look uneasy, which is how I feel,* thought Ida. Each passenger had a different purpose and destination. Eventually, the ticket desk came into view. When it was their turn, Ida and Ernst stepped to the counter. The man peered down at them through his thick glasses.

"Well, folks, where are you going today?" boomed Mr. Williams, as his name tag boasted. The ticket agent had already guessed the couple was traveling westward. It was a private game he played after years of working at a train station and reading people. He sized up the man first, noting his rough and calloused hands. Some of his clothes were new, but his shoes were ragged and worn. He was not a city man. *He was probably a farmer.* The wife at his side was thin and wore a simple dress with little decoration. Her modest hairstyle and plain hat were not of current fashion. The pallor of her face made him wonder if she was well. *They're searching for a new opportunity,* he decided.

It was no surprise to hear Ernst declare, "We are making our way out to Los Angeles. We need two tickets."

After discussing travel options, Ernst decided to travel ahead to Kansas City on the Santa Fe line. After the agent figured out the price of their tickets, Ernst opened his wallet and carefully doled the money.

As Ernst was tucking the ticket into his pocket, the clerk cleared his throat to catch Ernst's attention. He spoke sternly, "One must be cautious about your suitcases and wallet as you make your way down the train lines. Lately, we've seen a rash of scandals and pickpockets. Several passengers have been careless and lost some of their possessions even today. Remember, you are not in Minnesota anymore."

Ernst nodded in understanding as he remembered some of the vulgar people he had encountered on his journey from Sweden to America. He was young then, barely 16, but he saw and heard some things that made his skin crawl. *I must warn Ida*, he thought. *She is naive about these kinds of things.*

———

"Well, if the train comes through as expected, we should be able to board later this afternoon. We could have spent the night here, but I think it would be wiser to keep moving. Ida, I hope it will be all right; we will sleep on the train."

"Whatever you think is best, Ernst. I am so sleepy right now, I could fall asleep anywhere."

Spotting an empty bench down the way, Ernst suggested, "Ida, why don't you wait over there? I will go get some food. I promise not to be long."

Settling their belongings, Ida perched on the bench. It was a relief to have a few moments to herself. As she watched Ernst stroll away, she noted a few souls were milling about on the platform. Ida exhaled as she leaned back on the bench and closed her eyes. She willed herself to imagine she was some-place else, like leaning against a tree under a calm blue sky.

Suddenly, a distant conversation stood out. "Leave me alone!" were the insistent, loud words that caught her atten-tion. Ida bolted up to look around. A short distance from her, a young woman wearing a trim traveling suit of dark burgundy was having a heated conversation. Her companion, or what appeared to be her companion, was a man. He was standing close and leaning toward the woman in a somewhat intimate-looking way.

When the lady turned to walk away, the man stepped in front of her. Ida saw the woman's eyes flash dangerously when he tried to take the valise from her hand. While Ida could not hear the words distinctly, her tone of voice suggested anger. Ida's heart began to beat rapidly. Ida sat up, her body stiffening with apprehension as her heart began to beat rapidly.

She watched the man continue to harass the woman. Fortunately, the woman turned out to be resourceful. Ida saw her reach up and finger her large hat. The fancy plume of blue feathers bobbed twice, then the young lady found her mark. With great presence of mind, she turned on the rogue. What followed was a vulgar gasp of surprise from the man. Ida watched the unfortunate chap recoil and then stumble before falling awkwardly to the ground. Grabbing his arm and grimacing in pain, the man scowled up at the woman from his seated position. *She jabbed him with her hat pin!* thought an amazed Ida.

The episode quickly concluded as the woman gave him a steely glare as she skillfully reinserted the pin. Smoothing her bodice, the woman reached down to pick up her valise, stood straight, turned on her heels, and marched toward Ida.

Ida could not help staring at the advancing woman who held her nose in the air and carried herself with a perfectly calm demeanor. The woman nodded and gave the wide-eyed Ida a satisfied smile, saying as she passed, "And that is how to handle a masher!"

CHAPTER 17

Mrs. Sunderlin

I see she is off exploring again!

Two days later, Ernst still fumed at his decision to travel the extra miles to Chicago. But with the city now behind, and steaming in a southerly direction to Kansas City, it felt as if they were finally beginning westward progress.

"Come with me, Ida. I want to show you something." It was late afternoon, and Ida was stiff from sitting on the hard seat.

"But, our things?" yawned Ida sleepily.

Overhearing the brief conversation, a fellow passenger sitting nearby spoke up. "Go on; I will watch your things. My children will probably nap for a while now that they finally fell asleep." Her children were sprawled out on either side of her with their heads anchored in her lap.

Back in Chicago, Ida, Ernst, the woman, and her two young children had settled into seats nearby. Both Ida and Ernst had helped entertain the children with conversation and stories over the passing hours.

Ida quietly mouthed "Thank you" as she rose from her seat

and picked up her pocketbook. Ida trailed Ernst as he led the way through several passenger cars. Finally, he came to a pause and pointed to a sign that read, "Lounge Car." He was amused at seeing Ida's face light up in delight as they stepped inside.

Entering the lounge car was like entering a lavish Victorian parlor. The walls were dressed in emerald green fabric, and gold braid trimmed the window drapes. A dark mahogany bookcase, stocked with reading materials, stood at the far end of the compartment. Hanging lamps with ornately painted globes and richly upholstered chairs added to the ambiance. Several passengers were sitting at tables and benches located near the windows. One man was reviewing a stack of papers while an older woman was knitting. Moving about the rocking room, a porter expertly served hot coffee or tea in china cups. Ernst directed Ida to an empty table and assisted her into a chair. Then, he signaled for the waiter. In exchange for dropping a nickel on the doily-lined serving tray, they each took a steaming cup of drink. Ida admired the fine bone china cup as she inhaled the fragrant and soothing smell of the tea.

As she finished her tea, Ida looked up and realized an older woman was staring at her across the way. It was not an uncomfortable exchange but more of a recognition. "Look, Ernst, that woman is acting as if I should know her."

When Ernst turned to see, a grin came over his face. I see the old woman is off exploring again, noted Ernst. "Ida, I think I need to introduce you to Mrs. Alice Sunderlin." When Ida returned a questioning look, he added. "I met her earlier today. She is quite a jolly sort of woman."

Ernst went on to briefly explain that earlier, he and Mrs.

Sunderlin had an unfortunate encounter when she stumbled while walking in the train cars. Ernst, just behind her, took the brunt of her fall and caught her before she fell to the floor. And learning that she was unaccompanied, Ernst assisted her to an empty seat. "I told her to sit fhere until she felt ready to move on." I had gone only a few

steps when she called me back. She was upset." Ida listened with rapt attention.

"'My purse is gone,' she says. I guess she dropped it when she fell. I finally found it just out of view under one of the seats. When I gave it to her, she held it like a baby. Anyway, we got to talking."

"It looks like she is signaling. I think she wants us to join her," observed Ida.

"Then let us go and visit. I think you will find her a lovely person, and it will help spell the long hours of travel ahead."

As they approached her table, Mrs. Sunderlin's face lit up. "I am so glad to see you again, Mr. Ottoson. Please join me" as she signaled for the dining steward to bring refreshments. After exchanging introductions, the lady warmly remarked, "My dear, forgive me for staring. You look a lot like my daughter, Julia. She was to travel with me but could not at the last minute."

"That must have been a disappointment," remarked Ida.

"I am used to making plans on a whim with her that consequently fall apart. Julia lives in a constant state of activity and commitment. So, you understand how pleased I am to be here with you," declared the woman.

As the waiter moved about the tiny tables, he paused to offer the guests a selection of small sandwiches stacked high on the silver tray he carried. Ida watched as Ernst gingerly picked up a sandwich with his large calloused fingers. Under other circumstances, he would have eaten a mountain-high plate of the dainty morsels. "Have you recovered from your earlier incident?" inquired Ernst kindly.

"I'm quite right again. Seems I needed a prince to rescue me today. Your husband, my dear, was such a timely blessing."

"Not a prince, Mrs. Sunderlin. Just a steady arm!" Ernst replied lightly.

After a jovial afternoon tea, Ida grew weary and tried to stifle her yawning. With a nod to Ernst and a return look of understanding, he thanked their host for the company and began to excuse himself and Ida.

Mrs. Sunderlin agreed, "I am getting stiff and will lie down for a nap. I still have more questions to ask of you about Sweden. My late husband spoke so fondly of the country but never was able to make a trip back."

"We must go and check on our things," Ida insisted.

"After we have all rested, would you consider joining me in the dining car for supper? They serve excellent meals, and I would enjoy your company," implored the lonely widow. Ida and Ernst glanced at each other, then turned to assure Mrs. Sunderlin they would be delighted to dine with her.

Later that evening, Ida found herself seated in the luxurious dining car. Like the lounge car where she was earlier, this place was also embellished on all sides with plush green drapery and trimmed in gold fringe. The rest of the décor was opulent. Oil lanterns with ornately decorated glass globes hung between the windows and swayed gently as the outside world rushed by. Starched white cloths set off the elegant tables outfitted with china, crystal goblets, and vases of dried roses. If it were not for the ever-present rattling coming from wheels on the tracks below, people would think they were in a fine restaurant.

Their hostess, Mrs. Sunderlin, looked regal. She seemed to fit into the posh atmosphere of the dining car. Sporting a silvery gray suit trimmed in black, she also wore a plum-colored turban. The hat was trimmed with feathers pinned together with a gold broach. Ida looked with admiration at the woman who carried her age with easy dignity. Ida was greatly impressed with her confidence in traveling solo since she couldn't help but recall the trepidation she'd felt ever since leaving home.

Under other circumstances, Ida might have been self-conscious, surrounded by the better-attired passengers. But, finding Mrs. Sunderlin to be personable and kind, Ida soon felt entirely at ease. Ernst was surprised to hear Ida, ordinarily silent, ask questions when Mrs. Sunderlin recalled a traveling adventure. The woman had encountered the famous outlaws Jesse and Frank James in recent years, and the retelling of the event was entertaining.

As their meal ended, Mrs. Sunderlin spoke in a kind tone to Ida, "My dear, I know I am still a stranger, but you look quite exhausted. Please come to my sleeping car and rest for the night. I have traveled this way many times, and the journey ahead will be tiresome."

"Thank you," Ida replied, "but I could not possibly do that."

Turning to Ernst, the woman reiterated, "It will do your wife good to have a restful night. Don't worry; I will take care of her."

Ernst surprised himself when he said, "Ida, I agree. You know what another night in the passenger car will be like. You hardly slept at all. I think you should accept Mrs. Sunderlin's thoughtful offer."

"At least come and see my compartment to reassure you that all will be well," persuaded the woman. After the trio traveled through two cars, Mrs. Sunderlin came to a stop and announced, "This is it! I am alone, and as you can see, there are two beds—just as I said."

After peeking in and seeing that everything was in order, Ida finally agreed to the arrangement. She was extremely fatigued, but leaving Ernst so she could stay with a stranger did not seem right.

On the other hand, Ernst was relieved. He gave Ida a quick hug and pushed her into the compartment. "I'll go fetch your bag and be right back."

Upon returning, Ernst gave Ida a reassuring kiss. "Sleep well, my dear, and I will see you in the morning."

As soon as Ernst left Ida with Mrs. Sunderlin, he returned to the dimly lit passenger car where they had spent most of their day. Walking through, he could make out the bulky shadows of fellow passengers curled up in their seats. Some were snoring in a deep sleep despite the roar of the rumbling, drafty train car. Tucking himself into a corner seat, Ernst pulled his hat over his face and turned up the collar of his jacket.

As his spirit quieted, a subtle sense of liberation washed over him, as he tried to fall asleep. For once, he realized, *I do not need to worry.* Ida will gain some needed rest under Mrs. Sunderlin's care. It surprised him to realize just how much constant attention his wife had required since their departure from Grafton. *Whenever I go for food or check some of our travel arrangements, she becomes anxious, and I feel uneasy. Everything about the trip has been stressful for her. I wonder if she is even enjoying this journey?*

Crestfallen, Ernst finally realized he was mildly disappointed to discover his wife's lack of grit for adventure. *She mostly sits at the window and looks out or dozes for hours until it is time to eat or change trains. Then she seems nervous, afraid of getting lost or being left behind.* Grappling with his thoughts, he recalled how he recently suggested to Ida that she visit with other women on board. Ida merely shook her head. Lacking pluck, she said, "I can't do that, not strike up a conversation with a stranger, not without you."

Unable to sleep, Ernst finally got up and restlessly paced through the passenger cars until he came to the men's smoking car. He sighed; it was deserted. Standing by a window and looking out at the moonless night, he reflected, *I will pray that things work out and Ida will get better. She is homesick, and maybe this trip is overwhelming her.*

Meanwhile, when Ida first entered Mrs. Sunderlin's Pullman sleeping compartment, her eyes grew big in amazement. The tiny room was made up as a cozy bedroom. Overhead, a gas lantern lit the space, radiating a warm and welcoming glow.

"I did not expect so much comfort," remarked Ida as she sat down on the spare bed with her small bag at her feet.

"See, there is plenty of room here for both of us. I am glad you are here." returned Mrs. Sunderlin. Ida watched as the older woman opened her traveling trunk and pulled out a flannel nightgown and matching nightcap. The gown was pure white and heavily adorned with beautiful lace. *At least my gown is new,* thought Ida. *The one I left behind was ready for the rag basket.*

After changing, Ida snuggled into the bed and sighed in contentment. Four days had passed since the start of their journey, and tonight she knew she would rest. As she lay comfortably stretched out, Ida visualized that Ernst was probably sitting upright in the corner of the passenger car with his feet propped up on their suitcase. His hat would be set down over his eyes. *He is probably already asleep,* she thought. Early on, Ida had discovered her husband could sleep anytime and anywhere. She just worried he was not cold and missing her by his side.

"Do you mind if I say my prayers out loud?" came a voice from the dark.

Turning her head toward the voice, Ida said, "Of course. Do you mind if I listen?"

"Please do; we seem to find more things to worry about instead of gratitude for the things we treasure. At the end of each day, I try to list all the graces that came my way."

As she prayed, Ida followed along, concentrating on the petitions. Mrs. Sunderlin concluded, "Bless our travels, and thank you for bringing Ida and Ernst to me on this journey. Amen."

"Amen," Ida mouthed, thinking how strange it was to have someone else praying for her. She remembered prayers being said at her confirmation, but this was personal. It made her feel good, even tranquil instead of awkward. Lying quietly in the dark, Ida whispered, "Thank you." She was touched to be so kindly included in the woman's prayer.

After a pause, Mrs. Sunderlin spoke up, "As you heard, Ida, I use my prayer time differently than others. I consider my prayer as having a conversation with a friend I trust and depend on."

"A friendship with Jesus?" questioned Ida.

"Oh my, yes! I often find I need to sort through and try to unlock an understanding of what is happening in my life, situations that press on me with worry. It is also a time I set aside to express gratitude. Every day, my heart is moved by different events, and I attribute those moments to Him at work in my life."

As Ida drifted off to sleep, she considered what Mrs. Sunderlin had shared, and it stirred her heart.

The following morning, Ernst was awakened by Ida gently kicking at his toes. She had easily located him sitting in the corner of the passenger car. His head bobbed against the window. Sitting down beside him, Ida shoved him gently, "Ernst! Are you awake? I'm hungry and wondered how long before we can get something to eat."

Sitting up, he planted a kiss on her cheek. Ida blushed, glancing around to see if anybody noticed. Ernst smiled and kissed her again, delighted to find her fully rested.

"I slipped out. Mrs. Sunderlin is so kind. I had a comfortable bed to sleep in. It even had a pillow. She is still asleep, but I missed you and didn't know what I would do if I could not find you."

"I won't let that happen, so don't worry." He yawned. He pulled out his watch, "It is barely 6 a.m. You must wait an hour until the dining car opens. Do you have anything left in your bag?"

"Only some sorry-looking apples. I'll wait." Then, looking out the window, she commented, "Look how the land has changed. It is all rolling hills and so different from the flat land at home."

"Yeah, I also noticed how much more distance between farms." They looked out together, taking in the sunrise as they waited for breakfast.

——✠——

Mrs. Sunderlin was already sitting at a table near the window when they entered the dining car just after seven. She looked up from the paper she was perusing, and upon noticing them, she smiled broadly, waving for them to join her. Looking Ida over, she smiled. "When I woke, you were gone. I did not hear you stir. I trust you slept well?"

"Oh my, Mrs. Sunderlin, indeed I did. Thank you so much for inviting me to stay in your car last night."

"No need to gush on, Ida. I want you and your husband to have a good trip, and it is hard to rest on a train chugging along at 25 miles per hour. I am pleased to see you this morning. I still want to learn more about your plans when you get to Los Angeles."

Ernst assisted Ida into a chair and then sat down, too. When the waitress came over, she offered hot coffee and handed out menus.

"Have you been to Kansas City before?" asked their companion. When they said no, she offered a suggestion. "Check the Florence schedule when you arrive. I remember there is usually a long wait before the train connection at that station. You might enjoy a meal at the Harvey House."

"I've heard about those places," recalled Ernst.

"The food is usually excellent and fairly priced. You could eat, and travelers often take food away for later. It is a busy place, a little too much for me, but my daughter enjoys going there."

"I'm up for seeing it. What do you think, Ernst?

"Fine by me; we should order toast to hold us over."

Having traveled extensively, Mrs. Sunderlin was well informed about the routes of the train lines. "I prefer to get home to Los Angeles on the southern Santa Fe route. It is more scenic, with long stretches of the western desert. It is not my kind of place to live but certainly worth passing through just to see the barren land filled with cacti."

"So, you don't suggest going through Salt Lake City?" asked Ernst.

"Sometimes, that route has trouble with the mountain tracks, landslides, and snow during the winter. They keep up the tracks, of course, but I prefer a more level grade myself," Mrs. Sunderlin returned.

"Are you returning home straightaway?" asked Ida, hoping the answer would be yes. She has so enjoyed the company and kindness of their new acquaintance.

"No, I will be stopping for a few days in Kansas City to see a friend. Then I will continue on home to Los Angeles."

"Oh," answered Ida, hiding her disappointment.

"Now, it might be useful if the two of you plied me with all the questions you must have about the city," she invited.

CHAPTER 18

Concerning Longhorns, Harvey Girls, and Mesquite

They imagined the thundering of 1000 hooves...

After breakfast, Mrs. Sunderlin rose from her chair. "I need to pack, so it is time to say goodbye. I wish you safe travels and hope you will find everything you seek in California."

Ernst and Ida watched as their cheerful traveling companion made her way through the busy tables to exit the dining car. In their short time together, they had discovered a kindred spirit and were saddened to see her go.

The couple returned to their passenger car, and after taking opposite seats, they watched the passing countryside through the window. The announcements for Kansas City soon began. Ida had counted more than 50 potential stops along the tracks since they had left Chicago, though the train proceeded without stopping if no passengers waited to board or they had no business to conduct.

Once they crossed the Hannibal Bridge over the Missouri River, they were suddenly moving into a city with more buildings and homes in view out their window. The activity on the train began to increase as people prepared to depart.

As Ida and Ernst sat by, they overheard a man comment, "It won't be long before we get to the stockyards."

His companion replied, "Someone told me that Kansas City will have more cattle yards than Chicago before the end of the decade."

"Yeah, I hear you can have a job for life, but it's hard to take all this. I mean, what else does this cowtown offer its citizens? I'm here for a business meeting with a broker, then I can't get away fast enough," disparaged the man.

They watched with fascination as the train slowed to a crawl as the tracks looped through the West Bottom area, the center of the livestock and meat-packing industry. The stock pens that ran up to the edge of the Kansas City River held cattle from all parts of the West, waiting to be herded away for processing. The beef and meat from other animals like hogs and sheep were sent eastward by refrigerated cars. Ida, eyes wide open, was dismayed by the sheer number of animals that would meet their gruesome fates in such an organized way.

When the train stopped, Ida and Ernst stood up to stretch and to get a better view out the window. They had agreed to remain on the train for the short layover, and they did not want to get caught up in the confusion of the people rushing about on the platform. The Kansas City station was a conglomeration of multiple tracks coming in from all directions.

As the couple watched, Ida spotted Mrs. Sunderlin. Their

new friend was making her way toward the door of the train depot, walking arm in arm with another woman. Both women were wearing large hats, and each held dainty handkerchiefs to their noses.

The train horn blared an hour later before slowly rolling out of Kansas City, fully loaded with passengers. As the conductor passed through the train checking tickets, he stopped momentarily to talk to them. The couple was disappointed to learn that Florence was 150 miles west of Kansas City. Ida caught Ernst rolling his eyes and smiled back. With hungry stomachs growling, they realized their breakfast plans to eat at the Harvey House would have to wait.

"After we arrive, the delay will be two hours for resupplying. Many of the travelers enjoy partaking of a meal," he suggested. Ida and Ernst glumly sat back in their seat to wait.

Twenty minutes later, Ida sat up and asked, "What's that?" pointing to a wooden object rising from the prairie.

"It's a windmill, Ida," replied Ernst. "As the wind drives the blades around, a mechanism pumps water up from the ground so ranchers can water their herds." Just then, Ernst noticed something approaching on the horizon.

When Ernst heard Ida exclaim, he could tell they were looking at the same thing; a herd of cattle was rushing over the crest of a hill. Even though they were out of hearing range, it was easy to imagine the thundering beat of a thousand hooves hitting the ground.

"Those must be the Texas longhorns," admired Ernst.

The animals were unlike any they had seen before. Their formidable long, thick horns extended outward from their mighty heads. The tips were turned up at the ends, gleaming in the sunlight. The massive herd picked up speed and finally disappeared in a great swirl of dust. It looked like a giant dust devil moving over a newly plowed field. Eventually, the thirsty herd reappeared and streamed toward a distant watering hole marked by another windmill that glinted in the sunlight.

Later, when they recalled watching the longhorns, they realized it was a marking point of their journey. The Midwest farming communities were now behind them. Yet to come were the remote lands over the longest portion of their trip to California. Ahead lay the southwestern region of the United States, including New Mexico and Arizona.

Many hours later, the train chugged into the Santa Fe Depot outside the modest town of Florence, Kansas. After making arrangements with the porter to reserve their seats, Ida and Ernst finally stepped off the train. Though they felt stiff and the feeling of the train motion persisted, walking the platform was a relief. As a passing passenger came toward them, Ernst called out the question on their mind. "So, is the Harvey House nearby?"

The man stopped and grinned. "Oh yes! Just on the other side of this building, across the road. It is the only place to take a meal around here." Then tipping his hat to Ida, he moved on but turned and thundered, "Try the pie. You won't be disappointed. They make perfect pie at the Harvey House."

In short order, Ida and Ernst pushed their way through the doors of one of the famous Harvey House restaurants. The dining room was bustling with waitresses darting between tables and attending to customers, and all of them wore identical long, black dresses and spotless white aprons. And every waitress's head was adorned with a sizeable white bow.

A young woman arrived and greeted the couple, saying, "Welcome. We are quite busy now, but a table just opened. Come this way." Once they were seated, she handed them menus.

"Any specials today?" asked Ernst, ever aware of their limited funds.

"The lunch special is a hot roast beef sandwich. The lunch crowd ate most of the pie, but more is baking in the oven. Now, what would you like to drink?"

Ida could hardly hold back a chuckle as she noticed the bow in the young woman's hair bobbing up and down as she spoke. "I guess a glass of milk, please," Ida ordered, cringing to think she would pay for milk when it was so abundant at home. Ida and Ernst both ordered the special of the day and cleaned their plate with the last crust of bread. They ordered a slice of pie à la mode and found it delicious. In fact, the entire meal service was efficient and tasty.

When they finished their meal, an hour remained before they needed to reboard. Ida encouraged Ernst to take a brisk walk, claiming, "You need the exercise. I look forward to sitting quietly without a rumble beneath me!" As she moved to a platform bench, she noticed someone had abandoned a tattered, almost coverless novel. Intrigued, she sat down, stretched out her feet in front of her, and began to read. When Ernst returned, Ida looked up sheepishly, realizing she had been engrossed in the book. She smiled and raised the book for him to see. "Look what I found."

By the time they re-boarded the westbound train, they felt rested and eager to get moving. Having read the first chapter, Ida handed the book over to Ernst, saying, "This is a western adventure, the kind Eddy reads. Maybe we could pass the time…."

The next few days, as Ida dozed and listened, Ernst read the engaging story about Buck, a rugged and invincible rancher living in Texas. In the saga, Ida and Ernst imagined joining a cattle drive for a desert crossing under the dire urgency to move 300 head of livestock to water before the herd perished. Another chapter in the book concerned Buck's search for stray cattle that had been "rustled away" and hidden in a canyon. Under the blistering heat, Buck had to contend with a rattlesnake and a panther before meeting Emanuel Alverdo. "Manny" was a jovial old monk from Mexico who eked out a subsistence living in the wilderness. He helped Buck snag the rustlers. The tale was immensely satisfying, and the view of desert wilderness out their window made the experience twice as thrilling.

Ida found herself thinking about the description of the desert in their book. She sat up and announced, "I want to go and see it up close."

"What do you want to see?" puzzled Ernst.

"Cactus. We have passed them for days, but reading about the desert makes me want to see the real thing up close."

"The sky is as blue and vast as at home, but this place is not like anything I've ever seen before," agreed Ernst.

"How can one judge how big these things are without getting closer? See that cactus out there? The distance fools me, I think."

Ernst followed Ida's gaze to a giant cactus in the distance. Her plea made him smile. *Rarely did Ida express her feelings about things. If she wants to prick her finger on a cactus, I'm not going to get in her way.*

When the train stopped to resupply in Winslow, Arizona, Ernst stood up and suggested, "Let's go have a look."

Some passengers headed into the town to eat or see the sights, including the old Hubbell Trading Post or the St. Joseph Church. Ida and Ernst headed in the opposite direction along with half a dozen fellow travelers. They strolled to the end of the short wooden platform. With their backs to the buildings and the converging tracks of the Atlantic and Pacific Railways, they looked south. The barren terrain seemed endless. As Ida stepped down into the sand, a smell she did not recognize wafted toward them on the slight breeze.

"What is that smell?" murmured Ida.

"That, little miss, is the mesquite you be smelling," spoke up a rugged-looking man wearing a sweat-stained sombrero bleached by the sun. Pleased that his words had caught the attention of the small group of travelers, he smiled. Raising his cane, he pointed to a stand of scraggly-looking trees a short distance away. "That is the mesquite," he explained. "Out here, mesquite is vital for survival; it is tough and stubborn, growing where it wants."

With piqued curiosity, the group clustered around, eager to listen to the wizened old man. "If you have never seen it before, I suggest walking out and looking. Mesquite grows everywhere in the desert. The ranchers aren't too happy when it gets in the grassy areas. If you want to go out, I best walk with you."

"Yes, please," piped up a woman dressed in a smart suit and holding a frilly parasol. Her skinny teenage son accompanied her.

"Come on, then, while there is still time. Don't worry about the train. We're in plain sight. Besides, the conductor knows me, and he would not dare leave without you," reassured the old-timer.

Despite the oppressive heat, everyone in the group moved with the man as he set out to walk in the sand. Ida and Ernst joined the group but hung back slightly to talk. As they walked, Ida commented to Ernst how she could feel the ground's heat rising through her dress.

Ernst nodded sympathetically. The heat reminded him of standing next to the steam engine while it ran during threshing. *Her wool dress must feel like a hot oil stove!*

"Ida, do you know who he reminds me of?" asked Ernst.

Ida giggled. "I was thinking the same thing, Emanuel Alverdo. It is as if he stepped right out of a chapter in our story."

"I don't remember seeing him on the train. I wonder where he is from," teased Ernst in a low voice.

The desert cowboy was an older, wiry man. Though he might have towered over most people at one time, now he was bent with age. In one hand, he carried a peculiar walking cane that appeared to be covered in snakeskin, except for the handle, which was ornately carved and trimmed with silver. His other hand, withered and leathery-looking, twitched occasionally.

Ida observed his dark, wool jacket, roughly mended Levi pants, and boots as they walked behind him. *He must be a cow-*

boy; his boots have...spurs. So that is what they look like. I'll have to write to tell Eddy about him.

As the group moved along, "Manny" stopped to point out the different desert features, including several unusual kinds of cactus plants. "That is the prickly pear," he said. "The flowers are pretty, but those spikes are not."

"We saw some tall spikey trees on the trip. What are those called?" asked someone else.

The cowboy grinned, "I expect you noticed the saguaros. Some of those cactuses, the Indians say, have been growing for more than a 100 years. Some of them can rise more than 50 feet in the air. Most important, the saguaro can be tapped for water out in this dry land."

"How long are the spikes?" the teenager piped up.

"Near three inches and sharper than steel needles."

Ernst was amazed. Grappling to put the enormous cactus tree into perspective, he recalled that most farm silos are never more than 30 feet tall.

As they neared the mesquite stand, the cowboy put out his cane and said harshly, "Hush." The group froze in place, listening. They heard a rattling buzz vibrating somewhere, but their untrained ears could not determine the direction from which it came. They turned questioning faces to the pock-marked face of the cowboy. "That be what a rattler sounds like. Don't fret; it isn't close. Just keep your eyes open as we move along." The group came to a halt once again as he pointed out a small scorpion. The sinister-looking shiny black creature with a curled-up tail scurried across the sandy path. Manny calmly advised, "Those tend to be fatal. Best avoid them."

Ernst felt Ida slip her shaking hand into his, and he squeezed it reassuringly. She seemed to be both excited and nervous. He noticed her looking around carefully as though half expecting to step on something menacing like a snake or a cactus spike.

A quarter-mile distant, they arrived at the mesquite grove. Eight-inch pods hanging from the mesquite trees caught the group's attention. Manny spoke up, "That's desert food for humans and livestock alike. It is also a favorite of the coyotes. The pods can be ground into a sweet flour. Other parts of the tree are even used for medicine. That wood makes a good fire that burns without smoking."

Nearby, one of the trees had been uprooted, sending a thick root jutting upward. Curiously, the exposed root was twice as thick as the tree was round.

Suddenly, the train whistle sounding off broke the silence of the desert. The group hastily walked back to the platform. Still leading them, Manny suddenly stopped at the trail's edge. Lifting his large hat from his head, he turned it over and held it out as the passengers walked by.

As Ernst fumbled for a coin in his pocket to drop into the hat, it dawned on him that giving tours was the man's gig. Ernst guessed that "Manny" showed up whenever a train rolled into Winslow and offered a local tour. He considered it a well-spent coin. Later, Ernst told Ida that their impromptu excursion reminded him of an entertaining circus ring act. It was a "desert" variety with "Manny" as their eccentric showman.

SECTION 5

Los Angeles

CHAPTER 19

The Hamilton Boarding House

What will it be like to live in a big city?

The whistle sounded soon after the conductor announced the train's imminent arrival at the Rio Grande Station. As they approached, the train began to crawl slowly through the outlying neighborhoods of Los Angeles. Ernst and Ida caught glimpses of the downtown skyline with multistoried buildings. The days of perching on uncomfortable seats and looking through smudged train windows would soon be over. Ida sighed in relief. She would not miss the noisy rumbling of the cars moving over the iron tracks, the frequent stops, erratic meals, or uncomfortable sleeping conditions. Ida tried to quell her apprehensive thoughts. *What will our new way of life be like in the big city?*

As the train eased to a stop at the large platform, Ida stood up, pulled at her tight sleeves, and adjusted her bodice. She also tried to smooth out the wrinkles in her skirt made by long hours of sitting. Returning to the bench, Ida carefully tucked her errant curls into place. At just the right moment, Ernst, familiar with her routine, retrieved her hat from the overhead rack.

After securing her bonnet with two long hat pins, Ida looked up to meet the tired eyes of her husband. The journey had been a blur of time spent reading train schedules and worrying about transfers, meals, and money. Already they had paid out more money for sandwiches and coffee than they had planned along the way. *Oh, well, it can't be helped. We can be more frugal once we find a room,* thought Ida.

Ernst smiled at her reassuringly as he put out a hand to help her to her feet. "Come, my Ida, we are here. Our trip is over, and here is where we will make our new start!"

———

Ida and Ernst decided to begin their new life in Los Angeles by first seeking accommodations. "A boarding house would be more reasonable than staying at a hotel, Ida," said Ernst.

"If we could stay in the same place for a while, you could look for a job, and we can get to know our way around the town," reasoned Ida.

Sitting nearby, a fellow passenger leaned over and interrupted, "I overheard you talking. I can recommend a boarding house if you are looking for one."

Interested, the couple listened eagerly as the man cautioned them about choosing a place to stay. "I've stayed at the Hamilton Boarding House several times. It is a respectable place in a good location. Of course, you must expect things to cost more in the city, but the rate usually includes a daily meal, so you won't need to cook."

So, with directions in hand, they walked the necessary number of blocks to their destination. They were pleased to learn a room was indeed available, but dismayed that the clerk insisted they pay ahead, a week at a time. As he carefully laid out the dollars, Ernst reminded himself that a room was a necessary expense.

When registration was complete, one of the staff showed them the way to a second-floor room. The man handed the room key to Ernst, reminding him, "Please leave the key at the desk when you go out." It was a relief to have a room of their own. Ida unpacked their suitcases, hanging her dresses and Ernst's shirts, while Ernst arranged for baths.

The following day, Ida and Ernst wandered the busy streets. Under sunny skies, they took in the sights, including a close-up view of a horseless carriage. They shopped at the nearby market, buying fresh bread and fragrant oranges. Later, they ate at a lunch counter and treated themselves to a scoop of ice cream.

Exploring Los Angeles unfettered with luggage and the wonderful knowledge that they could leave the train schedules, soot, noise, and constant motion behind was a relief. As they walked, it was hard not to notice the drawbacks of city living. The pungent and unavoidable odors of the city filled their noses. The horses moving on the streets also contributed manure in the gutters with other refuse, breeding flies and making for poor sanitation. It was not exactly a perfect postcard picture of California. Nevertheless, Ida and Ernst enjoyed their time and carried on with light spirits as they recovered from traveling fatigue.

On the third day, Ida started to cough uncontrollably. "I just need to rest. I'll be okay," she insisted. Ernst realized that Ida was probably still feeling the effects of the trip, so he guided her back to the room and insisted she rest.

The following day, a note appeared, having been slipped under their door during the night. The words on the paper still burned him: *It has come to our attention that we will need your room. Please arrange to vacate today. We will refund the remaining balance of your stay.*

When Ernst marched down to the front desk, demanding an explanation, the clerk offered sheepishly, "We need the room—just like the note says."

When Ernst pressed on that he needed to speak to someone else, the clerk called a man in a suit of fine clothing from a back room. "You are obviously not from around here," he sneered. "We can no longer accommodate you here. You should have known that." When Ernst insisted on more details, the arrogant man finally admitted that one of the other guests had complained about hearing Ida coughing. "The management does not allow sick people to stay at the Hamilton House."

"But where are we to go? I'm looking for work as it is." An unsympathetic, silent, and cold stare was the only reply. Outraged, Ernst waited until the clerk slid the money he was due across the counter.

Upon overhearing the discussion at the front desk, another staff member, an older man, flagged Ernst as he headed outside. Motioning Ernst to follow him, they moved out of view of the front desk. Glancing around to make sure he could speak freely, the man began, "You were treated poorly and rudely.

So many are quick to vilify the victims, afraid of catching the plague themselves. It is not right. I saw your poor wife; she looks as young and innocent as my daughter. My brother works up the hill at Duclane's. I think they help people in your situation."

Ernst glared at the man, still steaming from the recent encounter. But as he started to focus on what the man was saying, he judged him to be genuinely kind. Ernst then recalled a memory of Arne mentioning the name *Duclane* at one time. *Is this a sign?* Ernst wondered, then clarified, "Is that the sanitarium you speak of?"

The man nodded. "You should try to go there. I advise you not to argue to stay here at the Hamilton. It could turn nasty. I have seen what happens when others have been shown the door."

Ernst looked at him with alarm thinking that something dreadful could come of this situation. The man added adamantly, "Your wife doesn't deserve such treatment. No one does."

After considering his options, Ernst quickly made a plan. *We have no choice,* he thought ruefully. *I must believe this encounter is perhaps from God, as I don't know what else to do.*

After breakfast, he announced to Ida that they would be leaving. "I've heard of that place of which your father spoke. Duclane's is close, just up the hill. I think it would be good for us to go there."

"Oh," her voice dipped. "The sanitarium?" questioned Ida in a confused and quivering voice. "Are you sure we need to go there? I thought we talked about remaining here at this boarding place for at least a few weeks until you found work."

Ernst replied softly without revealing more details than necessary, trying to rouse his confidence in the plan. "Yes, Ida, it is for the best. Now let's go back and pack our things. We can look forward to a pleasant walk. We will be going up a hill, probably the biggest hill you have ever climbed in your whole life!"

CHAPTER 20

Rules of the Sanitarium

No Spitting.

"*This has to* be the place," said Ida, huffing. It had taken more than an hour to reach their destination. As soon as they got started, Ernst regretted not hiring a ride. Halfway up the hill, they discovered the roads were not straight. After zigzagging in the neighborhood streets and finally feeling like they were getting closer, the road ended abruptly at the edge of a ravine.

Ultimately, Ernst asked for directions on how to circumvent the way. Finally seeing a newly painted sign marking the entrance to the Duclane Sanitarium was a great relief. They could see only a hint of roofs hidden behind a small rise in the land from their vantage point. The area had a sense of newness, and rather than housing, it was open meadows and rolling hills.

"Please, Ernst, I need to catch my breath before we go on," Ida entreated. Ernst responded by turning the suitcase he carried on its end and placing it in a sliver of shade near the gate, instructing her to sit. While she rested, they surveyed the area. As they waited, a friendly black lab trotted up to greet them.

After Ida had rested and the gentle dog had been sufficiently petted, they continued the trek up the driveway. At the top, they came to an office sign with an arrow pointing to the building ahead. Ernst turned and smiled encouragingly, "Come, dear, let us see what this place is about." When they entered the door, a man working at a desk raised his head. The sign on the desk read, "Mr. Wilcox, Manager." The man quickly assessed Ida and Ernst. From their worn faces and the luggage they carried, he knew they were seeking help.

Ernst walked over to his desk, announcing, "Good morning, sir. We are Mr. and Mrs. Ottoson," extending his hand in a friendly handshake gesture. "We are here because…."

Mr. Wilcox listened as Ernst explained their presence in a halting manner, seeming to search for the right English words to use. By her thin and frail appearance, it was evident that the nice-looking young woman at his side was sickly. The wistful look she carried in her eyes filled him with compassion.

When Ernst began to ask, "Do you have any lodging…?" Mr. Wilcox immediately put up his hand. Shaking his head side to side, he informed them. "No, we do not have any available rooms. You will have to move along. I'm sorry, but we cannot help you."

Even as he said it, Mr. Wilcox groaned inwardly. *How many times must I turn away hopeful folks?*

In desperation, Ernst persisted, "I see by the sign in the window that you need help. Perhaps it is work that I can do? I'm strong, and I need a job."

"Well…" Mr. Wilcox drawled, "I just put up that notice this morning. We need someone to run errands and perform general handyman repairs."

Ida spoke up for her husband, firmly boasting, "This man, he's a hard worker. He knows horses and has helped my pa build a house."

Mr. Wilcox chuckled. "She gives you quite a recommendation, but I would need a reference from someone else."

Ernst's shoulders started to droop, and then he looked at Ida. With a sense of urgency, he pleaded, "We just arrived from the Dakotas. I am a farmhand. Unfortunately, I did not think to get a reference before I left. We do not know anyone here yet."

Ida spoke again. "If you would be willing to give my husband a chance, he will show you he is the man for the job."

"Well, this is highly usual, but I would be willing to take you on for a trial period as we have been left short-handed rather abruptly. It is hard to find someone with experience and motivation."

Ida looked up at Mr. Wilcox with hope, and he felt her relief.

"There is a cabin-like accommodation on the back lot. If you are serious about working, you and your wife may stay there for the present. It is in a sunny location, and the air is good."

Ernst turned to Ida, and she nodded agreeably. *Maybe this is the next step in our journey.*

Mr. Wilcox went on. "The place is one of the resting cabins, just like we provide for our guests. It is a simple accommodation, but it is open for this position. You must be available at all hours as you may be summoned if an emergency arises. Would that be agreeable?"

"Of course, I understand," Ernst replied firmly, "We are most grateful."

"You also must understand we will not ask for rent but rather in-kind labor. You must offer free labor hours if your wife stays with you in the cabin. Of course, you will also receive the usual wage and board allowance. Meals can also be obtained from our cafeteria for a small fee."

"But, about my wife, she needs medical care. That is why we came. We read that you help people with her condition," implored Ernst.

Mr. Wilcox put his fingers to his chin in thought. Then, sighing loudly, he announced. "There are some rules for our patients to follow. However, I think I can work around what is generally required. We are proud of our treatment programs and have had great success. Maybe later we can arrange for your wife to be seen by our specialist, Dr. Duclane."

Mr. Wilcox then stood up and excused himself as he left the room. Ernst and Ida were uncertain of what they should do, so they waited. When the manager reappeared, he had a young man at his heels. "This is Simon. He will take you to the place I described. Mind you, the cabins are spare. Mr. Ottoson, you come back here in the morning at eight. Talk it over with your wife tonight and decide if you are interested in taking the job."

Then, addressing Simon, Mr. Wilcox instructed, "Give Mr. and Mrs. Ottoson the usual tour of the place as you take them to the caretaker's cabin. Ensure there is oil, and then show him where to get water."

Turning to the waiting couple, he added, "I will arrange for a food basket to be delivered to you at the cabin."

Before they left, Ida overhead Simon being admonished, "What have I told you about your dog coming on the property?"

———∿∿∿———

Come on, miss, let's get you sorted." Simon's words were kind and straightforward. For the first time in weeks, someone else walked with them along an unknown path. So did Remington, Simon's dog. "I hope you don't mind him; Remmy hasn't learned to follow my command to stay at home very well."

Assuming Ernst had been hired to fill the vacant job, Simon fully intended to ply the couple with questions. *Who are these folks that seemed to show up from nowhere at the gate of the sanitarium? Their clothes are of heavy cloth, outdated but new...and their curious accent?* Simon led them along a walkway that threaded through the palm tree-dotted campus. Eagerly he pointed out the different buildings and their purpose, including the medical offices, cafeteria, and laundry. He also began to speak about the rules of the place. Ida was appalled when he said, "I have to tell you there is to be no spitting on the grounds, miss." When he pointed out the doctors' offices, he instructed, "Never go there without an appointment. It is against the rules just to show up."

Simon came to a stop and pointed to the most prominent building on the campus. "That is the infirmary. If you look up to the second floor, you can see our guests on the balcony. They spend the daylight resting there on beds; when they get stronger, they can go to work or sit in the gardens. That building is also where the baths are located."

Ida, now completely exhausted, started to feel dizzy and reached to take Ernst's elbow. Simon, seeing her falter, halted. He then pointed and said, "Those are the cabins over there."

Ahead, capping a rise on a nearly treeless hill, was a cluster of 20 brown-colored canvas tents. Except for the colorful blankets and shawls laid across the porch rockers set out in front, each "cabin" was identical in shape and size. When Ida saw them, she was overcome with uneasiness. *This is what I imagine a military camp would look like. It is not what I was expecting.*

Getting closer, Simon explained, "You will be staying in number 11. Inside, you'll find a table, oil burner, and beds. The buckets are to be used only for hauling water. I will show you where the pump is before I leave you."

Ida could see no one else milling about or sitting out on the porches. The stillness of the place was broken only by the chirping of a small bird sitting in a nearby newly planted tree. "Are we the only ones here?" she asked.

"It is the quiet time of day, Mrs. Ottoson," explained Simon, "Most of our residents are over at the bathhouse." Simon then commented on another rule involving cold baths needing to be taken frequently. Ida and Ernst looked at each other dubiously as they thought that was a ridiculous rule.

When they reached the porch, Ida leaned into Ernst. Wrapping her in a supportive embrace, he helped her step up onto the plank porch of number 11. After settling in a wicker rocker, Ida insisted in a trembling voice, "You go ahead with Simon and find out about this place. I'll sit here on the porch."

The men entered the cabin, and Simon went directly to the kerosene heater, where he trimmed the wick and added some fuel to the base of the apparatus. He noticed Ernst surveying the hillside from the door. Simon offered encouragingly, "It is not much, but you will find you are welcome here. The place is still under construction. Mr. Wilcox will be sending someone over to help get your missus settled. In the meantime, we can go and draw some cool water from the well, and you can help me open the porch awning."

Ernst, glad to be told what to do, reached for the empty buckets and a pottery crock. "I'll be right back," he told Ida. She nodded from her chair. He could see her eyelids growing heavy. "Simon says someone will come shortly to help us settle in." In a lowered voice, Ernst joked, "I have no idea what that could mean."

As the men walked away, Ida noticed Simon reach over to pat Ernst on the back. She saw his head drop over his drooping shoulders. *Ernst is discouraged.* Ida felt the same. *Thank You, Lord, for the kindnesses we have encountered today, even if it is only for a while.*

An hour later, an older, robust woman with rosy cheeks and a cheery disposition arrived. She was carrying a heavily laden basket and a broom. "Hello, folks, I am Sally." Her loud greeting roused both where they sat dozing. "I've come to help you. I will be needing to sweep out this cottage. I like to call them that; it sounds better than "the cabins." While I am here, we will go over the sanitarium rules. Most people have questions about how we do things around here."

Ernst raised his eyebrows. Again, there was a puzzling

reference to "The Rules." He had already noticed a sign posted behind the door concerning them but did not deem them
worth reading.

Addressing Ida, Sally questioned, "There isn't much to our
cottages, but are you ready to get up for a look inside?"

Ida squared her jaw and set her hands to the armrest of the
rocker to rise. Seeing she was weak and unsteady, Sally stepped
up to assist as she adjusted Ida's shawl around her shoulders.
Then, with her arm wrapped around the sickly girl's waist, Sally encouraged, "Come on, I've got you; there is no hurry."

The lodgings of the two-room tent were spare. One area
was set aside as sleeping quarters, and the other had a table,
two chairs, and a kerosene heater. Along one wall was a long
shelf upon which a washbasin resided beside a towel hook. The
small windows vented the tent and brought light to the musty-
smelling space.

Ida wrinkled her nose and sneezed. Sally reassured her that
a good sweeping and airing out was in order. Looking into the
bedroom, Ida could see two narrow cots with a bedside table
between them. On the opposing wall were two shelves for storage. Having spied their luggage still sitting on the porch, Sally
stated, "You didn't bring much. Did you leave a trunk at the
train station? We can fetch it for you."

Ida shook her head, "No, we traveled light. There were
many train transfers along the way. We decided to bring no
more than we could carry."

"I will see about some blankets and sheets then. Usually,
we ask our residents to provide them, but don't worry. I'll have
this place ready for you in no time; you wait and see." Then,

turning to Ernst, she suggested, "Why don't you take your wife over to the flower garden while I straighten up here. I will unpack and put your things in place."

"Oh…no, that is not necessary. I prefer to take care of my things," Ida quickly piped up. "I think a walk will do me good." Ida directed her next comment to her husband, "Come, Ernst. Walk with me."

Giving instructions on how to get to the garden, Sally pointed as she said, "Go down the rise until you get to the brick wall. The smell of the jasmine will lead you to the gardens. Take your time. I will be back later with some food."

Sally, anxious to get on with her work, waved the couple off. After opening the cabin for airing, she swept the floor. When the dust settled, Sally made up the beds with fresh linens and added two patchwork quilts left behind by other patients. Spread out, the quilts added cheerful colors to the otherwise drab space.

On the kitchen counter, she laid out one white metal cup, a dozen handkerchiefs, some wash rags, and a bar of sweet-scented soap. She also supplied the travelers with bread, cheese, and oranges.

When Ida and Ernst came back from their walk, Sally began to instruct them about the rules. "Here at Duclane's, we keep the disease contained." Then, directing her eyes to Ida, she said, "There will be no spitting on the ground. This white cup or these hankies are to be always kept at your side. The hankies will be collected for burning every other day, and you will be resupplied. Never wash them out and reuse them out of frugality. They are riddled with the disease."

Overcome with rising panic, Ida thought, *Why do you look at me like that? Do you also consider me as being "riddled" with disease?*

Sally then began rattling off a litany of Duclane Rules. "The main meal is available in the canteen every day between 11:00 a.m. to 2:00 p.m. You may cook on the stove, but mostly folk make only coffee and toast." She directed Ernst, "You may bring food to your wife, but all dishes must be returned promptly for proper washing."

Ida's insides felt twisted in knots. *This kind woman standing in front of me is trying to offer help and advice. Yet...there is judgment in the pointed way she looks at me—just like at the hotel we were asked to leave.*

Later that night, as they watched a fiery sunset from their porch, Ida mentioned her feelings to Ernst. He flatly downplayed the interaction. "Ida, you are still weary and recovering from the long train trip." Ida said nothing. Rising from his seat, Ernst insisted, "It has been a big day. Let us go in, and I'll help you get ready for bed." Putting out his hands, he helped her to her feet.

Once inside, Ida began to unfasten her dress. When she tried to remove her shirtwaist, she lost patience fumbling with the fasteners. "Ernst, can you help me undo these last hooks?" she pleaded.

Ernst came to her side and undid the troublesome hooks at her throat. He then tugged at her shirt cuffs as she shrugged her shoulders out of the confining garment. Relief washed over her to be free of the tightly fitted top. Ida sat on the bed and closed her eyes, feeling the welcoming, warm breeze filtering through the open window near their beds. Ernst knelt and untied her shoelaces and pulled off her leather oxfords. Ida wiggled her toes and stretched her feet. Finally, she stood and unhooked her traveling skirt and petticoat, which billowed to the floor. Ernst took her outstretched hand as she stepped out of the circle of fabric. He bent down and picked up the 15-yard bundle of dress goods and looked around, puzzled.

"Just hang them over the chair for now," suggested Ida.

When Ernst turned around, she heard the dismay in his voice as he remarked, "I thought you were not going to wear that blasted thing anymore!"

Flattening her hand to her chest, Ida glanced down and blushed as she returned, "I had to wear it. I could not arrive in this big city dressed improperly. You don't understand."

"But you promised. You said it made it hard for you to breathe, especially when you're feeling so poorly," replied Ernst, softening his voice.

"I don't want to talk about this right now," returned Ida irritably, turning away to struggle with the laces of her corset. The forbidden clothing was designed to trim a woman's waist and at the same time throw her chest forward to create the fashionable "S" shape.

"Here, I will help you with that," offered Ernst; he could see she was frustrated and tired.

As soon as she put on her nightgown, Ida lay down on the narrow cot, sinking her head onto the pillow. Then, curling into a ball facing the wall, she closed her eyes.

Ernst thoughtfully retrieved the ragged blanket from their things and spread it over her. *Hannah was so right to insist we bring this quilt with us.* How often he had reached for it along their train journey.

After settling Ida, Ernst sat on the front porch. For the first time in many days, he found himself in a quiet moment. Since they had begun their journey, his mind and senses had been continuously wrapped up in all the trip details. In addition, he had suffered the continuous noises, erratic meals, the search for places to sleep, jostling crowds, and always the constant worry for Ida. The trip was too much for her.

Ernst willed himself to breathe deeply and let his thoughts roll over and over. *We made it...California...this place will give us a new start...a better place for Ida.* Ernst whispered a prayer for his wife, recalling the reassuring words of the prophet Isaiah: *They that hope in the LORD will renew their strength, they will soar on eagles' wings...and not grow weary* (40:31). He implored, "Lord, we will need Your help; show us the way."

Ernst drew out his pipe. He filled the chamber with a meager pinch of tobacco and lit it. Watching the smoke float away and disappear into fading twilight brought a sense of relaxation. Then, just when he finally started to relax, the morning's events came flying back into his head and gave him a start. Ernst again felt the sting as he recalled what had happened at the Hamilton. *I wonder if Ida heard their remarks?* He could do nothing more to buffer his anger and embarrassment at being turned away. Just the memory of it made his stomach flip and churn.

CHAPTER 21

A Letter Home

But I did not tell them we were here!

Ida awoke and felt immediately confused. *Where am I?* She called out, "Ernst, are you here?"

Ernst had risen earlier and started a pot of coffee to brew on the small oil burner. When Ida got up, she found him sitting on the porch. His head was cast down in thought as he studied the cup he held in his hands.

"Good morning, Ernst," she announced brightly, "I'm feeling better today. What time is it?"

Pulling out his watch, he opened the case. "Almost eight. I need to go meet Mr. Wilcox. Will you be all right? I will try to come back midday if I get a break."

"Of course, I will be just fine. What a lovely day it is!"

"It will be good to be outside and be busy. But I wonder what I will be working at today," pondered Ernst.

"We are indeed fortunate Mr. Wilcox offered you a job. Don't worry about me. I look forward to sitting here and writing a letter home."

"I will go, but before I leave, give me a kiss that will hold me all the workday," Ernst teased. He loved how that request always seemed to make her blush and beam.

———∿∿∿———

Ida furrowed her eyebrows and stared at the blank piece of paper. Her hand was clenched around a pencil stub poised to write. If only the voice in her head would stop scolding, *You have put this off for too long. You know they are waiting every day for a letter.*

Determined, Ida began: *Dear Mama and Pa.*

After listing the names of her siblings: Caroline, Alfred, Oscar, Laura, Alma, and Clarence, she also included Uncle Anthony's name. He had supported them with his money and made their trip possible; he deserved to have his name in the letter. Spurred on by imagining everyone's excitement to receive word from California, Ida wrote rapidly.

> *We arrived in California Thursday past. The train journey was long and dirty. I spent days with my smudged nose pressed to the window. The tracks carried us across farmlands, settlements, and through the bigger cities of Minneapolis, Chicago, and Kansas City. It was not until after we reached Kansas City that we finally headed westward and seemed to make progress. The desert is dry, barren land. Instead of trees, there are large strange plants called cactus and sagebrush. The cactus doesn't have leaves but is covered by fierce-looking spikes. The train stopped many times, every 300 miles, for water and fuel. Every time the engine whistle let out*

steam, it sounded like a scream. When we finally arrived
in Los Angeles, we went to a boarding house near down-
town. Unfortunately, the journey was more costly than
we planned. Our room costs $2 per night plus our meals,
so our purse is lighter now.

That said, I must say California is lovely. Bloom-
ing flowers everywhere, as well as palm trees. They look
just like the sketches in the dictionary—tall and skinny
with bushy tops of feathery leaves. Here in the city, many
people rush around. There are many horses with bug-
gies and wagons in town—also bicycles and cable cars
that look like single train cars but run on overhead wires.
Let Alfred know that sometimes there were thirty cars or
more attached to our train.

Mama, I miss your bread and soup. The food at the
boarding house is poor. I am fine. I know you worry, but
we will make our way. People say the city is growing.
Some people even have oil wells in their yards; it is true!
They look like a thick black forest of tall metal church
spires. Ernst found work straightaway. He insists I must
rest, so I sit outside in a chair as I write. Do not worry
about us. We will be fine...

Ida began to cough at that moment, and before she could
cover her mouth, a blood drop splattered her letter. She hastily
dabbed at the spots with her handkerchief and water. The letter was now watermarked and wrinkled. Then, too frustrated
and too tired to rewrite the words, Ida folded the letter, shoved
it into an envelope, and laid it aside. Shifting in her chair, she

closed her eyes and pulled her shawl over her face. Her lips were trembling, and her eyes started to fill with tears.

Later that afternoon, Ernst found the letter lying beside the porch. He commented, "Oh, good, Ida. Can I see what you have written?" Ida grimly nodded. Scanning the contents, he commented, "You write a fine letter. I'll ask Mr. Wilcox where to post it."

"But I didn't tell them we were here," Ida confessed, despondently sweeping her limp arm out to gesture at their surroundings.

"I'll add a little note, so they will know where to reach us. Your mother and Caroline are waiting to hear from us, so they can write back. Besides, we also need to ask about Hazel. What should we say?"

With his encouragement, Ernst wrote the words as Ida dictated. When they were satisfied with the letter, Ida said, "Give me the pencil. I'd better address it, or they will think something is wrong. Can you please get a stamp from my sewing box?"

With the letter complete, Ida felt she had accomplished something worthwhile. Next time, Ida thought, *I will write to just Mama and let her know more. By then, we will know if this job of Ernst's will work out and if we are still here.*

CHAPTER 22

Adjusting to Life at Duclane's

The definition of torpid is to be slow, sluggish, or inactive.
Ida felt torpid.

Sally arrived almost daily to replenish supplies like hankies and deliver fresh bread, fruit, and cheese from her basket. Midday, Ernst would come with a meal from the dining hall or make arrangements for someone else to check in on her. Ida assumed that she was not welcome to mingle with the other guests as they continued to wait to be summoned for a doctor's appointment. It was another rule they had agreed to follow.

As the days went on, Ida and Ernst adjusted to living in their spare accommodations. Sometimes they called it a cabin, other times a tent, but never "home," as they held onto the positive thought that they would not be here for too long.

In the beginning, when Ernst left in the morning, Ida stayed near the cabin. In the late afternoon, she would sit in one of the porch rockers, waiting for him to come walking up the hill. The idea of idleness in all its forms was almost more than Ida could endure. Within the time between resting and waiting, she tried to keep busy. She sewed on the quilt top, tidied their quarters, and visited the garden and the large chicken coop. Ida explored the extensive 25-acre sanitarium grounds in ever-widening circles from their cabin-tent site when restlessness set in, and she had the energy.

Ida found that being isolated in the tent location and having so few encounters with others since their arrival at Duclane's was unnerving. In the beginning, she had been told not to socialize with others, so she complied. When someone would pass her on a path or walk in front of her cabin, Ida hoped they would initiate a conversation. Therefore, Ida would smile or wave, and the moment would pass. *I cannot put my husband's job in jeopardy.*

She resolutely whiled away the hours in self-imposed seclusion, hoping her lungs were healing. She patiently waited and watched her surroundings. Sometimes, Ida questioned why so few people lived in the cabin tents but concluded few would put up with the rude accommodations for very long.

Probably they became patients in the infirmary and are sitting up on the balcony with the others.

Ida's quiet mannerisms made her approachable to a few wild creatures nearby. Of course, her conversations were one-sided. Still, she was cheered a little by a robin or the ground squirrels. The best companion was when Remington showed up. He would come right up to her and lay his head in her lap. After the cordial greeting, he lay at her feet.

Remmy often remained close until Simon whistled for

him at the end of the day. Simon asked again if she minded his presence, and Ida insisted the dog was welcome. Since the cabins were away from the main building, nobody took notice, and Ida gained comfort in talking to the dog as if he were human.

The supposedly beneficial climate that had brought them to California was agreeable. On most days, it was sunny and mild. Occasionally, the weather turned from pleasant to gray and overcast, and with it, so did Ida's mood. When a drizzle of rain and thick fog made the air feel heavy to breathe, she became irritable.

On one such day, Ida snapped when her husband arrived home late from running errands for the sanitarium. She was still in her nightgown when he arrived. When he asked if she had gone to the gardens that day, she became irritated and responded angrily.

"No, Ernst, I did not. You know the rules. I have been told not to breathe on anyone. So, I will just stay here. You have your work and can go where you want. I miss that. If we had our own place, somewhere with a kitchen, I could be busy making meals and taking care of things. Here, nothing is expected of me," grumbled Ida. *Why did I say that?* thought Ida dismally. *Ernst is just trying to take care of me.*

In response to her litany of complaints, Ernst sighed, saying, "Ida, I am sorry that you are here alone. It has been a tough day for me too." Ernst explained how the roads were muddy, the stench from the gutters unbearable, and he had trouble finding his way around the city. In the end, the conversation eased the couple's spirits. They reminded each other that, as complicated as the present circumstances were, they were temporary. "We must believe that it will only get better," reassured Ernst, even as he thought glumly, *I hope that will be so. These are indeed trying days to test the soul.*

But as time went on, Ida grew more despondent. She felt listless and became irritated at the slightest nuisance. Because she was prone to dwelling on and expressing thoughts of home and of missing their little girl, Ernst became worried. *Is Ida giving up? Will she demand to go home?*

Sometimes, she would twist her wedding ring on her finger as she began to question her fledging marriage. *Ernst is attentive and patient with me, but he always looks worried. Is he happy? Why should he be? He wants to get on with things, and I am doing little to help. Is our relationship crumbling, or am I just imagining and magnifying problems where there are none? It is unfair to me and Hazel and Ernst. Why should I dream about making a future with Ernst and Hazel when I know it will not happen?* She had never felt so alone in all her life.

"Tell me what is the matter, Ida?" pleaded Ernst. Ida had been silent since he had arrived home from working all day.

"Nothing, Ernst, I'm just tired."

Ernst pressed on and asked again. Ida's lip began to tremble, and finally, she confessed, "I'm not getting better; I know I'm not. I cannot bear that I am failing you and Hazel."

Her words left Ernst discouraged. He, too, wished for some outward indication that their sacrifice was making a difference. "I'm bringing home a little wage every week," he reminded optimistically. "I'm sure it will begin to add up."

But then, when he had to purchase groceries from the list she gave him, their meager funds dwindled. The reality was that they were barely making ends meet.

CHAPTER 23

The Chinese Medicine Shop

"Remedies prepared for ailments of all kinds,"
declared the advertisement.

Ten days later, Mr. Wilcox pulled Ernst aside, saying, "I need you to go to the freight yard with Simon today. We have a large order coming in, and it must be picked up as soon as it arrives."

"Yes, sir!" replied Ernst eagerly, brushing off his hands and setting aside the shovel he was using to put in fence posts. "I'll run over and tell Ida I will be gone the rest of the day."

"No, that isn't necessary. Sally can tell her later when she drops off the supplies. You need to get going."

The men soon had the four-horse team hitched to the long-bed freight wagon. Ernst climbed up and took a seat. He watched as Simon walked around the rig pulling at straps, checking the wheels, and adjusting the horse blinds. Finally, as he started to circle a third time, Ernst impatiently insisted, "Let's get going, Simon."

Simon climbed into the driver's seat and picked up the

reins. Carefully he threaded them through his fingers and timidly tested them. When he pulled back, the horses stepped back. Ernst grew alarmed when Simon, staring ahead, remarked in a slow, halting voice, "I bet it is hard to ease this wagon down the hill."

"Have you taken this rig out before?" demanded Ernst.

Simon responded, "Sure, I rode into town all the time with Jim…but I never done the driving."

Trying not to sound exasperated and at the same time moved with a feeling of sympathy for the young man's inexperience, Ernst proposed, "How about I drive on the way down? On my word, you can manage the brakes. I'm used to driving an outfit this size."

Relieved, Simon said, "I suppose you should try out the equipment, being new and all,"

Ernst agreed with obvious relief. "Those look like experienced horses that know what to expect. Just show me the way."

Simon immediately stood up and climbed over Ernst to slide next to the brake handle. Ernst set his hat, picked up the reins, and clucked to the horses. On the way downhill, Ernst instructed Simon on managing the wagon outfit by paying attention to the horses. He also reminded Simon to be alert for the approaching traffic. Simon listened intently but soon returned to his usual talkative mood as soon as they were off the hill. Ernst thought to himself, *He seems to relish being in charge and telling me where to go.*

"What are we picking up today?" asked Ernst.

"Let's see what's on the list," said Simon, pulling a slip of paper from his pocket. "Furniture, lumber, bed frames, a kitchen stove, and some other smaller items. Looks like it will be a full load if everything comes in today."

After threading through the city traffic, they arrived at the yard just before ten o'clock, the train's expected arrival time. Knowing there would be a wait before the freight was unloaded, they pulled the team out of the main thoroughfare. The men fell into conversation about the growth of the city of Los Angeles. Ernst learned that Simon had come to the city 20 years earlier, "Before they started pumping oil."

"I find it peculiar how people put up oil platforms in their yards," commented Ernst.

Simon shrugged. "Yeah, it doesn't look good, but people need to make a living. The city didn't try to stop it. People are always dreaming of making money."

"But what will all this oil be used for?" asked Ernst.

"That's the funny thing. There just isn't a great need for it beside using it for lubricants and lamp kerosene…at least, not yet," puzzled Simon.

They watched as the station master stalked over to them. He lifted his chin, saying, "Sorry, boys, there is a delay. The word on the line is it will be about two hours."

Simon looked at Ernst, "Happens most of the time. I just make the best of it."

Ernst pulled out his watch, then looked up. "It will be at least a couple more hours before we can load. Do you mind if I walk around the city? I'm still trying to get my bearings."

"Do as you wish. I am responsible for these horses. I plan to stay here and catch a nap," Simon yawned. "Just don't get lost, or you'll have to get back to Duclane's on your own."

"Don't worry, I'll be back," Ernst assured the man as he headed off in the direction of downtown. Reaching Main Street, he found it thick with commotion. An electric streetcar blared its horn as it made its way through horses, loaded wagons, and pedestrians. Sidewalk vendors were hawking their goods to passing customers beside their wheeled carts. He even noticed a few brave bicyclists maneuvering through the horse rigs and around another waiting trolley car.

As Ernst neared the heart of the Los Angeles shopping district, the crush of people on the sidewalk thickened. Suddenly, Ernst heard a slur aimed at him by a passing bicyclist. The man was obviously in a hurry and irritated by navigating around people. And Ernst just happened to be in his way, causing him to have to slow down. Ernst strode on, unfazed. *I will just have to get used to this, I guess.* Finally, after covering several blocks, he decided to circle back toward the train yard at a more leisurely pace.

When he crossed the street, the smell of cooking meat filled the air. His stomach enticed him to surrender a nickel, and he bought a sizzling sausage wrapped in a slice of bread. "Here, try that with mustard," the salesman suggested. "It makes it tastier." Ernst took a bite and agreed it was good. Before polishing off the treat, he moved on to keep himself from buying another.

A colorful display of fresh fruits caught his attention at the next corner. The sign on the door indicated it was a grocer. On a whim, he stepped inside, deciding to buy a few things for Ida, including an orange, a banana, a bar of soap, and some tins of milk and peaches. The grocer had baked goods, and he bought a dozen soft rolls and some oatmeal cookies. *Ida will enjoy these*, he thought as he picked up the items wrapped in brown paper and tied in string.

Ernst pulled out his watch when he heard the tower clock begin to chime the noon hour. Calculating he had about one more hour in the city before getting back to the wagon, he decided to venture into an area called Chinatown. All at once, the streets narrowed and became even more crowded. Suddenly, Ernst felt out of place. The people around him spoke Chinese, a language he could not understand. It was impossible to tell by the tone of the voices if the exchanges between folks were friendly or otherwise. Feeling like the stranger he was, Ernst retreated toward Main Street. But he stopped suddenly when a sign in a window caught his attention: "Remedies prepared for ailments of all kinds."

Driven by curiosity and a vague flash of hope, Ernst pushed through the heavy red enamel doors and stepped into a Chinese medicine shop. A bell over the door jingled, announcing his presence.

Immediately, the smell of wood and decaying leaves mingling with burning incense overwhelmed him. His eyes slowly adjusted to the dimly lit space, and he was amazed. The shelves and countertops were neatly lined with glass containers of all sizes. They contained all kinds of unfamiliar items. He saw bottles filled with dried plants, colorful powders, and the skeletons of insects and small animals like snakes and scorpions.

Near the entrance, in a prominent position, was another sign. It was written in English and was, in fact, the only thing in the entire shop that he could read:

We welcome you to the world of ancient Chinese med-icine practiced for more than 2,000 years. Please wait here for Dr. Wong and his staff to greet you. Please do not touch anything. We are happy to assist you.

Ernst waited and listened to the echoes of a heated discussion in the back room. Finally, a small elderly man leaning on an ornate wooden cane shuffled over to greet him. He was dressed in a long robe of worn silk brocade. With its threadbare spots, the robe seemed as old as the man.

He wore a black hat, and a long, ebony-colored braid hung over his shoulder. Upon reaching Ernst, the little man stopped, put his hands together, and bowed slightly in greeting.

Ernst paused, feeling awkward and unsure of how to re-spond, so he smiled and nodded, wondering *Will we be able to communicate?*

He was relieved to hear the man's first words, though spo-ken with care, were, "What brings you into my shop today? I am Dr. Wong."

Ernst began, "My wife, she needs medicine. She has con-sumption."

The man looked at him and said, "Consumption?" and nodded in understanding.

"Yes," returned Ernst. "She is so troubled, especially at night." He demonstrated this by pressing his hand to his chest and pre-tending to cough. "She cannot breathe well and has fevers."

Ernst stopped speaking when Dr. Wong raised a finger in the air. After a pause, Dr. Wong confidently said, "Yes, yes, yes! I have something for your wife. I will make a special medicine. You will wait. Okay?" Ernst nodded.

Ernst stood where he was and watched with keen interest. After retrieving a stone cup from an area behind a screen of red beaded curtains, the doctor selected ingredients from several jars around the room. The doctor mumbled to himself and periodically sniffed at the contents of the containers. When he appeared satisfied with the mixture, Dr. Wong picked up a pestle and ground the concoction into a smooth mixture. After diluting the mixture with some unknown liquid, he poured the cloudy yellowish solution into a glass bottle and corked it securely.

"Your wife takes this every day, two times a day," said Dr. Wong, holding up a spoon and two fingers to show him how much. "She can mix it with water if it is too strong."

"All right, we will try this. It should help with breathing?" questioned Ernst.

Doctor Wong nodded and then held out his open hand, saying, "That will be 75¢."

When Ernst laid a dollar bill on the counter, Dr. Wong suggested, "You also buy tea for her. It will help her relax." Then, reaching under the counter, he brought out a bottle of dark-looking tea leaves.

Ernst, suddenly wary, asked, "What is in the tea?"

"Leaves of anise," replied the doctor. "Smell it." Holding it up to Ernst's nose, he continued, "Sick people worry much and need rest from worries. This tea good for that, only 25¢."

At that moment, Ernst heard the town clock strike the first hour. He needed to be somewhere else, and it was not Chinatown. He added the medicine packages to the groceries to leave the store, but not before saying, "Thank you." As Ernst walked away, while he was hopeful the medicine would be helpful, he wondered if it was worth a day's labor and if it was even safe for Ida to try.

Fifteen minutes of brisk jogging brought Ernst back to the train yard. Simon was just gathering the reins in his hands. He waved to Ernst, "I just got word; we can load the supplies."

With the assistance of two experienced freight movers, the wagon was efficiently loaded high with the bulky items. Ernst and Simon tied down the wagon contents securely by pulling the ropes taut. When they turned onto Alameda Street, Simon was driving. Ernst felt it had been a very productive day.

Later, when Ernst presented his package of goods, Ida was delighted to find the treats from the grocers. "I'm glad for the soap," she exclaimed. "It is past time to wash our things!"

She was less enthusiastic about the bottle of Chinese medicine and tea. "What are these?" she asked suspiciously, recalling a certain feeling she had the last time her Pa brought home a new bottle of cod liver oil.

Ernst then told her about the visit to Chinatown and his impression of the medicine shop and "Old Doctor Wong." As he handed her a business card, he recalled, "The place was like an unusual library. Instead of books, there were many jars lined up and filled with twigs, leaves, and colored powders. The sign I read in the store said that the medicine is 2,000 years old." Ida looked dubiously at the card and later placed it into her sewing box. "The doctor told me he is willing to see you if we can go back together."

Stoically, Ida examined the bottle before pulling out the cork. She took a whiff and promptly wrinkled her nose and frowned. Then, looking at Ernst with resignation in her eyes, she said, "Well, I'm willing to try it if you think it is really for the best. I hate keeping you awake at night."

"Here," Ernst encouraged as he reached to open the bottle of tea flakes. "I cannot place what it smells like, but I think it is pleasant."

Ida took a tentative whiff, and this time she smiled. "It smells like licorice candy!"

SECTION 6

Passages

CHAPTER 24

A Perfect Day at the Seaside

*There was a light in her eyes he had not seen
for many days.*

Finally, the day arrived that Ida and Ernst had looked forward to, even before leaving the farm back in Nash. Setting out early in the day, they boarded a fast line car to take them west…to the ocean. At first, only a few other travelers rode with them, but more like-minded people heading to the water got on with each stop. Ernst finally stood to offer his seat to a silver-haired woman. A feather from her large ornate hat brushed Ida when she sat down.

"I know you, my dear," a kind voice asserted.

Looking up, Ida was startled to see the face of the woman from the train. It was the kind soul who had entertained them and invited Ida to sleep in her private Pullman car, giving Ida a brief respite on their journey westward.

"Mrs. Sunderlin!" Ida bubbled brightly, "How unexpected to see you again!"

Ida reintroduced them by name and reminded her how

grateful she was for her kindness. She added, "Ernst is taking me out to the water."

In response, the older woman smiled at the girl's good manners. "You will enjoy your time at the beaches. It is a lovely day indeed. Will you be taking the new Balloon Route Trolley?" Mrs. Sunderlin inquired. "I hear it is quite popular with the vacationers."

Ida looked at her husband questioningly. Ernst picked up the conversation, "This is our first trip to see the ocean. We shall spend the day in Venice."

"Your first time?" Alice replied in surprise. "How long has it been since we journeyed? Most travelers cannot wait to view the ocean." As the woman paused to study Ida's face, she became alarmed. The young girl appeared to have lost weight, and her eyes were heavy with dark circles. Turning to glance up at Ernst, she observed he seemed to have aged from what she remembered, causing her to wonder, *How are they getting on?*

"We are still finding our way around," offered Ida feebly as she thought about their tenuous circumstances. They had searched their pockets for extra coins for the present outing.

Quickly formulating a plan, Mrs. Sunderlin decided she wanted to give them something more for this special day. She cheerfully offered, "How about we spend the day together? I know this place, and I would love your company."

Over the din created by the train's motion and the passengers' buzz, Mrs. Sunderlin explained how she made periodic trips to the shoreline to visit her brother. "I usually ride out in the morning, browse the Main Street shops, and walk out on the beach."

"It sounds like an enjoyable day," returned Ida, smiling and pleading with her eyes to Ernst to accept Mrs. Sunderlin's invitation.

"It is quite good for the soul to watch the water and breathe the air, as you will soon see. Afterward," she continued, "I go to my brother's house, have a tea and some conversation, and catch the 3:00 train back to the city."

Meanwhile, Ernst was taken aback by the friendly exchange. It seemed the simple day he had envisioned with his wife could potentially evolve into something complicated. *Perhaps an outing we cannot afford.* But seeing Ida's face light up with interest and then remembering how entertaining they had found the woman's company, Ernst affirmed. "Thank you. We would love to join you, Mrs. Sunderlin." *Besides, we can go our own way later if we need to.*

When they arrived at the end of the train line, Mrs. Sunderlin stood up and, with purse and umbrella in hand, looked at them smiling as she commanded, "Come, follow me."

Upon stepping off the train, a gust of wind seized Ida's hat and lifted it from her head. It happened so suddenly that Ida missed it when she grabbed for it. Instead, they watched it tumble away. Ernst dashed down the block in pursuit. Unfussed, Mrs. Sunderlin remarked, "I forgot to mention that it is breezy down here, and sometimes one needs to adjust our hatpins."

Ernst returned, carrying Ida's now dilapidated bonnet. Ida bit her lip in dismay. She only owned one hat, and it looked ruined. Taking it from Ernst, she sighed as she dusted it off and tucked the frayed netting deep into the hatband.

"Don't worry, my dear. I will take you to a hat store for a repair. And it will look good as new," assured the woman.

"Come this way," Mrs. Sunderlin urged once again, moving out to take the lead. "We will begin our day with a bite to eat; I know the perfect place." When Ida started to protest that they were not hungry, the woman responded, "A least sit with me while I have some tea. I despise dining alone." Taking Ida by the arm and patting gently, she added, "This is my treat, dear girl. Remember I told you once you look like my own daughter. It does me well to see you again." Ida looked at Ernst helplessly.

Smiling, he leaned over and chirped, "It seems you will get the day you always dreamed of at the ocean."

Mrs. Sunderlin wanted more than a cup of tea. When the waitress arrived with menus, she confiscated them. After asking for their drink preference, the woman ordered a bewildering amount of enticing food. Ernst ate heartily until his belly was uncomfortably full and satisfied. Mrs. Sunderlin looked on, pleased. *My children never relished the food as he does.*

Between the meal and dessert, Ida began to appear sadly distracted.

"You look like your head is heavy in thought, Ida. Is something wrong?" questioned Mrs. Sunderlin, concerned.

Ida looked up and apologized. "I'm sorry, Mrs. Sunderlin. This is a lovely meal, but I was just thinking about our daughter."

Ernst then added, "This is our little Hazel's first birthday, and we are lonesome for her."

Mrs. Sunderlin could hardly bear the thought as she considered Ida's sorrow at being separated from her child and pulled out her hanky to dab her eyes. Then, grasping for some comment, Mrs. Sunderlin offered, "It is good you are doing something special for her birthday. You can write about it in a letter home. Then, your family can tell her how her Mama and Papa celebrated for her."

After finishing their food, their waitress asked, "Mrs. Sunderlin, is there anything else?"

"Elsie, it is a splendid day for a picnic. Would you please ask the kitchen staff to prepare some sandwiches? We will take them along."

"Ham or beef," queried the waitress, who knew Mrs. Sunderlin.

"I think two of each kind would be about right."

"And pickles and some cookies too?

"Oh, but of course!" responded the generous woman, imagining her new friends relaxing in the warm sand later enjoying a treat.

After the meal, at Mrs. Sunderlin's suggestion, the three casually strolled down Main Street, stopping to look at the display windows to admire a novelty or an article of clothing. After a while, Mrs. Sunderlin remarked, "My, isn't it hot for a September day!" Concerned, Ernst directed the women to a nearby bench under a shady tree.

"This heat is not something we are used to. Ida, you must rest also," Ernst instructed tenderly.

Smiling, Ida reassured him, "Stop worrying; I'm fine, Ernst. We are having a lovely day. If you like, you could walk on. I still need to fix my hat. I am sure you would prefer to look at anything other than dress goods."

"There is an excellent bookstore and shell shop at the end of this street," recommended Mrs. Sunderlin, pointing down the block.

"That is a good idea, Ernst. We will meet up later," said Ida.

As Ernst sauntered off, Mrs. Sunderlin remarked, "He is an attentive man. Most men must learn how important it is for womenfolk to spend some time together!"

"Yes, he rarely gets a chance to enjoy himself anymore," commented Ida.

After Ernst left, Mrs. Sunderlin pointed, "That shop, The Women's Emporium, is the place that can help you. Go show them your hat, and I will come shortly to meet you there."

Upon entering The Women's Emporium, a fascinating display of hats caught Ida's attention. Stylish hats, simply trimmed but with rolled and angled brims, were nestled next to flamboyant and oversized picture hats. These creations, designed to frame a woman's face, were ornamented with large flowers, ribbons, chiffon, lace, and feathers. When Ida spotted some hats with stuffed robins and other songbirds sitting in nests, the fashion statement left her sad and confused.

Finally, a saleswoman stepped up to greet her. Ida pointed to the hat on her head and explained, "My hat needs a repair."

The young saleswoman directed Ida to sit in a nearby chair that faced a mirror. After removing the pins securing her hat, Ida handed it to the woman for inspection. As she watched through the mirror, Ida was horrified to see the sales clerk grab and tear at the netting and the ribbon of her hat. In one swift jerk, she pulled off the lot.

Ida turned around and gasped, "What are you doing?"

The clerk replied condescendingly, "This hat is sorely out of date. Let's try on something that will suit you better, something new."

Ida watched in shock as the woman retrieved a similar-sized hat from the display and then returned to plop it crookedly on her head. When Ida's eye caught the price tag of four dollars, she panicked. Finally, a feeling of outrage began to wash over her. With rising anger, Ida realized, *She is mocking me! How dare that woman destroy my hat! She knows I cannot afford a new one.*

Then, the bell over the entry door jingled, announcing a new customer. The saleswoman looked up to see an older woman enter the shop. She quickly sized up the new customer, thinking, *Look at her fashionable dress…she is just what I need today, someone with money!* She told Ida curtly, "I'll be back shortly."

When the saleswoman approached, Mrs. Sunderlin was fingering an ostrich feather on an expensive hat. She commented, "My, isn't this lovely? I have not seen one styled with velvet rosettes before."

"Oh, it is lovely and how perfect it would look on you, madam," gushed the saleswoman. "I am finishing with another customer, then I will be right back to assist you." The clerk had often resorted to using flattery to influence a sale.

"Oh, no hurry. I will look around, and as you know, every woman deserves your full attention," replied Mrs. Sunderlin agreeably. Then as she turned around to survey the room, she saw Ida sitting in the sales chair. Immediately she took in Ida's blazing eyes and followed their direction to her destroyed hat.

Then, as Mrs. Sunderlin listened, she heard the shrewish clerk say, "If that hat doesn't suit you, perhaps I don't have what you need."

Mrs. Sunderlin stepped up and spoke sharply, "Oh, I am surprised, but how kind of you to suggest we go elsewhere. Come along, Ida."

Ida rose from her seat and smugly smiled at the red-faced clerk. Then, she swept past the stunned woman, gathering up her tattered hat and tossing the new hat to land upside down in the chair.

Back on the boardwalk, Mrs. Sunderlin pulled Ida aside to apologize. "I'm sorry, my dear girl. I did not send you in to be treated like that."

"It happened so fast," sniffed Ida, dabbing a handkerchief to her pooling eyes. "I was mortified! I have never encountered such a rude person nor been at a loss for what to do. Thank you for rescuing me."

Shaking her head, Mrs. Sunderlin retorted, "That ill-tempered, arrogant clerk does not deserve her commission today or any other day. I advise you not to let this incident ruin your day."

"Yes, you are right. I'm still shocked by her reprehensible actions. Just look at what she did to my hat."

"Never mind, I will make this right. Follow me." A few steps farther down the boardwalk, the older woman came to a halt. The glass door in front of them was embossed in gold paint. Ida read "Cooper Millinery est. 1887" in ornate lettering. "Here, we will find what you need."

"Mrs. Sunderlin!" came a cheery greeting from across the way. "It is such a fine day for a visit, even if it is warm. I trust you are well." The petite woman moving toward them was similar in age to Ida's new friend.

"Hello, Millicent. This is my friend, Ida. I hope you might assist her with a repair. She had a gusty misfortune earlier today."

"Of course, Alice. Flyaway hats frequently happen here."

Ida offered her dilapidated hat to the clerk. "Let's have a look at this. Yes, this repair will not take long at all. Why don't you look at my display of accouterments?" she suggested, placing Ida's straw hat on the counter. "There are scores of ribbons to choose from; perhaps you would like a different color this time?"

Before long, with Mrs. Sunderlin's input, Ida decided on a new striped ribbon in burgundy and black for the hatband, along with a matching bow and a small nosegay of dried flowers.

When the clerk returned to them, she said, "Alice, I've been changing the displays and putting out some new styles. Please enjoy looking around while I stitch these into place."

Millicent then picked up Ida's new selections and her ramshackle hat. She carried them to the window to sit beside her large sewing basket. In minutes, she secured the last knot and clipped the thread. When she presented Ida's hat for approval, the kind milliner asked, "Does this please you?"

"It looks brand new!" admired Ida. "It is lovely, thank you." Ida opened the little purse she carried and reached for some coins, hoping she had enough to cover the cost.

"It is already paid for, Ida...hardly came to anything," her new friend spoke up. Then changing the subject and pointing to an Edwardian-style hat, Mrs. Sunderlin asked, "Now, Ida, tell me, what do you think of this bonnet? Is it too wide?"

"It is lovely. I think it suits you," said Ida brightly.

Mrs. Sunderlin chuckled, "I am rather fond of hats, especially since my hair isn't as lovely as when I was younger. Someday, I will perhaps be able to show you my collection. It is somewhat embarrassing to own so many."

Ida laughed, "Well, this one matches your eyes and looks smart. Since I left home, I have never seen so many kinds of fancy hats."

In return, Mrs. Sunderlin said, "I find it is worth it to enjoy a few pleasures at any age!"

When they collected their purchases and were once again walking down the street, Ida commented, "That was enjoyable…I do like my new hat!"

"Millicent keeps a fine shop and enjoys many returning customers. She is a real lady whose courtesy is inborn, just like you, Ida." Mrs. Sunderlin's compliment made Ida blush.

The afternoon sun continued to bear down on them. When Ernst finally rejoined them, he was pleased to see Ida enjoying herself and her company. Mrs. Sunderlin was furiously fanning her face using a silk fan. Finally, she pulled out her umbrella, saying, "I'm surprised it is so hot this late in the season. Ida, would you mind managing my umbrella as we walk?"

Ida took the umbrella from Mrs. Sunderlin, looking at it with a perplexed frown. Ernst reached over and, taking it in hand, demonstrated to Ida how to open it. Then, holding the umbrella high and with Mrs. Sunderlin's hand on her elbow, Ida proceeded to walk along in their circle of shade, discussing the sights as Ernst followed. Finally, they came to a seashell display; Ida stopped short in fascination. "Look at these, Ernst," she exclaimed.

"You never know what the ocean will send up in the tides. You can, of course, buy these for a few pennies, but it is more exciting to find them for yourself in the sand," declared Mrs. Sunderlin. "I collected seashells as a young girl. When I came back from our beach outings, my mother never complained about all the sand I brought in my pockets!"

After lingering at the display and picking up and examining the wide assortment of shells, Alice announced, "It is time for me to leave you and go to my brother."

Pressing the parcel of the picnic sandwiches into Ernst's hands, she encouraged, "Do enjoy the rest of your day. It has been most agreeable to spend it with you. If you require anything, I insist that you come to me."

Ida and Ernst thanked the woman for the delightful day, including their lunch. Their gratitude was all they could offer to the generous woman.

"Here is your umbrella," Ida reminded, extending her hand.

"You keep it for the day. The sun will seem more radiant down by the water." When Ida protested, Alice shook her head. "No, I have no use for it after I get back on the train, and I have my hat."

With that final comment, Mrs. Sunderlin pressed a folded slip of paper into Ida's hands, securing it by closing Ida's hands together with her own. "Here is my address. Do not hesitate to pay me a visit soon. I will be honored to welcome you to my home. Perhaps the next time we meet, you will call me by my given name, Alice."

Alice leaned in, dropped an affectionate kiss on Ida's cheek, extended a nod to Ernst, and then turned and walked away.

Mrs. Sunderlin had left them near a crude wooden walkway marked with a sign that read, "Beach." They could hear the roar of the ocean, but a sandy dune in front of them prevented them from seeing the water.

Ernst took up Ida's hand, and together they crossed over to the walkway. Stepping into the shifting sand, Ida was surprised to feel the trim heels of her shoes sink. *"Uff da!"* she exclaimed, "I wish I could take off my shoes!"

And with the same thought in mind, Ernst said, "Let's do it!" as he knelt to help Ida unlace her shoes.

The couple explored the shoreline for hours and played at the water's edge. They roamed about looking for shells and anything else that had come in on the tide. Each find brought a novel sense of discovery. For a little while, the mesmerizing motion of the ocean waves kept their worries at bay. They knew the day away was drawing on their critically low funds, but neither would have put a price on that splendid outing. Later in the afternoon, under the shade of the borrowed umbrella, they feasted on the picnic thoughtfully provided by Mrs. Sunderlin.

"Ernst, do you realize more than three months have passed since we said farewell to Mama and Pa at the train station in Grafton?" asked Ida soberly.

"I've been thinking about that, too. I wish it was easier, Ida. It is unsettling that we are not making progress yet."

"But we should be encouraged knowing we are doing the best we can. I'm sorry my condition keeps causing difficulties. I also worry all the time that we are running out of money."

"Hush, Ida, we are managing. This is not the day to worry.

We must be grateful for the little things," chided Ernst, smiling and raising his sandwich.

"Seeing Mrs. Sunderlin again was a pleasant surprise. I want to return her umbrella," Ida remarked.

Ernst teased, "I believe she intended you should keep it."

Ida shook her head, saying, "No, I would not even consider it."

"Let's see where Mrs. Sunderlin lives," suggested Ernst.

Ida reached into her handbag to draw out the piece of folded paper. Upon opening it, two quarters and a tightly folded five-dollar bill fell into the sand. "Oh my," gasped Ida, staring down.

Taking the note from Ida, Ernst examined the neatly written address. "I've seen the name of this street. It is close by. I think she lives in the neighborhood right below the sanitarium."

"Then we must plan to go see her again. She is a kind woman and the only new person I have met since we arrived that I would call a friend."

Returning an Umbrella

Gratitude turns what we have into enough.

The opportunity to return the umbrella to Mrs. Sunderlin came unexpectedly just a week later when Ernst needed to go to the lumberyard to pick up some building supplies for the sanitarium. Seizing the opportunity that he was to make the trip alone, he asked permission to invite Ida along for the ride.

Leaving the sanitarium grounds, Ernst edged the team of horses slowly downhill to town. Ida gripped the edge of the large freight wagon tightly. Ida knew Ernst was a skilled horseman, but the route up and down the hills of Los Angeles was not easy.

"Will it be out of the way for us to see her?" questioned Ida, checking for the third time, ensuring the borrowed umbrella was still stowed in the wagon.

"No, by her address, it is only a few blocks from here. Just keep in mind that we cannot stay long. I am working. I need to get those supplies straightway and return," reminded Ernst.

As they rounded the corner to enter the street where Mrs. Sunderlin lived, Ida gasped in delight. The wide street was lined with palm trees. The homes on the boulevard were stately. Sitting back from the road, they displayed colorful flower gardens and ornamental statues. Ida looked at Ernst, "I cannot believe she lives here."

"It sure is a grand place," agreed Ernst. "Now help me look for the house number. It will be on the door, the porch, or the mailbox."

It wasn't long before Ernst pulled back on the horse reins and came to a stop. He pointed out a three-story house. Though more modest in size than others on the street, it was a mansion in Ida's eyes.

Ernst climbed down and secured the wagon rig to the hitching post before assisting Ida down from her seat.

Suddenly, she felt nervous, "Do you think I should have sent a note that we were coming?"

Ernst shook his head, reminding her, "We are not inviting ourselves to tea, just making a delivery."

The Victorian house looked freshly painted in ivory with brown highlighting around the windows. Stars, dominoes, and curlicues were attached as gingerbread accents in every conceivable place.

A cobblestone walkway led to the wide porch steps. Walking toward the house, Ida caught the sweet smell of jasmine hanging in the air and looked around until she located the trailing vine on a side fence. Pink roses and bougainvillea climbed the trellises that surrounded the porch. Lined up on the steps were pots of red and white geraniums in full bloom.

226 | IDA'S TRUNK: A Dakota Farm Girl Goes West

The front porch itself was a wonder. Ida promptly decided it was like a well-decorated room. A wicker chaise lounge resided in one corner, flanked by two matching and comfortably cushioned rockers. A table was set between them near the doorway. Finally, a fat calico cat slept contentedly in the sun. The heavy front door was accented with colored glass cut into oblongs and squares surrounding a centerpiece of transparent glass etched with a flower spray.

Ernst tapped lightly on the door before noticing a button that would ring a bell. Instantly, a young woman opened the door slightly and peered out before asking gruffly, "Can I help you?"

Ernst began to speak, saying, "We are looking for Mrs. Sunderlin. Does she live here?"

"I don't recognize you," came the terse reply.

"We are friends. I have something to return to her," said Ida, holding up the umbrella in front of the narrow doorway opening.

Upon recognizing the parasol, the young woman changed the tone of her voice. She opened the door wider, politely saying, "Mrs. Sunderlin isn't here right now. I expect her back in an hour. You may wait here for her if you like."

They could now see the girl was about Ida's age and wore a freshly starched apron. On her head was a bright scarf that covered her blonde hair except for the long braid trailing down her back.

Ida looked up at Ernst, and he saw the disappointment in her eyes. "I need to go on with my errands, Ida. I can come back for you later."

"Yes, miss, please wait. The missus gets so few visitors. I

know she will be sorry if I let you go. You can stay right here. It is lovely here in the shade."

Knowing that this was the right house and assured that it was acceptable for her to wait, Ida sent Ernst onward to the lumberyard.

After he left, the girl came back with a glass of lemonade for Ida. "I am Mary. I help Mrs. Sunderlin with the housework," she offered, telling Ida that she came twice a week. "I also need to apologize. When you and your husband knocked on the door, I thought you were trying to sell something. I saw you pull up in the wagon and all."

"I know that feeling, Mary. Back home, peddlers were coming around to our farm. Sometimes they were pushy, and it was hard to get them to leave," shared Ida.

"I grew up on a farm too. We had a garden and chickens and everything. After my folks passed on, there was only me. My relative sent for me, so now I am here," rambled Mary.

"Do you miss the farm?" asked Ida before continuing, "I do; I miss it. I liked growing our food and cooking things in the kitchen. Now, I can't do either."

When Mrs. Sunderlin came strolling down the street, she was delighted to see Ida sitting on her porch with her cat, Rosie, curled up in her lap. Even better was catching her in an animated conversation with her young housekeeper. Mary was startled to see Mrs. Sunderlin coming toward them. She abruptly stood up and began to apologize.

Alice smiled and raised her hand to hush the words tumbling out of her mouth.

"Never mind, Mary, you can get to it later." Handing the

shopping parcels over to Mary, Mrs. Sunderlin continued. "Be so kind, Mary, and make a plate of sandwiches for us and one for you as well. Also, please bring some more lemonade. This is a perfect day for a porch picnic!"

Ida Begins to Fail

"On the day I called for help, You answered me."
– Psalm 138

"*Ida, are you* all right?" whispered Ernst. It was the middle of another restless night. In the dark, he reached out to touch her. She felt clammy, and her nightgown was soaked from a fevered sweat. He groaned silently. Of late, Ida had been having night fevers that left her weary during the next day. Rising, he went to retrieve her spare nightgown, where it hung from the back of a chair drying on the porch. Ernst gently helped her slip into the dry gown in what had become a sort of silent ritual, knowing it would make her more comfortable.

At least the coughing isn't too bad tonight, he thought, drifting back to sleep. Occasionally, the relentless hacking grated on his nerves so badly that he covered his ears with his hands. But mostly, his attentive compassion for his sickly wife made him able to bear the disturbing noise.

When morning came, the daytime routine began. Ida roused long enough to exchange a goodbye with Ernst as he headed off to work. She spent the rest of the day, as she described it, "lounging about aimlessly." Sometimes, she fell asleep and had "real-feeling" dreams about being back home. Upon waking, a wash of disappointment would roll over her spirits.

She found it troubling that she lacked energy for everyday things like writing a letter or sewing on her patchwork quilt. In addition, Ernst and Sally constantly tried coaxing her with food. Still, with no appetite, Ida ate little. It was evident she was growing weaker and losing weight. Ida was also becoming frightened by the sharp chest pains she felt regularly now. Sometimes the pain was so intense she could not do or think about anything until it passed.

Ernst was becoming frustrated. As he walked away each morning, he left with a prayer sent from his groaning heart that Ida would be all right when he returned. Leaving her to go to work meant she had to fend for herself for many hours at a time.

On a good day, Ida could move about the cabin and stroll slowly to the gardens. She was not exactly an invalid, but she was limited. Ernst did everything he could think of to make Ida comfortable. He would settle her in a porch rocker if she was ready to get out of bed in the morning, leaving food within reach. When her coughing started, he sat beside her, willing her to breathe.

Working at Duclane's was not entirely without cost. Soon after Ernst started, his pay was docked for every minute he arrived late if he needed to give Ida extra help in the morning or when he went to check with her during the day. Another deduction came from a "service charge" for food Ernst brought Ida from the canteen. It was explained that each week Ida did not provide sufficient hours of service, she would be charged a small fee to cover the labor cost of the meal. He also had the cost of Ida's medicines and the little incidentals that seemed to come up, like the purchase of food tins, stamps, and work gloves.

When Ernst had returned to Dr. Wong for more anise tea and "the yellow stuff," he found the prices had doubled. At first, the herbals seemed to help, but now he and Ida were convinced they were useless. When Ida worsened, Ernst approached Dr. Wong about pain medication. Even though he had not met the man's wife, the doctor knew Ida was probably failing. He shook his head sadly and produced a bottle of laudanum to "make her sleep better."

Reluctantly, Ernst purchased the sedative. *If Ida could rest a little during the day, it would help pass the time while he worked.* The reality was that Ida was growing weaker, and both he and Ida knew it. In addition, as the couple's funds were dwindling, they were slowly becoming destitute. In the end, Ernst faced the reality that getting ahead was impossible under their present circumstances.

A timely opportunity came when Ernst was offered a few extra working hours as a landscape laborer at Elysian Park, less than half a mile away. While he did not like to be away from Ida for so many hours, it had become necessary.

He finally went to the office to appeal for help. "Surely, Mr. Wilcox, someone can come and stay with her? I don't have much to pay, but I can work extra hours," he pleaded.

"Well, I'll arrange to have Martha come and stay a little while, but no more than an hour each day," Mr. Wilcox grudgingly agreed. Clearing his throat, he added, "If this situation is no longer working, we must reconsider your boarding status. Perhaps you need to find a better and different place to meet your wife's needs."

"I don't understand. Isn't this a place for people with her condition?" asked Ernst, frustrated.

"Yes, but this is a business, after all. We have a reputation to get patients better, and if—"

Ernst let the door slam on his way out. All prior indications of sympathy and goodwill from the sanitarium office had vanished. And those cold words had been spoken in a tone devoid of emotion or compassion. It stung to hear, "This is a business."

After Ernst stormed away from the office, he delayed returning to Ida's side. He did not want her to know of the words he just heard or his fury. He began to walk. Leaving the sanitarium grounds, he turned out of the driveway to climb to the highest point of the Chavez Ravine. Trying to contain his stirring anger, he pleaded, "Please, God, I don't want Ida to be in this unwelcoming place any longer." Unexpectedly, an image of Hannah's holding their child, Hazel, flashed across his reeling mind. His heart began to ache. *Lord, send me help. I do not know what to do. Ida is getting worse.*

In despair, Ernst dwelled on his personal responsibility, including the guilt and injustice of taking Ida so far from her home in North Dakota. *They don't know how sick she is now. If only she were back there, it would be better…now it is too late.* In this mindset, Ernst forgot the vision that he and Ida had created together that brought them to California. They had traveled west with high hopes for their bright future.

As he was leaving, Ida told him, "Something is wrong. Ernst, I'm afraid." Hearing those words and feeling the pressure to leave for his new job with the city parks department was hard. But he knew he must not be late, so he rushed around, trying to make her as comfortable as possible, covering her with blankets and setting hot tea beside her chair on the porch. "I'll come back at lunch to check on you," he reassured.

"I will be fine, Ernst. Now you need to go," she insisted weakly. "Alice will come later. She always does. Don't come back at lunch. They dock your time. We need you to work."

Ida tried to go back to sleep but could not get comfortable, and her ribs hurt from coughing as her lungs screamed for oxygen.

When Alice arrived, she knocked lightly before entering the cabin, calling out, "Ida." Alice was alarmed to find the girl doubled over in pain and gasping for breath. *She shouldn't be left by herself!*

Soothing the girl, shaking out her blankets, and changing her gown again, Alice resettled Ida on a porch chair. She insisted, "You need the fresh air." The frail woman smiled feebly in appreciation of being so ably mothered. Alice took a seat next to Ida and waited the rest of the day until Ernst returned.

As they waited, Ida rested. When she stirred and felt compelled to talk, she wanted to recall memories of home. Alice listened with interest as she looked out from the vantage of the hilltop to the city view below. *Poor child,* she acknowledged. *So far from anything familiar. If my own daughter was in these circumstances, I could not bear to be separated from her.*

Much later, when Ernst was nearly back to the tent after his long workday, he spied a figure seated next to Ida on the front deck. Panicking, he sprinted the rest of the way. After one look at his pale-faced wife, Alice's presence told him the worst.

"Oh, no!" wailed Ernst as he reached to take Ida's thin hand to rouse her.

Ida, opening her eyes to his voice, listlessly gasped, "This is…worse…this time…Ernst. I can't breathe."

"She must go to the hospital. I have been afraid to leave her, Ernst," Alice explained, adding, "I'm sorry."

In short order, arrangements were made, and Ida was admitted to St. Vincent's Infirmary, commonly known as the Sister's Hospital, three miles away. In their pristine white habits, the Catholic sisters swept in to care for Ida, telling Ernst, "Go home and rest. We will attend to your wife. Come back in the morning about ten o'clock when the doctors make rounds."

Ernst found his way back to their accommodations at Duclane's in the dark of night. Exhausted and stunned, he lay on the cot, trying to sleep. When he did drift off, he woke with a start, remembering that Ida was not there with him. *She is at the hospital.*

In the morning, Ernst was ushered to Ida's bedside in the contagion ward. The room was large and airy, with many cots lined up in a row with a small table separating each bed. She was sitting up in bed and, when she saw him, beckoned him to her bedside. In his eyes, he thought Ida looked much better. She had been bathed, her hair was braided, and the hospital bed was made up in fresh linens. Ernst perched on the edge of her cot; taking up her hands, he tried to contain a sob of relief.

When the doctor arrived, he listened to Ida's story and then to her lungs using a stethoscope.

"How do her lungs sound today?" asked Ernst.

The doctor's report was grim. "I don't think your wife will be able to withstand another episode. Her lungs are nearly destroyed—the toll of the disease. She is fragile and needs rest."

"What more can I do?" questioned Ernst in a broken voice.

"Mrs. Ottoson can remain here for a week. I hope she will recover her strength. I am sorry, but the effects of tuberculosis are relentless. You need to prepare for the inevitable."

Ida reached out to her husband, "It will be all right," she said with a shaky voice that trailed off, "We knew that this... was coming."

For the next few days, Ida rested. When her meals came, she ate with enough appetite to regain some vitality. Ernst worked long hours at both jobs but came as often as possible and stayed until the nurses sent him home. Alice, ever faithful, came daily to visit. While there, the two women talked, read the newspapers, and walked the ward. Ida learned that Mrs. Sunderlin was a benefactress of the hospital and commanded a certain amount of leeway in her visits to St. Vincent's. Usually, visitors were barred from the consumption ward, but the sisters allowed Alice to see Ida without a challenge.

The bills for Ida's care were an immediate concern for Ernst, but he kept the matter to himself. When Ida would ask about the expense, he reassured her, saying, "Ida, you must not worry." Mrs. Sunderlin also put effort into trying to bolster Ernst, but they often missed each other between his work schedule and the time of her visits.

One day Mrs. Sunderlin left a note at Ida's bedside summoning Ernst to dine with her at a local restaurant. Ida encouraged, "You must go. She is our friend and keeps asking about you." Ida was also worried about Ernst and thought some time with Alice might lift his spirits besides giving him a good meal to eat.

On the same day Ernst received the invitation for supper, he also heard more bad news, which was almost too much for him to bear.

When he arrived at the restaurant as requested, Alice found Ernst much changed. He looked haggard. Her first attempts at conversation seemed to go nowhere as she watched him despondently push carrots around his plate. Finally, Alice raised her voice, pleading, "Please, Ernst, you must think well enough of me by now and of our friendship to trust me with your worries."

"I think Ida is looking better now. It is a relief for me that you go and see her. It seems to cheer her on," replied Ernst glumly as he stirred his coffee with a spoon.

Alice responded more directly, "I'm talking about you, Ernst. You are deeply burdened. You have been steadfast in watching over Ida ever since leaving home. But frankly, you are wearing out."

Ernst looked up and weakly smiled, admitting, "It has not been easy."

"Tell me about your plans. Do you know them? I may not be able to help, but I can advise you if you so wish."

"My apologies, Alice. You are right. Something happened today, and I am at a loss of what to do," began Ernst.

"Did something happen at your new job?" asked Alice, concerned.

"No, that isn't it at all. My job at the park is going well. I enjoy pushing the dirt around. In some small way, it reminds me of home. No, my problem is something else. I went to the sanitarium office today to check if we had received any mail."

Alice nodded, "Did someone say something to upset you?"

Ernst looked at his hands and frowned before saying, "Mr. Wilcox asked about Ida. He knew Ida was at the hospital and that she was gravely ill. But then he told me, 'Mr. Ottoson, I am sorry, but if your wife is doing poorly, you will need to move on. We ask you to vacate your accommodations.'"

Alice was shocked. "How callous! How could they say such a thing to you?"

Ernst rubbed his temples. "When I asked them why, they told me someone else needed the cabin. Mr. Wilcox also reminded me that I knew it was not a permanent place from the beginning. It was all a ruse to get me to work for them. They never did plan to let Ida see their doctor."

"That is terrible!" snapped Mrs. Sunderlin.

"Mr. Wilcox also accused us of not following their rules. He said Ida had not participated in the sanitarium routines as expected because she hasn't been for her cold bath for weeks or contributing hours in the work program."

"I'm baffled. Ida told me she was asked to stay away from the others until she had been seen by the physician," said Alice.

"I asked them what I was to do," reported Ernst, trying to steady his voice and squelch his rising anger.

"What did Mr. Wilcox say?" asked Alice, her outrage growing.

"The man just shrugged his shoulders and said, 'We will give you until the end of the week to remove your things.' Then he gave me a list of some other boarding homes."

Indignant, Alice stormed, "This, after all the work you have done for them. How un-Christian!"

"Maybe we made a mistake giving up following their rules. But Ida hasn't been strong enough to be up to it. Maybe they were angry I took on that extra job, though I don't think they really cared."

"Don't make excuses for their actions. No one should be treated like this, especially now when your wife is in hospital. Let me see that list of places from Mr. Wilcox," insisted Alice.

Drawing the paper from his pocket, Ernst handed it over. Alice looked at the list and concluded, "I see these places are all rather pricey, but they are in excellent neighborhoods." She paused and added, "What does Ida say about all this?"

Fiddling with his hands, Ernst answered, "I have not told her yet. It will just set her to worrying."

Mrs. Sunderlin nodded in agreement. "Good, Ernst; she needs to focus on resting. Now, I have a proposition for you. Please hear me out before you say a single word."

CHAPTER 27

The Good Samaritan

God appoints our graces to be nurses to other men's weakness.
–Henry Ward Beecher (1813–1887)

At the end of the week, Ida felt much improved, and the doctor said she was ready to leave the Sisters Hospital. She was surprised that Mrs. Sunderlin had arrived with Ernst to take her home.

"It will feel good to put on your own clothes again," commented Alice as she helped Ida pull her skirt over her head.

When Ida tried to fasten her skirt, she realized the waistband was loose. Ida sighed, "I guess I will need to move the button again."

"You can gain your weight back now that you feel better," encouraged her friend.

As the trio left the building, Ida was struck by the warmth of the sunshine on her face. It felt soothing after her long days of confinement in the contagion ward.

"How far do we have to go, Ernst? I don't remember from when you brought me here," Ida confessed.

"It won't take long. We have just a mile or so," replied Alice, motioning for her carriage to pull up to the hospital entrance.

"Thank you for coming, Alice. I would have been so lonely if you had not come to visit me every day," offered Ida once she was seated between them.

"I thought you might like a short drive in the neighborhood. Ernst has offered to stop and purchase a few items at the grocer before we go home."

Ida looked up sharply. She could tell something was up. *Never had that place at Duclane's been called home.* "What are you two holding back?"

"Tell her, Ernst, I can't wait any longer!" returned Alice mysteriously.

Ernst happily announced, "Alice has invited us to stay with her. She has a room that she normally rents, and she wants us to take it."

"Oh, my! That offer is so kind of you, but it is such an imposition," Ida stuttered as she put her hand to her mouth to stifle a sob.

"Hush, child! It is all arranged. Ernst has moved your things. There is no need to ever go back to that place again."

Ida settled back into the carriage seat and let the news wash over her as she murmured in gratitude, "You bring the best solutions of all. Thank You, Lord."

When Ida crossed over the threshold of Alice Sunderlin's home, it was as if her tired spirit was embraced in hospitality. The feeling was unexpected. Entering through the decorative front door, Ida drew in a breath of astonishment. The ample entry and hallway floors were laid with heavy oak planks, polished to a shine. Oak paneling and touches of elegant wallpaper covered the walls. Two lovely paintings of flower bouquets hung down on golden cords beside an oversized mirror. Both the mirror and pictures were surrounded in similar, gold-trimmed frames. A tall grandfather clock stood by the stairwell, ticking softly in rhythm to the long swinging brass pendulum.

The first room off the entrance hall was a large alcove. "This is our library," announced their hostess. A large desk commanded a corner of the room. Two matching tufted chairs had been thoughtfully placed near the window and turned to catch the light perfectly. In one of the chairs, a yellow cat slumbered away.

Ida noticed as she looked around that one entire wall was lined with shelves full of books. She was dumbfounded. Ida had never seen such a quantity of books assembled in one place. *Papa would love this,* she thought. Ida recalled how Caroline had recently written, "Grafton is building a library. It will be the first Carnegie Library in North Dakota. Anyone can come and borrow books for free." *Maybe this is what it will look like.* Next to the library was a stairwell. The steps were covered with a lush oriental carpet runner, held in place with brass rods. Midway up the wall, a window lit up the area and shed light downward, bathing the front hallway in sunlight.

As Mrs. Sunderlin continued to show them around, Ernst and Ida were struck with astonishment at the luxury and comfort of the home. They already knew Mr. Sunderlin had been an innovative businessman, but nothing had led them to expect this kind of abundance from their friend.

Ida timidly asked, "Alice, do you live here alone?"

"Yes, I do. I manage with Mary's housekeeping help and my gardener. My husband always insisted I must keep help to run this household," she explained. "Our first home, though, was much smaller. I took care of things myself."

"Your home is lovely," commented Ernst.

"We finished building this place shortly before Mr. Sunderlin passed. He was proud of how well it came out. We were living in Los Angeles before the oil pumping started. That enterprise, along with others, brought the city's rapid growth. My husband had foresight. His many enterprises all seemed to turn a solid profit."

"I would be lonely in this big place," mumbled Ida.

Mrs. Sunderlin smiled at the remark. "I agree with you, Ida. Some days, being here by myself seems foolish, but I will stay for the present. I am engaged in some community projects and manage to stay quite busy. Currently, I do not yet have a second plan for this time in my life."

"This room will be yours, Ida," said Mrs. Sunderlin, ushering the couple into a large bedroom near the kitchen. The cheery room was painted in ivory, except for one wall papered in a print of tiny flowers. The bed, pushed up to the open window, looked inviting. The chenille bedspread was cream-colored and patterned with soft tufts. A cheerful patch quilt lay folded at the foot. The other furniture in the room included a small cot, a rocking chair, and a dresser.

Mrs. Sunderlin frowned when she noticed one of her cats curled up on the chair. "I hope you don't mind the cat?" she inquired. "His name is Karrot. The calico is Rosie."

"Not at all!" exclaimed Ida, bending down to touch the silky fur of the purring feline.

"The washroom is down the hall," explained Alice. When Ida looked puzzled, she quickly explained indoor plumbing had recently been added. "I will show you how everything works," she reassured.

Ida found the Sunderlin home a welcome refuge as she grew weaker. Never complaining, Ida was content to move between her bedroom, the porch, and the kitchen. Although she was alone much of the time, Ida claimed she did not mind. Lacking energy, she spent many quiet hours daydreaming, trying to satisfy a longing for her own home.

In her mind, Ida created pictures of her little girl at play. Often, she saw Hazel running through a wheat field playing with Clarence or the dogs while grasshoppers scattered in their wake. In another image, Hazel was in the barn, carefully playing with the baby chicks and ducklings in a pool of sunshine while sitting cross-legged in the straw. The imaginings sometimes framed her mama at work in the kitchen or Papa on his horse reaching out to take Hazel for a ride, encircled by his strong arms.

To shorten the miles between California and her family in North Dakota, Ida wrote letters recounting these images and revealing her longing for home. The task often proved too difficult for her weakened hands, so Ernst or Alice would help finish the letters Ida had started.

After Ernst walked away from his job at the sanitarium, he increased his job hours with the parks department. The strenuous manual labor of working in Elysian Park on the footpaths and helping with the landscaping suited him. While the orderly Avenue of Palms lined the way to the 600-acre park, once inside, the terrain became more rugged with eucalyptus, cypress, and cedar trees. Ernst walked back to Alice's each day in good spirits, even after a grueling day.

Before entering her home by the back door, Ernst paused to shake his clothes and empty the dirt from his boots. Using a bucket of water and soap, he washed up and then went directly to Ida's side.

Alice, realizing that Ida rarely saw her husband grubby from work, inspected his clothing. If there was necessary mending, she brought it to Ida's attention and cheerfully took over and offered to make the repairs. In addition, Alice gathered up any dirty clothes Ernst could spare and the bed linens to send out to be cleaned every week. When the laundry returned, pressed, and folded, Ida shook her head. *What would Mama think?*

Whenever Ernst tried to give their hostess money for rent or food, Alice graciously accepted, never pressing the issue. Later, she dropped the money into a fancy china teapot. Alice reasoned the struggling couple would need the funds later. Somehow, she would figure out how to return the cash.

Ida did not regain her health. But under the care of Mrs. Sunderlin and her ever-watchful husband, Ida's fears and apprehension dissipated. Alice offered everything she could to comfort the young couple she had grown to love.

Like the other households in the neighborhood, she would have had a hired cook, but she preferred to run her own kitchen. Relishing the challenge to tease the appetites of her guests, she often tried new recipes. Then, hoping to stir Ida's appetite, Alice prepared tiny portions of food served on dainty china plates for the invalid. On the other hand, Ernst enjoyed a robust amount of food and began to look better again under her care.

One day, Alice knocked and pushed open the door of Ida's bedroom. Softly she asked, "Ida, are you awake?"

"Yes, I've been thinking of getting up, but this bed is so comfortable I don't want to move yet."

"I have brought some warm washing water. And maybe after breakfast, I could help you wash your hair; it won't take long. We can use the kitchen sink," offered Alice.

"What day is it?" asked Ida softly.

"Saturday…and I just sent Ernst on an errand to buy some groceries. It is just the two of us here in the house."

"You are right. I should get up and dress. Maybe I could sit out on the porch to dry my hair. I know it still smells of hospital disinfectant."

"That is a good plan, my dear," Alice encouraged as she set down the pitcher and stepped forward to help Ida rise to perch on the edge of her bed. Then, handing Ida a washcloth, Alice said, "I brought a kimono for you to use. It is one my daughter left behind."

When she draped the dark blue wrap around the girl's thin shoulders, Ida looked up in appreciation as she examined the garment embroidered with bright flowers. "This is lovely. I did not think to bring my flannel one when I packed. But, then, our space was limited." Catching a whiff of cinnamon and vanilla, Ida commented, "Something smells good!"

"That would be the scones baking in the oven."

A short time later, Alice settled Ida on a porch chair, propping her up with extra cushions under her thin arms and covering her with a soft blanket. Then, standing behind her, she tenderly combed out Ida's long hair and patted the sections to damp dry. Ida leaned back, closed her eyes, and inhaled the flowery fragrance of her now clean hair mingled with the nearby blooming jasmine. It was intimately soothing to have someone else work out the snarls from her wet hair. "Sometimes, Ernst combs my hair. It takes more effort than I have these days, so I thank you, Alice."

"Well, I enjoy doing this. I'll just weave it into a braid when it is drier," decided Alice, smiling as she remembered fixing her own daughter's hair in the past.

Ida shook her head. "You are an earth angel, Alice. Your kindness is a gift. I think you are crazy to take us in, but I am grateful. Ernst is having a terrible time dealing with my illness, but he is better now because of you and being here."

"Let's not hear this any more. The good Lord is my teacher, and the holy Word repeatedly addresses how we need to be kind." *And we are not genuinely loving if we allow others to go astray.*

"If He was good, He wouldn't put this illness on me, or if I was a better person, I suppose I would get better," remarked Ida flatly.

Mrs. Sunderlin tilted her head in concern. "Ida, did your folks raise you to know about God?"

"Certainly, Alice, both Ernst and I are confirmed. Although we attended the Lutheran services every Sunday at home, we have not sorted that out since arriving here."

"The Lutherans have a church on the other side of town. Maybe one day, when you feel stronger, we will drive over," offered Alice, greatly comforted to learn that Ida was churched. She suspected that the girl's faith might need a boost with the gravity of her illness looming ahead.

With a solemn face, Ida assured her, "My mother raised us to be God-fearing people. But Mama also taught me that we bring on our troubles. So, if we do not practice the virtues, all manner of problems will come to us."

Ida's response made Alice's thoughts whirl with uneasiness. *Does she think her sickness is because of something she did? Does this dying girl know the merciful Father? Has the couple come to terms with twhat is to happen?* Turning to prayer, Alice silently asked, *Dear Lord, give me the words to help her sort through this spiritual confusion.* Then she prompted another question. "Ida, have you thought about the future? I mean, beyond this life?"

"Are you asking me if I know I will die?" clarified Ida. "Yes, of course. From the beginning, when I first learned about having this sickness, I knew it would take my life."

"Oh, Ida, what a burden you have carried."

"Did you know I tried to make Ernst go away before we ever courted? There is so much I will never get to do in my life. It just isn't fair, especially for Ernst," fumed Ida.

"Have you and Ernst talked about this?" probed Alice, sensing her deep pain.

"What do you mean? My death? What is there to say? I will never get home again, and I will never see my little girl. What is there to talk about, Alice?" Ida sniffed. Alice went to the distraught girl's side to console her, pulling her close. Emotionally exhausted, Ida started to cry as she gulped for air.

Alice sat quietly by until Ida regained her composure. Finally, she changed the subject, asking, "Ida, I want to know more about your home in North Dakota and where you grew up."

"I'm just a 22-year-old farm girl from North Dakota. Where I come from, we are poor, except for our land, which provides what we need. We milk the cow, plow the land, and plant the garden. We never talked about the future. Mama used to say, 'This day is all we can face.'"

"Did you go to school?"

"Sure, I did. And after I finished the eighth grade, I went to be a housekeeper for my uncle. You should understand that nothing more was expected of me. So, you can see, I never did anything mighty."

"Oh, Ida, my dear, do not belittle your place in this world. You are young, but that doesn't mean your life experience has any less value in God's eyes than someone who lives to be 100 years old."

"But, what do I have to show for my life?"

"Ida, you are a woman of substance and are bearing your affliction with grace."

"No, I'm not!" retorted Ida.

"But you are," countered Alice. "Our lives should not be measured by the number of hats, shoes, or other bobbles we own or the size of our accomplishments. Instead, the measure is in our efforts. Christ, by His actions, modeled how we are to act in all circumstances. His words provide the guidelines for aligning all decisions and choices we must make."

"The only good thing I have done was marrying Ernst and having Hazel," Ida noted.

"Yes, and you love them both with all your heart," Alice stressed. "And God knows and loves you even more deeply and profoundly than you love them. In that knowledge is absolute comfort," reassured Alice, looking into Ida's face as she patted away her own gathering tears with a dainty handkerchief.

Ernst returned from the grocer's. Arriving in time to hear Alice's last sentence, his countenance hardened. Without forethought, he harshly blurted, "I wish I believed in what you say, Alice, but what loving God would ever allow my wife to suffer like this?"

"Ernst!" Ida responded in surprise, "How can you say such a thing?"

"I say it is not fair. I am taking care of you the best I know how, but nothing is working," Ernst said with emotion as he set the food bundles aside to come to her. Taking her hand, he whispered, "Ida, when we came to California, you were supposed to get better."

"We did not know that moving here would help," reminded Ida softly.

"Ida, do you want to go home?" Ernst asked.

"No, it is too late for that. Alice has given us a home. My days on the porch with the flowers and the warm weather are all I need. I am content." What she did not say was, *I am too weak to make the trip, and we have no money.* "Ernst, we have much to talk about, and this is the time."

CHAPTER 28

Conversations of Consequence

When you face the fear, it backs off.

The image of the young couple in their sorrow over-whelmed Alice. Rising from her seat, she gathered Ernst's packages and disappeared into the kitchen.

Ida and Ernst spent the next hour confronting their heart-ache and the reality of what was to come. When Ida turned the conversation to more practical issues, it took Ernst off guard. When she began instructing Ernst on her wishes for their little girl, he began to shake his head in misery. Ida reached out to clasp his hands, saying, "You must listen to me. I have some-thing I must say." Satisfied she had his full attention, Ida con-tinued, "I want you to get on with things when I am gone. We talked about getting our own land and building a place to raise our children. You wanted to train horses. I still want you to go after all of that when I am gone."

Hearing Ida speak so frankly lifted a burden for Ernst, but not at the time. That "lifting" would come later after the sting of sorrow had eased. Ida insisted, "Ernst, I expect you will go back for Hazel, but I think it will be all right if you wait. My parents love her, and I am more at peace with her under their care. Mama was right; I would not have been able to care for her like she would have needed if she had come with us."

Ernst acknowledged this truth with a nod. Ida had anguished over the issue of leaving Hazel behind all the time since leaving home. He shuddered at the thought, asking, *What would I do if Hazel was along right now? Yes, Hazel should be with Arne and Hannah.*

"We must tell your folks how you are doing, Ida," advised Ernst. "Should I write to them now?"

"No, not yet. Pa and Mama do not need to worry. This is our time; we will spend it quietly, and all will be as it should. Now let me rest. I am tired." Ida wanted to unwind her feelings about something Alice had said, *"God knows me and loves me, and that is a comfort."* *Why exactly is that a comfort?* She wondered.

———

Ernst glanced at the front porch and sighed. Her chair was empty. More than a week had passed since she had greeted him from her comfortable chair surrounded by flowering vines. Too weak to walk anymore, Ida was limited to spending most of her time in bed. Ernst went around to enter by the kitchen door. Mrs. Sunderlin was stirring a fragrant pot of bean soup on the stove.

"Hello, Alice," he greeted. "I am sorry I am late. We were planting trees today, and I wanted to finish before coming home. My, whatever you are cooking smells good."

"Thank you, Ernst. I'm making bean soup," she announced.

"Ida has been in your room all day. Mary and I tried to encourage her to sit outside, but she refused. Another thing, Ernst, she has been asking for you. Something is on her mind. I almost sent for you, but I was unsure of where you were working today."

Concerned, Ernst headed down the hall and into the dimly lit room. Ida rolled toward him at the sound of his footsteps. "Ernst!" she mumbled so low that he hardly heard her say his name.

"Yes, Ida, it's me. I'm back from work. The foreman says it will rain tomorrow, so I won't go in. Anyway, he was pleased we got all the trees planted today."

"Oh, good! I thought we could write a letter home. I should do that, shouldn't I?"

"Of course! Your folks look forward to the letters just as much as we do theirs. Are you hungry? Alice made some soup that smelled good. When you are ready, I will take you to the table."

"All right, if you say I must, Ernst. I hardly have any strength, but I will try to eat something," replied Ida, struggling to pull herself into a sitting position. Then, reaching up, she felt her hair was in disarray and realized she was still in her nightgown. "Ernst, would you get my comb and help me with my robe? I think it is too late in the day to dress."

Ernst opened the nearby drawer and pulled out the comb as requested. As he held a hand mirror in front of her, he saw her frown.

"What is it, Ida?" he asked gently.

"I hardly recognize myself anymore."

He put down the mirror and said supportively, "You are brave, Ida. Don't worry about such things. I think you are as beautiful as ever." He smiled at his wife but groaned inwardly. Along with Ida's body growing alarmingly frail, her hair had become so thin. He tried to keep her brush from view each time they combed her hair until he could dispose of the long strands.

"Our supper is ready," Alice announced as she stood in the doorway. Seeing Ida sitting up in bed was a relief.

"I'll bring Ida along," replied Ernst. "Maybe we could eat on the porch if it isn't too much trouble."

"That is a good plan," Alice agreed. "Would you like me to run a braid in your hair?" Ida nodded in assent. Handing over the brush, Ernst watched as the older woman gently parted Ida's hair into three sections and began plaiting.

As Alice braided, Ida made an unexpected comment. "Remember when you asked me what I thought heaven would be like? I used to think it was like sitting quietly in a church and praying. I do not think that anymore," Ida said as emphatically as her weakened voice would allow, glancing at her husband. In her mind's eye, Ida was picturing the white-steepled church back home in Auburn, where she was confirmed.

Her curiosity piqued, Alice prodded, "What then, my dear? What is your vision of heaven?"

"I know it will not be a place of confinement. Not like this, where I hardly can move and breathe. A loving God will release me from this sick body."

"I'm so glad to hear you say that with certainty," Alice affirmed.

"And I understand now that it wasn't His fault this happened. I listened to everything you told me," reflected Ida, slowly going on, "I think God is using my pain to bring me closer to Him. My life has been meaningful, but it is not as important as what is to come. He waits for us to choose to be with Him. I am not afraid of leaving anymore."

"What a comfort and blessing to hear you say that," commented Alice as she finished the braid. Reaching over, she placed her hands lightly on Ida's thin shoulders. "You are right. I also believe heaven has no limits. God has prepared a place for us, but we can only imagine a glimmer until we are ready to meet Him. It must be a place of peaceful loveliness that we can only imagine."

After a momentary pause, Ernst moved to her bedside. "Come, Ida, it is time for sunset." Then he bent down and effortlessly scooped her up and carried her to the porch. They remained there until the first star appeared overhead. Gently rousing his sleeping wife, Ernst asked, "Where have you gone in your dreaming tonight, my dear?"

Ida, snuggled deeply in blankets, opened her eyes to his voice. Taking a short breath, she blew it out of her mouth, willing her lungs to work, "I was thinking about Hazel. Do you think she is walking yet?"

"The last letter home said she was getting around well now," reminded Ernst. "Caroline was having a time with keeping her shoes on. Our girl is 14 months old now."

Ida rambled on in short raspy sentences. "I was also thinking about…the kitchen at home. Remember…when Ma and I painted it blue and white…when we moved from the cabin? I always liked working beside Mama. The first thing she showed me was to make scrap crust little pies. Ernst, do you think… Ma will teach Hazel how to make pie?"

It was more words than Ida had spoken all week. "Yes, Ida," Ernst consoled, "certainly. She will show her how to make pies, bake bread, and everything else that is important."

"I wonder if Hazel will ever think to ask about me. I could not bear it thinking she would forget me as her mother."

"Now, Ida, where is all this talk coming from?" asked Ernst.

"I am dying, Ernst; you cannot think otherwise. We need to talk about these things…and it is also time to write home," she explained, her voice weak and raspy, "They need to know." By Ernst's hand, Ida finally wrote the words acknowledging her health was failing. With a sense of urgency, Ernst left to post it immediately.

Ida struggled to write the other goodbye note; it was a letter for Hazel. She wanted to leave a message with her little girl expressing all her motherly love and regrets. Ida labored over each sentence until Ernst gently announced, "Ida, you have said all that is important." Finally satisfied, Ida signed the letter: *Love, Your Mama.*

"Hold on to this letter. When Hazel is grown, if she asks about me, promise me, Ernst, that you will give it to her." Taking it from her hands, Ernst folded it and slipped it securely into his pocket. Later, she barely roused as Ernst gathered her into his arms to carry her back to bed.

Theirs had been a conversation of consequence. Within days of writing the letters, Ida began to fail even more, slipping into periods of deep slumber disturbed only by intermittent gasping for air or crying out in pain. To ease her discomfort, Ernst and Alice doled out small doses of laudanum, which seemed to help. They both knew that Ida's health had finally turned a corner from which she would not recover.

On Tuesday, the first day of December, it rained, and Ernst came home early from work. After washing up, he went to sit beside Ida's bed. In the dim light of the lowering sun from the window, her frail and fragile appearance shocked him anew. Full of utter sorrow, he gathered her up, blankets and all, and held her to his chest as he murmured, "I love you, Ida, my brave girl. You don't have to keep trying; it is too hard. You are tired." When he released her to lay back on her pillow, he felt her feebly reach to hold his hand. Ida's soul slipped away quietly with the golden light of the setting sun on her face. Ernst began to weep.

Later that night, Ernst left to seek a Wells Fargo office, per Alice's instruction. He felt it urgent to get word to Ida's family. When Ernst stepped into the telegraph office at such a late hour, the elderly man at the desk looked up and sighed. Just a glance at the man's face, awash in grief, revealed the nature of the visit. The operator handed Ernst a pencil and paper, instructing, "Here …ten words…keep it to ten, or it will cost you more." Ernst, suddenly feeling numb, stared at the blank form and groaned inwardly. *How on earth am I to share such news?* Upon noticing the young man's turmoil, the telegraph operator returned. After making a sound as if to clear his voice, he offered in a soft tone, "Let me help you. Now tell me what is important?" With astute experience, the man concisely wrote: *Ida died at 6:30 tonight burial Thursday EJ Ottoson.*

"Now, who do I send this to?" came the next question.

"Arne Oihus, Grafton, North Dakota," Ernst replied.

The telegraph cost Ernst dearly at eight dollars, but he knew it was necessary. Otherwise, it would have taken at least a week or two for a letter to reach home.

In just a few words, the telegram would convey to Ida's family that the California venture was a failure. Transmitted by Morse code, the words traveled over cable wires. By tomorrow morning, the sad news in the telegraph would be deciphered at the Grafton office. Ernst shuddered to imagine a lone rider going out to the farm to deliver the information that would inflict such grief.

When the notification business was completed, Ernst returned to Alice's. He quietly let himself in the back door. Alice was there to greet him. She lifted his hat from his head and helped him out of his coat. Drawing him to the warm kitchen, Alice insisted, "Now, Ernst, sit and drink this coffee. We will keep the lights on tonight in vigil."

"I sent the telegram; her parents will know tomorrow," he offered numbly.

"Good. I'm sure it was not easy, but it was necessary. Ernst," she paused, "while you were away, I laid her out. I picked her pretty flowered dress and fixed her hair the way she liked it."

Nodding, he stammered, "Thank you, Alice. I hardly know what to do." Ernst was numb. *Has this really happened? Is Ida really gone?*

"I should never have taken her from her family," Ernst blurted out the thought foremost in his mind. "They could have taken better care of her."

"Don't talk like that, Ernst. You have put in your best effort even though it has not been easy." Mrs. Sunderlin did not want the dear boy to be mired in guilt. "Ida told me that you planned your trip to California together. It was going to be a new start for both of you."

"Yes, that is true, but she is gone. But without Ida, I have nothing."

"Loving someone never leaves you with nothing. You are hurting. You need to allow yourself plenty of time to sort this out."

Ernst rose from the table, murmuring, "I'll sit with her tonight."

"I left a candle burning…light another if you wish." Then, Alice quietly added, "Ernst, I already sent word. The undertaker will come in the morning."

Two days later, Ida was buried in the Angelus Rosedale Cemetery. Ernst and Alice looked on as the funeral director recited a short Bible verse and commented about the tragedy of losing one so young. Without further ceremony, eulogy, or procession, the service was over in minutes. Ernst placed the white carnations that Alice had provided on Ida's grave. Alice then withdrew quietly, telling Ernst she would see him later.

Alone at the gravesite, melancholy thoughts churned through his mind. Their marriage vow kept repeating in his head, *In sickness and in health, until death does us part. So not only is Ida gone, but our marriage is over too.*

Ernst left the cemetery with his dismal thoughts too jumbled to make sense. He walked the neighborhood until he finally arrived back at Alice's house. Upon entering, he was relieved to find himself alone. In the kitchen, he found a note from Mrs. Sunderlin instructing him to eat. So, he did, blindly consuming but not tasting the fare. After washing his plate, he went to his room and closed the curtains. Then he lay on the bed, restlessly shifting until sleep finally claimed his weary body and mind.

CHAPTER 29

Ernst Makes a Decision

We expect love to be healing and whole and are astonished
to find it can create hollow gaps and empty failures.
–Thomas Moore, Care of the Soul

$\mathcal{E}$*rnst woke with* a jolt. As he stared at the ceiling, all that had happened the day before returned. Suddenly, the bedroom became a chamber of gloom. He rose to sit on the edge of the bed and think. *I'm not expected back at work yet. I don't want to be here.* Rummaging through a drawer looking for his comb, he encountered Ida's hairbrush, and a sudden sadness struck his heart without warning. On top of the bureau, he picked up a pile of assorted coins and inserted them into his vest pocket.

Ernst slipped on his coat and reached for his hat. Standing at the bedroom door, he paused to listen. He sighed in relief to hear only silence. *I don't want to talk to anyone right now. I need to get away from here. I just want to be alone.* After quietly creeping down the hallway, Ernst let himself out the front door.

Standing on the porch, Ernst found himself drawn to walk back to the cemetery. Walking briskly, he felt a sense of urgency to confirm all that had happened in the past two days was real. Entering the "Silent City," he saw Ida's gravesite from a distance with the disturbed dirt and the carnations of white. He stopped suddenly. Unable to make himself draw closer, he turned away. *It hurts too much.*

He began to walk south toward neighborhoods that, from a distance, seemed shrouded in pine trees. He knew it was just an illusion. The "trees" were the hundreds of oil derricks in the front and backyards of private homes. *I think it looks like a terrible infestation.* The air seemed heavier than usual, and the smell was stifling. *This could not have been healthy for Ida,* he frowned.

As he walked, his thoughts whirled. He imagined Arne and Hannah and how they would take the news. *Did they know how sick she was? Indeed, Ida had told them, or had she? And, what of Hazel? She has no mother.*

After walking vigorously, Ernst absently followed a rail track line. Finally slowing his pace as he approached a waiting streetcar, he pulled the coins from his pocket and counted the change. Seeing sufficient fare, Ernst impulsively climbed on board and took a seat in the nearly empty car. An hour later, he caught a glimpse of the ocean in the distance. Suddenly, the air felt lighter.

Upon arriving at Santa Monica Beach, Ernst felt his stomach stirring in want of food. Even though he felt no appetite, he decided he needed to eat. Walking toward the main street, he was flooded with memories. He recalled Ida's excitement at the prospect of seeing the Pacific Ocean and then her delight to encounter Alice. *It had been a good day.*

Ernst paused at the entryway of a café. It was the same place where he had eaten before. Peering in, he noticed the table where they had enjoyed their meal. Ernst placed Ida, Mrs. Sunderlin, and himself at the table in his mind's eye. He could see how Ida's eyes were big, smiling in appreciation of the lively and bountiful meal.

"Sir, can I seat you?" came a feminine voice.

The moment of his reverie was broken. Ernst turned to the waitress and pointed to the lunch counter. "Yes, I would like to sit over there, if I may." As he was led past the table, his heart thudded as he realized *This is what it will be like without her.*

Sliding onto a swivel stool, he felt alone. When the waitress came by, she smiled and laid a menu in front of him. Ernst pushed an empty coffee cup toward her, picked up the menu, and glanced over the prices. When he realized he had not planned the day with a clear mind, panic rose. Knowing he had barely enough to cover his train fare, he searched the menu for something he could afford.

When Elsie returned, she suddenly recalled seeing the man before. That time he had sat with a young woman and Mrs. Sunderlin, one of her favorite customers. *Something must be wrong,* she thought in alarm. Then she noticed the dark armband of mourning and understood.

Ernst ate the fried egg on toast and drank two cups of coffee. When Elsie returned with his bill, she put a package on the counter in front of him. "You might need some more food later. I fixed a sandwich for you to take along."

Ernst protested as he fingered his change, knowing he had only enough left for a return fare to the city. "But I cannot pay you for this."

Elsie shrugged and smiled kindly. "Our mutual friend has always been generous in her tips. It pleases me to extend a little kindness to others now and then."

"Tack för maten," returned Ernst, slipping back to his native Swedish words to show his gratitude.

"Now, go to the beach and sit by the water," she instructed. "Nothing is more calming when things are down than to feel the rhythm of the ocean waves."

Ernst conjured up a smile. He felt slightly revived by the unexpected kindness from the sympathetic woman who had no idea of the extent of his woes.

Walking out to the beach, Ernst was drawn to the same stretch of sand where he had last sat in the sun with Ida. At least we got to the ocean, Ida. *It was a happy day we shared, and it was the only thing you ever said you really wanted to see.*

Ernst wandered the shoreline as the drumming of the rolling waves anesthetized his feelings. He picked up one shell, lying half-buried in the sand. It was unbroken by the current, and he slipped it into his pocket. *I will take this for Hazel. Someday I will tell her of the time her mother and father visited the ocean.*

—◊—

Disillusioned and in debt, Ida's death left Ernst reeling. Ida's medical and funeral costs would have to be reconciled. In addition, Ernst was keenly aware of his responsibility to Ida's family and the care of his faraway daughter Hazel. What he needed to do was apparent.

Numb and grieving, Ernst immediately buried himself in strenuous manual labor. In addition to the park department job, he also took a temporary job unloading train freight during the weekends. By late spring, he had managed to pay off the bills and cover the cost of a one-way ticket back to Grafton, North Dakota.

During that time, Mrs. Sunderlin insisted Ernst remain in her home. Ernst knew he needed her friendship, so he gratefully accepted her continuing hospitality. They often sat on the porch late into the evenings. Ernst talked. Alice listened. When he asked, "Would it be possible for me to raise Hazel on my own?" the older woman bluntly advised him. Alice gave counsel from her own perspective and helped him sort out his feelings. Ernst also spoke of his discouragement and ranted in anger at losing Ida, asking, "What am I supposed to do now?"

It was early summer when Ernst decided to return to Grafton. He implored, "Please, Alice, tell me what to do with Ida's things. Perhaps I should give them away."

Alarmed by what she felt was a rash decision, she reminded Ernst, "When Hazel is older, she will want some of her mother's things." Taking charge, she offered, "Let me do this for you." It did not take Alice long to gather Ida's two best dresses, shoes, the sewing box, and a grooming kit that included a hairbrush, a comb, and a button hook. Finally, she added the unfinished quilt top to the small pile.

The day before leaving California, Ernst decided to purchase some souvenirs. He was pleased to locate several small ruby-colored glass mugs with little handles and crystal bases. Ernst had the cups inscribed with some family members' names for a few pennies more. For his daughter, it read, "Miss Hazel Ottoson, Los Angeles 1904." The next day, Ernst purchased an eastbound train ticket. Settling into a corner seat of the Santa Fe passenger train, Ernst sighed deeply and pulled his hat down over his face. He was a worn and weary man.

As the train neared Grafton, Ernst sat up and stretched. *Though I've only been gone for months, but it feels like I've been gone for years.* Looking out the window, he was struck with a sense of appreciation. It was good to be back on the open flatlands. *How I've missed the vast dome of this blue sky.*

After nearly two weeks of train travel, Ernst arrived home. Gathering up his luggage, he set out on foot to return to his daughter and to the farms of his family by marriage. His arrival was unexpected, but Arne and Hannah welcomed him home.

CHAPTER 30

Return to North Dakota

*At the end of the day, we must go forward with hope
and not backward by fear and division.*
– Jesse Jackson

"*Here, Hazel, hold* Kristine's wreath," instructed Hannah as the family settled into the sleigh. Sitting next to Kristine, the four-year-old carefully balanced the heavy sleigh blanket over the bridal crown of greenery in her lap. It was a sunny, brisk December day in 1907.

Arne picked up the reins, and soon the party glided over the snow heading into Grafton. Ernst turned to look at his little girl.

"I have an important job, don't I, Papa?" Hazel spoke up. Ernst nodded, wondering, *Does she understand that Kristine will be her new mother?*

Three years had passed since Ernst had buried his beloved Ida, and his heart still ached when he allowed himself to think of her. Their little girl was a constant reminder of his brief marriage. It was heartbreaking to think all Hazel would ever know about her mother was through family stories and mementos set aside until she was older.

After returning to Nash, Ernst lived with Arne and Hannah. He slept in the "boys' dorm" upstairs along with Oscar, Alfred, and four-year-old Clarence, working for both Oihus brothers. To Arne and Hannah, it seemed as if Ernst was drifting. Along with losing Ida, he had also lost sight of his prior ambition.

Then something changed. Ernst found friendship with Kristine, whom Uncle Anthony had hired as a housekeeper after Ida and Ernst left for California. The 21-year-old young woman from Norway spoke little English, but she and Ernst discovered a mutual attraction. Hannah and Arne encouraged Ernst, a man they had known for more than ten years, to try marriage again.

In the beginning, Ernst often had to stop short when he would catch himself comparing Kristine to Ida. Kristine however, was in love for the first time in her life. She saw Ernst as an upright and good man with the potential and desire to make something of himself, even though it might be slow to come. Ernest eventually proposed to Kristine, and she accepted. Finally, it seemed as if Ernst would know happiness again.

The brief wedding ceremony was to be held on December 17, 1907, at the Lutheran parsonage in Grafton. When the wedding banns were announced and published in the *Grafton Times*, the family laughed heartily to see the humorous article posted directly under their names entitled, "Selecting a Husband."

Within the first months of their marriage, the couple began planning a move to Saskatchewan, Canada. Lured by the opportunity to claim virgin land and farm their own place, they would, additionally, be living closer to Kristine's family. While it was still wintertime in North Dakota, they decided to leave after the spring thaw.

The question of Hazel's future was once again uncertain. Hannah dug in her heels when she learned of their plan to leave the area for good. "Hazel should stay with us. You are heading to unsettled land. You do not know what you will find when you move on."

His in-laws had given the same argument three years ago when he and Ida went to California. Perhaps they were both still angry and mourning the loss of their eldest daughter to the illness that claimed her short life. Yet Hazel seemed like a daughter more than their grandchild. "She will remain here— the home she knows," Arne insisted firmly.

"But…" Ernst argued weakly, "Hazel is not your responsibility."

"How can you say that?" retorted Hannah. "We all want the best for her, and being with you right now is questionable. Maybe in time, when you are settled, she can come to you. We shall see." It was all just words, and Ernst knew it. After two years of being reunited with his daughter, he would have to say goodbye to Hazel again. Kristine simply stood by, uncertain of the role she was to play in young Hazel's life. Though Hazel called Ernst "Papa," the child had also always referred to Hannah and Arne as Mama and Papa, which was easier than explaining otherwise.

Finally, the long-awaited day arrived for Kristine and Ernst to depart. Anthony readied the wagon as Alfred helped Ernst load their trunk and suitcases. The couple would travel almost 500 miles by train, heading first to Winnipeg and then west to the unsettled area of Niacam, Saskatchewan, in Canada.

When the time came to exchange a solemn goodbye, Ernst knelt in front of his little girl. Hazel's lips trembled as she clutched her mother's doll, Clarissa, tightly in her arms. His voice was thick with emotion when he simply murmured, "Goodbye, Hazel." Then he wrapped his daughter in his arms.

Silently he prayed, *God, let me know that I am doing the right thing.* Standing up, he handed Caroline a small envelope. "Give this to Hazel when she is older. It is a letter from Ida."

Arne spoke, "Better get going. The train heading north won't wait." Ernst straightened up and gently tugged at one of Hazel's flaxen braids, "Be good, my little one. Take good care of Clarissa."

Turning, he smiled weakly at his wife as he ushered her to the waiting wagon. As they drove away, Ernst looked over his shoulder. Caroline was standing behind Hazel, whispering reassuring words to the trembling child. Anthony clucked to the horses, and the trio ambled out of the yard.

———

Dear Hazel,

The day you were born, your papa and I were happy. As we held you close to our hearts, you changed us, and we became a family. Later we had to leave you with your grandparents; it was the hardest choice I ever made. We wanted you, but I needed to get better so I could be a good mama. Instead, I got sicker. The family will raise you with kindness, love you, and teach you all the things a little girl ought to know to get a good start in this world.

Sometimes I try to imagine what you will look like when you are older and what kind of a personality you will have. Will you be serious like me or playful like your father? I hope you are becoming a kind, loving, and faith-filled person. I firmly believe that God will grace your life for all the trouble that will come your way. When you are older, I hope you will ask your father about me and that he will tell you how much I loved you.

I am leaving two things that I want you to treasure. This first is a doll. I thought you might call her Clarissa, but only if you wish. By your side, she can be a friend when you have adventures or read a book. The second gift is our wedding clock. When you are older, I told Caroline to show you how to wind the clock carefully. I hope one day, when you get married, you will take the clock to your own home. When it chimes, maybe you will think of me.

Always look for joy and fun each day, and I will smile as I look down from heaven.

Love,

Your Mama

Epilogue

Hazel grew up in her grandparents' home, living there until her marriage. Ida's sister, Caroline, took a practical interest in her young niece. With 18 years between them, Hazel and Caroline always maintained a close bond.

Soon after Ernst and Kristine moved to Canada, the hardworking Oihus brothers pursued their dream of owning the equipment and operating a successful harvesting outfit. The Oihus and Oihus Threshing company continued as a business into the 1920s.

In 1913 when Hazel was eleven, sorrow entered the family. After years of ill health, Arne Oihus died on Thanksgiving Day, November 27, 1913. The following year, Laura, age 23, also passed away after a ruthless course of tuberculosis—the same disease that claimed Ida.

Hannah and her children continued to manage the farm without the family patriarch. But, in the natural course of life, the offspring began to marry and leave home. By 1928, when Hazel married, only Hannah, and Clarence lived in the little gray house.

About that same time, Hazel began to write to her father

Ernst. She first wrote to inquire about the location of her mother's grave, and Ernst responded with an informative letter about his wife, their four children, and their home life in Canada. As time went on, so did the letter exchange.

In 1928 Hazel married Harry Lykken, the youngest son of another early Norwegian settler, Hans H. Lykken. Harry and Hazel had been acquainted for years, ever since Hazel's Aunt Alma had married Luther Lykken in 1916. In one letter, Ernst wrote telling Hazel to greet her new father-in-law for him, recalling how he had met Hans many years before.

Ernst's troubles seemed to continue after he left North Dakota. Like most farmers during the 1920s and 30s, the times were tenuous. Once he humbly wrote asking if Hazel might spare ten dollars to buy hay to feed the horses. In the late 1930s, a chimney fire destroyed their home, including all the furniture Ernst had built. After sending his family to live with relatives, he camped out of an empty grain silo, "batching it" until the home was rebuilt.

In May of 1938, an unexpected letter arrived from Mrs. S. Ericson. The Boston woman wrote introducing herself as Hazel's Aunt Selma, her father's sister. Hazel was eager to discover more about her father's family. Over the following years, Hazel and Aunt Selma continued to exchange letters often.

In 1948, Hazel finally arranged for a modest granite headstone to be placed on her mother's unmarked grave in California. Later, when her daughter, Joy Ann, was in high school, Hazel and Joy Ann took a bus tour that looped along the famous Route 66. They saw Texas, Arizona, and New Mexico sights on the way to Los Angeles. Theirs was perhaps much the same route Ida and Ernst had taken half a century earlier by train. Hazel visited her mother's grave in the large Rosedale Cemetery during their stay in Los Angeles. The small granite marker read: *Ida Ottoson, Mar 10, 1881 – Dec 1, 1903.*

The year Hazel turned 50, she decided to visit her father in Saskatchewan. As Hazel drove north into Canada accompanied by Alma and her two children, Joy Ann and Lee, she anxiously considered how she would find her father both by location and by person. Many years had passed since the farewell between the younger Ernst and the little girl clinging to her doll. Despite years of exchanging letters, Hazel still wondered about the man who referred to himself as "your old man" or signed his letters "Dad" or "E J Ottoson." *I don't even know the sound of his voice.*

Hazel's impending arrival stirred anxiety for Ernst too. Sitting in his favorite chair *(pictured right)*, he mulled over the passage of time. His thoughts whirled. *Look at how old I am; she should have come before now.* Well past his prime, Ernst was now bent over. His bones ached, and he was frail with age. His hard life as a farmer was written in the lines of his weathered face and gnarled hands.

When Hazel arrived, she recognized some of the family from photographs. After introductions, Joy Ann and Lee went off with their relatives, Ivar, Carl, Oscar and Cora, to explore the area. Ernst gave Hazel a tour of the farm and house, and both relied on information gleaned from their letters for conversation.

The following day, having stirred the family connection but finding less and less to talk about, the family quietly parted. Lee took the steering wheel while Hazel settled into the passenger seat for the long drive home. Hazel turned to look back as they drove away until the Ottoson farm disappeared in a cloud of dust.

Author's Comments, Photos, and Memorabilia

For the curious reader, the following is an accounting of the significant items, facts, and helpful finds used to create the story of *Ida's Trunk:*

- Ida's baptismal certificate, dated 1881, Dakota Territory
- Pictures of the family home taken over the course of the twentieth century
- A worn family Bible containing Ida and Ernst's marriage license, a telegram, and the funeral program for Ernst J. Ottoson
- A ruby souvenir cup engraved with "Hazel Ottoson, Los Angeles 1904"
- A small red velvet-covered sewing box containing a worn business card from Dr. Wong, Los Angeles
- Two sisters, Ida and Laura, suffered early deaths due to tuberculosis.
- A pair of barely worn, trim-heeled black boots
- A scrap of wallpaper from Ida's bedroom

- Clarissa, a kid leather doll with a china face
- A Seth Thomas mantle clock belonging to Hazel
- Letters to Hazel from Ernst, Aunt Selma, and Caroline arriving from Canada, Boston, and Minneapolis, respectively
- A receipt for a gravestone to be placed in the Angelus Rosedale Cemetery, Los Angeles
- Reference information: *From the Valdres Valley of Norway to the Red River Valley of the North and Beyond: A History of the Oihus Family, 1580-2020.* Grafton, ND

———

Ida's Trunk would be incomplete without adding a few comments about tuberculosis. In the early 1900s, infectious diseases such as pneumonia, influenza, tuberculosis, and gastrointestinal sickness were the leading causes of death. Several different strains of the tuberculosis bacteria have been identified. It is plausible that Ida contracted the Mycobacterium bovis strain from consuming unpasteurized milk from infected cattle on the family farm.

A tuberculosis patient seeking medical help would learn their affliction was incurable. More than 40 years would pass before medical research could demonstrate the effectiveness of antibiotics for the treatment of active tuberculosis.

To ease the symptoms of coughing, pain, fever, and night sweats, comfort measures were suggested along with the promotion of rest and good nutrition. Over time, which was often years, tuberculosis patients suffered from weight loss as their bodies were slowly "consumed" by the disease—thus, the disease's nickname, "consumption." Tuberculosis was a public concern known to be contagious. TB patients were commonly ostracized socially. Around the country, sanitariums promoted climates with dry air and milder climates, especially in the southwestern areas of the United States.

Though Ida and Ernst's accommodations during their short time in California are unknown, this remarkable account of a young woman from a small Dakota farm is a tale of romance, hardship, and hope. Though the details are a work of fiction, *Ida's Trunk* is a true story as I imagined it might have unfolded.

Sisters Ida and Caroline, c. 1895

The Wedding Picture of Ernst and Ida Oihus Ottoson
May 25, 1901
Grafton, North Dakota

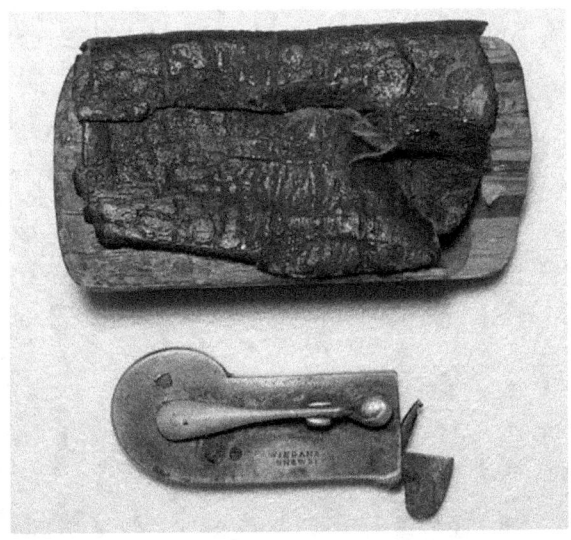

Above: Scarificator. Bloodletting was a common practice in the 1800s believed to be curative for many diseases in animals and humans. This brass-covered lancet belonged to Arne Oihus.

Below: Toluca Street oil rigs, Los Angeles, California, c. 1895-1901

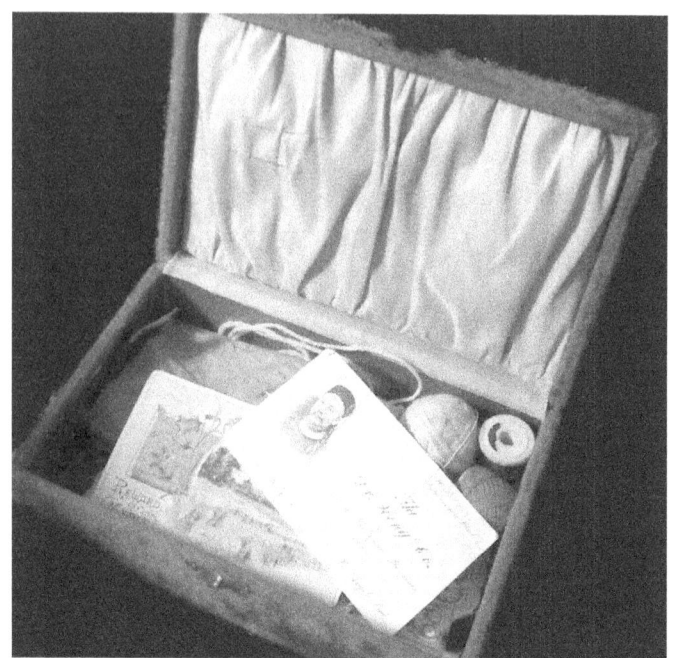

Above: Ida's sewing box with Dr. Wong's business card
Below: Telegram sent to Arne Oihus; Ida's date of death was December 1, 1903. The date on the telegram was probably a transcription error. Ida's and Ernst's marriage lasted only 2½ years, though they had know each other about nine years.

Form No. 1.

THE WESTERN UNION TELEGRAPH COMPANY.

INCORPORATED
23,000 OFFICES IN AMERICA. CABLE SERVICE TO ALL THE WORLD.

This Company TRANSMITS and DELIVERS messages only on conditions limiting its liability, which have been assented to by the sender of the following message. Errors can be guarded against only by repeating a message back to the sending station for comparison, and the Company will not hold itself liable for errors or delays in transmission or delivery of Unrepeated Messages, beyond the amount of tolls paid thereon, nor in any case where the claim is not presented in writing within sixty days after the message is filed with the Company for transmission.
This is an UNREPEATED MESSAGE, and is delivered by request of the sender, under the conditions named above.
ROBERT C. CLOWRY, President and General Manager.

NUMBER	SENT BY	REC'D BY		CHECK
1 F	Cw	p	8 Paid	

RECEIVED at 837 C ____ / ____ 190

Dated Los Angeles Calif

To Mr. Arne Oihus

Grafton

Ida died 630 tonight
buried Thursday

Ernest J. Attasou

Hazel Ottoson
1920 Grafton High School graduation

Above: *Harry C. Lykken, c. 1918*

Below: *Wedding record for Harry and Hazel Lykken, November 21, 1928. The hanky is inscribed "Ida Oihus, 1892." Perhaps this was the "something old" and cherished that Hazel carried on her wedding day.*

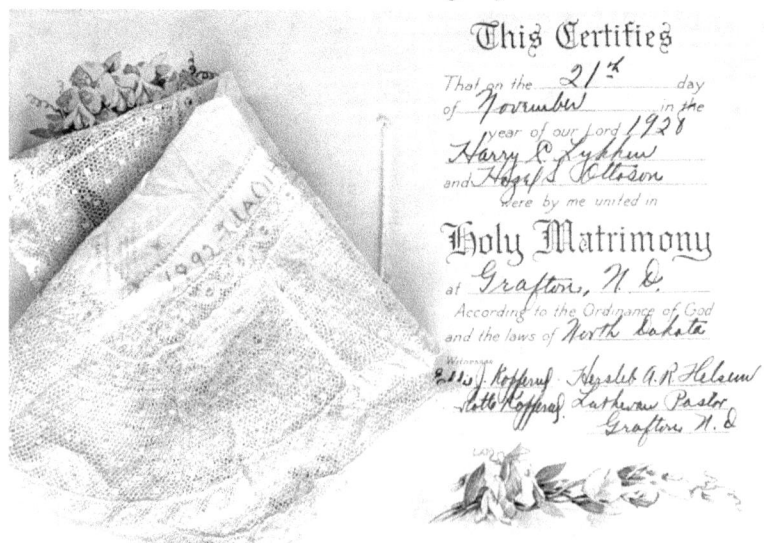

Above: World War II ration book and coupons issued
for Hazel's 8-year-old son Lee.

Below: Family gathering near Naicam, Canada, c. 1952
Left to right: unidentified boy, Kristine (Gudbrandsdatter),
Ernst Ottoson, Hazel Ottoson Lykken with her two children,
Lee and Joy Ann Lykken

Above*: Harry and Hazel, c. 1950s*

Below*: A wintertime scene of the 1896 farmhouse where Harry and Hazel Lykken lived out their lives.*

Acknowledgments

To my mother, I offer my love for her patience and affirmation of this tale. *We spent hours sitting in rocking chairs while I wrote and you crocheted. You listened to the story with your full attention, providing timely help with words and grammar.*

To Uncle Lee, for sharing your wealth of knowledge and candor in answering my questions concerning past agricultural practices, insight regarding the war years, and clarifying details regarding the Nash home. If we want to know about something, we turn to you.

To my niece, Connie Barrell, I am grateful for your eagerness to provide sketches of the actual doll Clarissa. In addition, thank you for your willingness to model our great-grandmother Ida's dress as pictured on the cover of this book.

To my dear friend, Rose Marie Murray, for your unbridled support of this project. Thank you for graciously reading the unedited version of *Ida's Trunk.* I used all your suggestions. Most of all, for your gift to continually lift and inspire me with your lively and deep faith.

To my editors, Linda Stubblefield and Angela Zachary, I

appreciate your expertise in helping me to complete this new book. I am a huge fan of your talents. Once again, you have polished the manuscript and offered ongoing words of encouragement that make me want to keep writing.

Finally, I remember in gratitude my great-aunt Hazel Sutterlin, "The Teacher and Storyteller," who instilled an appreciation of our Norwegian heritage and a love for words.

Landstad Lutheran Church, built in 1888.
The church, built in Auburn by early pioneer settlers, is now located in the Heritage Village of Grafton, North Dakota.

About the Author

Patty Cresalia *enjoys* developing endearing characters faced with baffling and seemingly hopeless situations. As in her first book, *The Eagle's Nest,* her plots tease out qualities of bravery and grit while demonstrating the strength of personal faith. Patty firmly believes writing about virtues is definitely not "old-fashioned."

Growing up in Utah, Patty now claims the Dakotas as home. She often finds inspiration for her stories by walking the same fertile farmlands of the Red River Valley that provided her great-grandparents' livelihood.

www.ingramcontent.com/pod-product-compliance
Lightning Source LLC
Chambersburg PA
CBHW051532260626
47170CB00003B/902